The
Biggest Liar
in Los Angeles

Books by Ken Kuhlken

Midheaven

The Hickey Family Series
The Loud Adios
The Venus Deal
The Angel Gang
The Do-Re-Mi
The Vagabond Virgins
The Biggest Liar in Los Angeles

With Alan Russell
Road Kill
No Cats, No Chocolate

The
Biggest Liar
in Los Angeles

Ken Kuhlken

Poisoned Pen Press

Library of Congress Catalog Card Number: 2009942190

ISBN 13: 9781590586976 Hardcover
        9781590587362 Trade Paperback

Poisoned Pen Press
6962 E. First Ave., Ste. 103
Scottsdale, AZ 85251
www.poisonedpenpress.com
info@poisonedpenpress.com

Printed in the United States of America

For my kids, Darcy, Cody, Zoë, Darren, and Nick—
who bring me a world of joy.

Acknowledgments

A thousand thanks to Barbara Peters for encouraging, reigning in, and generally keeping me in line; to Robert, Jessica, Marilyn, Nan, and all at Poisoned Pen Press who make these books happen; to my writing pals Alan Russell, Gene Riehl, Ron Argo, Lynne Kennedy, Mark Clifton, Dave Knop, Maynard Kartvedt, Barbara Hopfinger, Barbara Gardner, and especially to Gary Phillips for help finding my way around old Los Angeles; to the librarians downtown; to Jerry Bumpus, Charlie Brashers, Vance Bourjaily, John Irving, and other teachers; to all the novelists who made me want to be one; to Jackie Miller of the Foursquare Heritage Center; and to the writers of history, including Kevin Starr, J. Eric Lynxwiler, Kevin Roderick, Ben Proctor, Dennis McDougal, Cecil M. Robeck, and Daniel Mark Epstein, who made my stay in 1926 Los Angeles such a delight. For details about their books, go to www.kenkuhlken.net

Chapter One

Tom Hickey rented in a court near the intersection of Wilshire and Normandie, halfway between downtown Los Angeles and Beverly Hills. He shared the cottage with his little sister Florence. She was seventeen. Six years ago, Tom had snatched her away from their mother, Millicent Hickey, a seamstress for Universal Pictures.

He hadn't spoken to Milly since the day he and Florence left home with nothing but his clarinet and a suitcase of clothes between them. At first he believed their mother would track them down, have him arrested or beaten by a gang of her fellow spiritualists. But all these years, she had left him alone.

He credited Leo Weiss for that blessing.

When Tom was in fourth grade, Milly rented a two-bedroom bungalow on Orange between Highland and La Brea. The owners, who lived next door, were Leo and Violet Weiss. Leo was a detective with the LAPD.

At first, Leo and Vi appreciated Milly. She kept the house spotless, and her passion for gardening transformed the yard into a wild yet orderly scene reminiscent of Eden. But soon, Vi caught Milly whipping Tom with a rope while shouting in "tongues." Leo warned her, politely, hoping to keep Tom and Florence next door where he and Vi could observe and react.

Then Vi rescued Tom when Milly lashed him to a fence post in the back yard and left him while she ran errands. For that offense, Leo threatened jail next time. Milly moved them to Hollywood, several miles away.

Tom snatched his sister when he was sixteen, Florence eleven. A few days afterward, he reported to Leo what his mother had done to the girl. Then Leo informed Milly that although minors running from their guardians was illegal, torture was more so, and got rewarded by long prison terms.

Now, in 1926, Tom was a bandleader. Before he turned twenty-two, the other musicians drafted him, though most of them were twice his age.

Tonight they roamed around the vacant storefront owned by Archie the drummer's uncle, trading jokes and filling the room with a smoky blue haze.

Tom hoped a high C would grab their attention. He lifted the clarinet to his lips.

Then Oz came loping in. He carried the tattered case that protected his alto sax, and a fistful of leaflets. He shoved a leaflet at each of the boys. As Tom took his, Oz said, "None of you white folks go telling me the Klan don't be here out west."

The leaflet was a broadside entitled the *Forum*.

It declared:

```
LYNCHING. We who ask to live in peace; who
came to this City of Angels hoping to leave
the terror behind; who judge no man without
cause; who take only our meager share of the
promise this nation affords to those unbound
by color; who wish to believe that justice
will someday prevail, must now pause to weep.
    On Monday, the 11ᵗʰ day of October, a
gentleman who shall here go unnamed went
out walking in Echo Park just as sunlight
spilled over Angelino Heights. In the glare
of dawn, a vision appeared. So terrible it
was, the gentleman believed he had not risen
but was in the throes of a nightmare.
```

A dark man hung limp from the live oak not ten yards off Park Avenue, not fifty yards from Sister Aimee Semple McPherson's majestic temple.

Before this heinous act, the "Invisible Empire," resurrected by Mister D.W. Griffith's "Birth of a Nation," would have us believe that in our locale they limit their hooded activities to preserving the Good Book's values by smashing the furniture and windows of speakeasies, flogging the occasional adulterer, marching to protest the election of our first Negro assemblyman, and rallying voters to elect candidates opposed to unfettered growth. Now, with one act, despicable in both substance and symbolism, they have declared war against peace and decency.

The test of a community lies not in the occurrence of sinister deeds. Evil will always live among us. No, the test of our mettle lies in our reaction to manifestations of evil. In the case of this deed, more vicious than simple murder because it targets the spirit of a people, we who seek truth, peace and justice must mourn to our depths more than the loss of an innocent. The implications of the lynching go so deep, they mock the very concept of justice. When public servants attempt to obliterate the truth, they shatter our dreams of a world that could be.

Members of the Los Angeles Police Department carried off the body in such haste, only the one early-rising gentleman witnessed the shameful deed. Let the reader judge: has the briefest account of this heinous crime appeared in the *Times*, the *Herald*, or the *Examiner*?

To our knowledge, no publication but the *Forum* has risked offending the powerful by reporting the murder of Franklin Gaines.

The floor beneath Tom rose and fell, as if another earthquake had struck. He back-stepped and leaned against the brick wall. "Frank Gaines," he muttered.

Chapter Two

Tom would've gone directly from rehearsal to check on Florence. According to his rule, she was to walk straight home following her after-school job sweeping and ushering at the Egyptian Cinema in Hollywood. But the broadside changed Tom's plans. He caught the streetcar on Pico, transferred to the coach line up Western and Wilshire and hustled the several blocks through the drizzle on slippery pavement to the neighborhood where he once lived.

The Weiss home was a Craftsman bungalow with a low-pitched roof and a rock walled porch extending the width of the house. Leo came to the door in blue cotton pajamas, no robe. He rubbed his eyes and scratched his head through a tangled web of thinning hair.

Though Tom hadn't seen the man in months, since early summer, he didn't waste an instant on pleasantries. He gave Leo's meaty hand a quick shake and said, "Who put a lid on the Echo Park lynching?"

Leo peered at Tom as if to assure himself this was no impostor. He scratched his head again, then turned and flopped into a rose-patterned easy chair with doilies on the arms. "Sit down."

Tom entered and shut the door behind him.

"Lynching?"

From his hip pocket, Tom produced the *Forum*, which he tossed. Leo caught it, raised and held it close enough so he didn't need his glasses. While he read, Tom watched for a reaction but saw the profile of a poker face.

Leo folded the broadside in half and set it on the chair arm. He looked up and shrugged.

"How about it?" Tom said.

"Meaning you want to know did it happen?"

"Meaning I know it happened. What I want is to know what you cops are going to do about it?"

Leo stared above, as though tracing the route of a crack that bisected the plaster ceiling. "What's it to you?"

Tom folded his hands to keep from shaking a fist. "Besides that a man's dead, and no doubt a whole lot of colored folks are barricading their doors, and a murderer, or a gang of them, is on the loose?"

"Yeah, besides all that," Leo said. "See, last month a Chinese couple got robbed. The creep raped the gal and dumped both of them off the Santa Monica pier. You must've heard, but you didn't come running to me."

"Frank Gaines was a pal of mine."

"Musician?"

"An old pal," Tom said. "Long ago, at the mission on Azusa Street, Frank used to take me down the block to the Arkansas Diner, all those times Milly couldn't break away from the Holy Ghost long enough to feed us. Frank was a gentleman. Not a morsel of spite or bitterness in him. Good will toward everybody. "

"I see."

"Meaning you're going to tell me who put the lid on?"

"Who says I'm in the know?"

"I'm asking, are you?"

Leo shook his head.

"Okay then, are you going to find out?"

Leo drummed his fingers on the chair arms. "No."

"Oh," Tom said. "Orders from Two Gun Davis?"

The way Leo grimaced meant Tom had stepped out of bounds, which didn't stop him. "You're not a fan of his, are you?"

"He's my boss."

"Yeah, and I hear he's trigger happy as Billy the Kid."

Leo said, "The city's crawling with bad guys. Chief Davis is following the will of the people."

"Which people?"

"Most of them. Listen, back when you belonged to Milly, in one year, more than a hundred of us got killed. Maybe you recall?"

"So?"

"So when Davis sends the message about the crook you fail to kill tonight could be the one kills you tomorrow, we've got reason to heed his warning."

"And to follow his orders, even if he tells you to cover up a lynching?"

"Some would do just that." Leo waved the *Forum*. "According to this, police were involved." Leo stood and plodded toward the kitchen. As he passed a small marble topped table with a chessboard laid out, a game interrupted in progress, he slid the *Forum* under the edge of the chessboard. "Tom, I work for the city of Los Angeles. I don't run it. That's other men's job."

Tom had followed, a footstep behind. "And if you get uppity about it, you'll soon be out selling cutlery door to door. I'm aware of that. I'm no freshman. The thing is, as you have told me on more than one occasion, every man's got to choose sides. If you side with the rats just because they run the city, it'll prove you're not the guy I believed you were." Tom choked down the lump in his throat. He wanted to say, And that would break my heart. But a look at Leo's eyes told him he'd said enough.

They stood nose to nose. "You sound mighty righteous, boy."

The word "boy" pinched a nerve. He couldn't remember Leo ever calling him boy. He leaned on a wall and ordered himself to act civil. "Back when I was a churchgoing youngster, Frank Gaines and some other good folks pounded into my head I should do what the churchgoers say, not what they do."

"And what do they say?"

"Seek the truth, for one thing."

A smile broke slowly out of Leo's stony face. "And where would you go to start seeking."

Tom gave up the wall and stood straight. "Angelus Temple."

"Why's that?"

"Frank was lynched not fifty yards from the place, and I'll bet plenty of his brothers and sisters from Azusa Street are among Sister Aimee's flock. I could give you a few names. You can start there."

"I'm not going to start anywhere, Tom. You're the truth seeker. I'm just a cop."

After a few speechless moments, Tom said, "I've got to check on Florence."

Chapter Three

Tom's day job was selling meat. He serviced restaurants, meat markets, and corner groceries from Pasadena to Santa Monica and south past Anaheim. He drove a 1921 Model T Ford with a shed-sized icebox perched behind the cab. The route paid $38 weekly, more than what the butchers made. Because Tom signed new accounts and customers admired him for having been a USC fullback, even though he'd only lasted a year.

He'd started with Alamo Meat as a janitor, swabbing the floor, scraping blood and bone scraps off the cutting boards, scouring the knives and cleavers, and airing the place as best he could. Six years ago, the morning after he and his sister escaped from Milly, he'd gone there to give Bud Gallagher the news.

He'd known Bud as his dad's best pal. After Charlie Hickey vanished, when Tom was barely six, Milly set out to find him, carrying baby Florence and dragging Tom. Charlie had worked beside Bud as an Alamo butcher. The rare evenings he arrived home late, Milly accused him of carousing with Gallagher.

She raged into Alamo Meat. The way Tom remembered his mother's assault on Bud, if he hadn't stood holding a cleaver, Milly might've snatched up one of the knives and run him through.

Gallagher swore he knew nothing about Charlie's disappearance. Before Milly gave up, she paused for a dash into the ladies' room, which gave Bud a chance to wrest Tom's promise to come to him if troubles got bigger than even a tough little man could handle on his own.

A dozen times between Charlie's disappearance and the escape from Milly, Tom had gone to Alamo Meat. At first he believed he only wanted to visit sights and smells that recalled his father. Later he admitted, only to himself, that Bud gave him strength and fortitude. Like Leo did. They were formidable men. Leo had taught him to box and throw, catch and hit a baseball. Bud coached him to sling a football, one of the skills that earned Tom entrance to USC.

Six years ago, Bud convinced the boss to hire the sixteen-year-old. Tom went to work as apprentice to Seymour Asberry, the colored fellow who led Tom and Florence to the Jefferson Boulevard flat next door to his own, and whose wife Clara sat with Florence evenings while Tom worked. It was Clara, Tom believed, who convinced Florence her charms would one day fail, but her education wouldn't. Wild as she'd become, she made higher marks than Tom had.

Besides his wages, Tom found a measure of peace at Alamo Meat, even during his despair over leaving USC. And while swapping anecdotes and jokes with Bud Gallagher, he often got lifted by a distant hope that some offhand remark would provide the clue that might lead to his father.

The day following his visit to Leo, Tom used his lunchtime to detour off his route. He turned from Hollywood Boulevard onto Ivar, then crawled the truck up the block past the Knickerbocker Hotel, enduring horns and shouts. All the curbside parking was filled. Sidewalk crowds spilled between the parked vehicles and into the street. The Knickerbocker, a masterpiece of Beaux Arts architecture, was a stars' lair. Tourists and newcomers stood on tiptoes, leaned on cars, or paced in circles, awaiting a thrill.

As a native, to make sense of newcomers, Tom grew up sorting them into types. Aside from the few who'd found their pot of gold in films or finance, they were: folks, lost souls, and crazies.

The folks had found something here, maybe a tract home with a driveway for their Flivver, or faith in a God, raw food, rite, or regimen. The lost souls roamed the streets, staring with desperate hope for a glimpse of some movie idol or other grand vision, and in danger of joining the crazies. Not the soldiers who never escaped the war, whom Tom suspected remained lost souls forever. The crazies were born dreamers whose dreams got so viciously trampled all they had left was outraged vanity that sent them on a hunt for revenge.

Tom hadn't come looking for stars, but to chat with Raleigh Washburn, who shined shoes outside the Knickerbocker and remembered the Azusa Street revival as well as anyone, and never wearied of talking about those days.

As always, Raleigh looked weary but glad, as if he'd just finished a race. His hands were restless, so his trousers and red and green checked vest bore smudges of brown and black.

Tom didn't mention the lynching. He only asked, while Raleigh buffed his brogans, "You remember Frank Gaines, used to preach now and then at the mission?"

Raleigh gave him bug eyes, then shook his head and commenced a nervous titter. No doubt he'd read the *Forum* and wasn't apt to trust his thoughts to anybody white. Tom, assuming an offhanded manner, shifted the topic to the disappearance and resurrection that, every day since summer, claimed the headlines. "How about Sister Aimee? Do you buy her kidnapping story?"

"Hush," Raleigh said. "That gal been two months out on the town, is all. You know, Tom, ain't nobody pure holy."

Tom nodded. "Say, you've been to any services over at Angelus Temple?"

"Yessir. Quite a number of us from the mission find our way to the temple on occasion. Say, Mister Tom, you heard about a lady coming to town, a magician, she claim to be. Going to hold one of them séances, on the night of Halloween, call on poor Mister Rudolph Valentino. Mister Rudolph, he been a generous friend to me. Lady oughtn't to call on him. Ought to let him rest in peace."

A séance to contact Valentino would collect a sizeable mob, Tom supposed, rich as the city was in suckers. He would've bet on Milly's being part of the mob.

He said, "Those folks going to Angelus Temple, how about a few names?"

Raleigh supplied a half dozen names, which Tom memorized and jotted down upon his return to the meat wagon.

At the end of the workday, Tom ran to catch the 5:14 red car at Eleventh and Central into downtown. As he descended beneath the Subway Terminal Building to meet the Glendale Boulevard line, he listened to the low, polite voices of colored folks around him. He caught no mention of the lynching, or any hint of a lead. He noticed more than a few wary glances.

Chapter Four

Most of what Tom knew about Sister Aimee Semple McPherson, he'd learned from his sister. Whenever Florence came home wearing a dark and petulant expression, instead of tuning her bedroom radio to songs, she tuned to Sister Aimee's broadcasts.

He knew Sister Aimee was decidedly younger and prettier than most evangelists, and that her gospel was gentle, with hardly a taste of the Billy Sunday hellfire. He knew she had arrived in Los Angeles the same year Tom and Florence escaped their mother, after years of road show crusades in tents and rented halls. Still, she often toured the country and Europe, healing, baptizing, and raising loot. Upon returning from her journeys, she got met by larger and louder crowds than did President Coolidge or visiting monarchs.

Five months ago yesterday, on May 18, she went swimming at Ocean Park Beach and vanished, presumed drowned. Millions mourned. So when she staggered into Agua Prieta, on the Mexico side of the Arizona border, most of Los Angeles and much of the nation rejoiced, almost as though at the Second Coming. But District Attorney Asa Keyes and a boss of Leo's, Herman Cline, Chief of Detectives, didn't buy her kidnapping story. Now she faced a grand jury inquest.

Tom had spent pleasant afternoons across the street from Angelus Temple, rowing on Echo Park's lake. Twice with Florence. Once with a USC coed he'd entertained thoughts of courting until she balked at the notion of competing for third place against football and music, behind raising his sister and earning a living.

He admired the temple, with its round coliseum face and wide beckoning doorways. He'd heard about the plush and ornate interior, wondered what magical charms Sister Aimee must wield to enlist the army of devotees and star chasers who filled the five thousand seats three services daily. He'd often thought of going to witness her in action. But he'd yet to venture inside. Even six years after he and Florence escaped, he avoided places that boosted his chances of running into Milly.

He turned from Angelus Temple, gazed around the park for the scene of the lynching, and saw what he imagined was the hanging tree. A live oak, squat and broad, its trunk about a foot across, its lowest limb perhaps nine feet above ground.

He remembered Frank Gaines as a small man. Around five foot seven. Add to that height some inches of rope above and his feet turned down below. In the picture that came all too clearly, Frank's toes reached the tips of the highest grass. Tom stared at the image until it faded.

Worshippers and tourists poured off buses and trekked across Echo Park from their Chevys and Flivvers, and crowded the sidewalk outside the Temple. Even in October, after three weeks of rain, tourists appeared to outnumber the locals. The tourists shuffled, gawked, and wore summer clothes on the edge of winter. Tonight, though drizzly, felt pleasant compared to the recent stormy weather. Especially the deluge that pounded the rooftops and flooded the streets for three days beginning the day before the lynching.

Tom circled the tree. He scuffed his feet through clumps of grass. He scraped the dirt, his eyes keened for any object or morsel the police might've overlooked in their haste to cover up.

After the ground provided no clues, he looked above. He studied the branches and spotted a line a half-inch wide. Standing on tiptoes, he saw it as a groove, a semi-circle around the top of the lowest limb, about three feet out from the trunk. A rope burn, he believed.

He leaned against the trunk and hoped somebody might notice him there and wander over, feeling the need to talk. An early riser, a day sleeper, or an insomniac. A witness to the lynching of Frank Gaines. Maybe the source of the *Forum* report. Although he couldn't imagine anyone strolling at dawn in a deluge.

No one came. The only people who glanced his way were a few women and girls, clearly more interested in him than in the hanging tree. Aside from his large nose, Tom was a handsome fellow.

After promising himself to return and canvas the neighborhood, knock on doors until he learned something, he crossed the street. A half-hour before the service, the crowd reduced Park Avenue to a single lane. He scanned faces in search of one he'd known from Azusa Street fifteen years ago, and pondered: if he saw Milly, should he march over and question her, though she hadn't been a friend of Frank Gaines. She'd claimed Frank was wicked, and warned Tom away from him. But no matter her opinion, or jealousy, she might've kept up with his comings and goings. Like veterans of battles, folks who shared common experience as extraordinary as the Azusa Street revival often kept tabs on each other.

On the other hand, any contact with Milly was risky. The sight of him could provoke her into a crusade to regain her still underage daughter.

Whenever Tom glanced behind him, the crowd appeared to have doubled. He nudged his way around, peering more closely wherever he spotted a dark face. They were plentiful but far from the rule. This was no Azusa Street, where you found more dark folks than pale, and ample shares of the colors people called yellow and red.

Ushers eased open the dozen double doors, in unison. The multitude began lunging into the temple. At the doorway, Tom found himself squared off against an usher inches taller than his six foot one. The fellow appeared to have singled him out. Tom shook the offered hand. The man eyed him head to toe. But this was no admirer. He might've been a speakeasy bouncer. A ruddy, clobbered face, flattened nose, scar in place of a cleft on his chin, and squinting right eye.

"Welcome," the bouncer said, in a raw voice and with a thin smile that meant the opposite. Then he turned and walked away.

After the dubious greeting, Tom loitered in the foyer, backed against the interior wall, watching arrivals. He only gave up his post when the bouncer, staring over the crowd, rolled his hand and pointed to the archway that led into the sanctuary.

Tom obliged. A woman usher tried to lead him down front. He thanked her, veered off and made his way to the steps. He found a seat midway across the front row of the mezzanine balcony, supposing that vantage offered as strategic a position as any from which to study the crowd. Even before he got settled into the cushioned seat, he spotted the bouncer. Up front. Staring.

The fellow mistook him for a reporter or other antagonist, Tom supposed. With the reverend Sister standing accused of perpetrating a fraud most nervy and outlandish, the Temple had plenty reason to station a bouncer at the door. According to the last report Tom read, the prosecutors had exposed as a fraud the mystery woman who claimed she, not Sister Aimee, resided with one Kenneth Ormiston in a Carmel cottage during weeks Aimee claimed the kidnappers held her in Mexico.

Tom moved his Stetson fedora, the most expensive piece in his wardrobe, from his head to his lap, and continued to search the multitude for any face that would carry him back to Azusa Street. But once Sister Aimee came swooping down the ramp from the backstage mezzanine, Tom lost sight of all but her.

Though the Sister was no beauty queen, she was a looker, even with her thick brown hair coiled into a tight bun and her bosomy contour disguised by a nurse uniform and cape. Her bodily grace was more suited to sport than to dance. Still, she glowed. Not from any visible lighting, but as if she'd conjured a way to enshroud herself in moonlight.

When Tom had listened to the Temple choir over Florence's radio, he gave them high marks. He admired old hymns. No matter the lyrics, he could attend to the melodies, harmonies, and arrangements. Gifted vocalists of all sorts, unless they went too operatic, could make him shiver ear-to-ear. Most any rhythm set his feet and fingers tapping. The temple's drummer, Sister had lured away from the Pantages.

But tonight, no choir, no orchestra. Sister Aimee glided to stand beside the grand piano. A pianist in tails and top hat strolled out from behind a trio of potted palms. His trousers hadn't yet touched the bench when he commenced a two-barre lead-in.

The preacher opened wide her long, graceful arms and crooned:

"If I have wounded any soul today,
If I have caused one foot to go astray,
If I have walked in my own willful way,
Dear Lord, forgive!
If I have been perverse or hard, or cold,
If I have longed for shelter in Thy fold,
When Thou hast given me some fort to hold,
Dear Lord, forgive!"

Her vibrant contralto delivered the lyrics with such passion, they convinced Tom she meant them. She might be nuts, but she believed.

He felt eyes on him. He crooked his head around and found himself gazing into the watery dark eyes of a woman whose hands reached for the sky. Her bony arms quivered. Her tongue lolled back and forth.

Once Sister launched her sermon, as soon as Tom heard the word mother, he wanted to run. She was telling a story of an old widow who lamented that she hadn't spent a life winning souls, and of a friend who reminded the widow that her sons were missionaries, in China and Africa.

Sister would speak a few sentences, then repeat a line and pause for shouted amens and hallelujahs, which often came joined by white hankies waving. The woman behind Tom bellowed her amens so loud and jerked her uplifted arms with such fervor, and jumped up and down so often, Tom expected her to break into a babbling tongue.

The widow had born and raised, along with the missionaries, a younger son. Sister went to her knees, acting his part. "Mother," she vowed, "I am never going to leave our little home with the roses climbing over it until the day the Lord has taken you up to heaven. I am going to stay here and look after you, Mother."

Tom could listen no more. Instead he peered below, searching the pews for an even vaguely familiar face.

Moments after Sister concluded the sermon and opened the service to vociferous communal prayer, Tom heard his name called out. He turned and saw the woman of the loud amens flash him a grin.

A sizeable number of folks stood and pardoned their way to the aisles and fled. Probably tourists who'd had as large a helping of Pentecost as their schedules or psyches allowed.

Tom sat crooked half around, waiting for the amen woman to make her move. When she stood, so did he.

On the Park Avenue sidewalk, he found her waiting, leaning on the fence outside the parsonage. She was short and bone-thin, with knobby shoulders, and a milk chocolate face. She looked young enough so she might've been one of the Azusa Street children.

Out here, she acted timid. "You Tommy?"

"Tom Hickey."

"I know Hickey. I remember your mama. And a baby girl."

"Florence," he said. "Your name?"

"Mavis."

"How about Frank Gaines?" Tom said. "You remember Frank?"

Her head began wagging. "No sir. I don't know a soul called Frank. No, I surely don't."

She too had read the *Forum*. Rather than call her a liar, he asked, "How about other folks from the mission. Do you keep up with any of them?"

Her eyes brightened, and she reeled off a few names Tom didn't recall. But when she named Emma Gordon, he said, "Whoa. Does Miz Gordon come here?"

"Here to the Temple. No sir."

"You know where she lives?"

"I surely don't. But I believes she works at a laundry. In Chinatown. Ho Ling be the Chinaman's name."

A lanky dark fellow wearing a derby came stalking at them across Park Avenue. A fist swung at his right side as though preparing for action, maybe clutching a sap.

"Well now," Mavis said, "here come my ride. Lord bless you, Tom Hickey."

She clutched the man's hanging arm and hustled him away, no doubt explaining her acquaintance with the husky blond boy.

Across the park, a streetcar bell clanged. Tom might've caught it, but he couldn't quite make himself run, so absorbed was he with thoughts of Emma Gordon.

In a recurring childhood daydream, he got rescued away from Milly, who had stolen him from his real mother who looked like Emma with her angel smiles. Emma with the gleaming eyes he saw when the dirt floor and the walls of the mission shook and all around him folks thrashed, teetered and toppled, rolled on the ground, wept, and sang or hollered in fits of ecstasy, and Emma came running to scoop him up and deliver him out of there.

He hadn't seen her since Azusa Street. Once Milly changed her beliefs, anyone who didn't change with her became a pariah.

By now Emma must be seventy-some, Tom estimated. He imagined her plump as ever and with skin like velvet except on her hands. She would wear a dark cotton dress that smelled of lye soap and a modest hat with a flower on the side or no hat and the flower bobby-pinned into her stiff, shiny hair.

He ambled across the street, went to the hanging tree, and stood beneath the rope-gouged limb remembering Frank Gaines' ice-white eyes and crooked mouth that always looked primed to boom a laugh. In the mission, while others sang and shouted, Frank often whooped what they called holy laughter. Holy or not, Tom believed the laughter came from Frank's heart. Most anything could make Frank glad. Tom remembered him telling someone he came looking for God because he needed somebody to thank.

When Tom heard the next streetcar one stop away, he gave up his reveries. He was rounding the east end of the lake, passing a gaggle of ravenous ducks, geese, and mud hens, when he noticed the temple bouncer squeezing himself into the driver's seat of a Nash sedan parked at the curb across Glendale Boulevard.

Tom made a dash to the streetcar, hopped on, and pardoned his way into a seat on the right side of the aisle, across from a couple he'd seen going into the service. The man, though he wasn't a dwarf, could slouch and pass for one. His woman might've played tackle for USC. Before the service, from their sheepish and hungry stares, he would've bet they were lost souls. Now, they held hands, and their eyes appeared moist with gratitude.

As the trolley pulled out, so did the Nash. When the streetcar stopped at First Street, Tom watched the Nash pull over behind. Again, at the Beverly Boulevard stop, the Nash pulled to the curb. Neither of its doors opened.

Tom wasn't about to lead the man to his court on Virgil Street. So far as he could, he kept his home a secret, on account of the unpredictable Milly. Most of the USC football team, whom he wasn't inclined to trust around women, had met his gorgeous sister.

After transferring at the end of the Wilshire line, he kept the Nash headlights in view while he rode the bus to La Brea, a few short blocks from Leo's.

Running from trouble wasn't Tom's style. Besides, no matter how fast he could run, he wasn't going to lose the tail unless he scaled fences and cut through a yard or two. Instead, he strolled the blocks, then climbed to Leo's porch. He stood beside the front door under the porch light, and watched.

The Nash rounded a corner then sped up. As it passed, Tom smiled. He imagined the bouncer would return tomorrow, maybe accompanied by some Rasputin elder come to uncover Tom's sinister motives for spying at Angelus Temple. And he'd find himself facing off against an LAPD detective.

Chapter Five

The Nash turned the corner. Tom stood and watched the neighborhood long enough to decide the bouncer didn't intend to round the block and park for a stake out.

He was about to knock when the door swung open. Leo filled the doorway. "Bed time," he grumbled.

The whites of his eyes were flamingo pink. He slumped sideways to lean against the door jamb. His vest was unbuttoned. His tie, which sported a hand-painted cluster of purple fruit, hung loose to one side. Tom pointed to the cut glass tumbler he held partly hidden by the wrinkled shirttail outside his trousers.

"Nightcap?"

"What of it?"

"You want to stand aside and let me in, I'll tell you what."

Leo backed a step. "Don't bother telling me what I already know."

Tom entered and shut the door behind him. He followed Leo into the kitchen. "Just what do you know?"

"Where you've been. What's going to happen next, provided you don't change your ways. You old enough to drink yet?"

"Would be," Tom said, "if I lived where drinking was legal. Anyway, I'm not drinking tonight." The last thing Tom needed was to bedevil his already flummoxed mind. He returned to the parlor and flopped onto the sofa, trying to guess what Leo knowing his movements could mean. If police had watched for him at Angelus Temple, he supposed Leo must've reported his intention of going there. And the bouncer could be police. He might've known where Leo lived and recognized it when he drove by.

When Leo appeared, he was clutching the tumbler in both hands. He sank into his easy chair.

Tom asked, "Where was it I've been?"

"Getting religion."

"Okay, and the guy following me is?"

Leo raised his tumbler as if for a toast and drank it halfway down.

"Level with me," Tom said. "Are you sitting this game out, like you said, or playing for the Two Gun Davis team?" He waited for a reply. Leo only sipped his medicine.

On the wall above Leo hung a Charles Fries painting of an oak grove and clouds, the centerpiece of Vi's California Plein Air collection. The most gnarled oak reminded Tom of the hanging tree. His blood heated and rose to his head. "You think I'm some loose cannon?"

Leo made a pfft sound. "I think you're a kid who's got plenty to learn before he ought to take on the big boys. You say there's a hush on the newspapers, radio. Meaning the stakes are this high." He lifted his hand all the way. "Month or so back, Wobblies hold a meet up in Long Beach to gripe about the way labor gets treated by the oilmen and shipbuilders. A gang of citizens crash the party, a half dozen Wobblies come out as stiffs, and plenty more on stretchers."

"You telling me the cover up's about politics?"

"Sure, could be, but what I'm telling you is, the citizen party crashers, I know a couple of them, and I know they've got their eye on you."

"Cops?"

"Maybe."

"How about giving me their names."

Leo only scowled.

"Any of your cop pals also Klan?"

"Watch it, Tom."

"Say, Davis himself could be the dragon. Suppose he heard some brethren of his got too zealous, so he called a hush on the story."

Leo appeared to consider before he said, "If the Chief had a way to keep the news hounds hushed, I'd hear about it. Now, for the last time, lay off."

"You think I ought to let some wretches get away with murdering a pal of mine?"

"I'm saying you've got a future. So does Florence. Where would she be without you?"

"I'll watch my step."

"You do that." Leo heaved to his feet, set his drink on the chess table and tucked in his shirttails. He plucked his bowler hat off the rack, shuffled to the front door and threw it open. "I'll run you home."

"You might want to tell Vi? In case she wakes up."

"Gone to her sister's."

Leo's dour look broke through Tom's annoyance. "Want to tell me about it?"

"Not on your life." Leo threw back his shoulders, marched across the porch, down the steps, and along the path to his garage. Backing his Chrysler roadster out of the garage, he missed the driveway and uprooted a trellis draped in bougainvillea.

Before Tom hopped in, he offered to drive. Leo snorted. Thereafter, Tom kept his mind off the car's slight but constant weaving by keeping watch. He saw one tan Nash stopped at the intersection of Wilshire and Van Ness. As they passed, no matter how hard he peered, the driver looked like a shadow. The Nash swung a left and headed west, away from them, on Western.

The running board of Leo's roadster scraped the curb of Virgil Street in front of Cactus Court, where Tom rented the rear faux-adobe cottage on the east side. He had one foot outside when Leo said, "Get yourself a weapon. A sap, a length of pipe. Something that'll knock 'em out. And keep it handy."

"Knock who out?"

Leo yanked the steering wheel away from the curb. "If you knew how to use a gat, and if I didn't figure any shooting would sure get you hanged, I'd lend you one of mine."

"So it's cops," Tom said.

Leo grabbed the handle, slammed the door, pulled away, swung a wide turn, and weaved down Fourth beneath the hill of Moorish villas.

Chapter Six

Roger Villegas owned Cactus Court, which he called the final remnant of his heritage as the descendant of Spanish land grant nobility. Last summer, following the death of the scorched grass that bordered the walkway between the two rows of cottages, he planted more cactus. Tom had twice since gotten attacked by the jumping cholla. When the evil plant stabbed Florence, Tom complained.

Villegas only chuckled. "Tell her to start wearing denim, in place of those frilly items."

Tom had learned, no matter how tired, distracted, or agitated, to concentrate on his steps when arriving home. Besides, he had Frank Gaines, Emma Gordon, Leo's betrayal, and the infamous LAPD crowding his mind. So he didn't notice that his cottage was dark until he reached the door. Florence never slept without the light on in the hall between her bedroom and Tom's.

The cottage door was locked. He used his key. But just as he laid his hand on the knob, he got spooked by a thought Leo's warning must've prompted. He pictured the bouncer and another Palooka on the couch, with Florence gagged and squeezed between them.

He needed a pistol. Shooting couldn't be hard to learn. A sap wouldn't take out a guy across the room. He backed off the porch and picked up an egg shaped stone.

He turned the knob with his left hand, kept the stone in his right at ready, and used his foot to ease the door open. Nobody on the couch. All he heard was cicadas and a scratchy phono at least two cottages away. Al Jolson singing "Mammy," a number Tom detested.

He flipped on lights, peered around the parlor, then into the kitchen, and then each of the other three cramped rooms. For a minute, he sat on the edge of his bed and kicked air. From now on, he vowed, wherever he went after dark, Florence went with him.

He rushed out, avoided the chollas, turned left onto the sidewalk and double-timed to Vermont and on to Third Avenue. He hustled past the bakery, hardware, boot and saddle shop, and newsstand to the old livery stable. Max Van Dam had deodorized the place, touched it up with a smattering of chrome and neon, and christened it the Top Hat Ballroom.

Tom knew the colored doorman. This wasn't the first time he'd come to fetch his sister. He gave old Mister Hines the fifty cent admission plus a dime tip. "Florence here?"

The doorman leaned close and confided, "Lest she done slipped out while I gone to use the gents'."

Inside, a lifeless trio fronted by a bald, toothy fellow mangled "Bye Bye Blackbird." Tom passed through the ballroom without much bothering to look for his sister in the smoky blue glow. The gals ranged from too young to Tom's mother's age and beyond. Those who danced downstairs for a nickel couldn't play in the same league as Florence, no matter how bare, glittery, or painted they made themselves.

Upstairs, she could earn a quarter a dance.

At the foot of the staircase that led to the liquor and quarter-a-dance girls, Tom nodded at the tiny sentry who called himself Abe since some wag told him he resembled the president. His uniform was stovepipe trousers, a sky blue double-breasted jacket, and a high top hat. He said, "I told her what you think about her coming here."

"And she said?"

"She said, 'My brother changed his mind, with rent coming due and all.' Then she gave me that babydoll look. You know, I'm a sucker for the Janes."

Tom emphatically shook his head. "When I change my mind I'll come tell you."

Little Abe saluted.

The combo upstairs, livelier than the trio, commenced the second verse of "I Cried for You" just as Tom spotted his sister. She wasn't hard to spot. Even the waist-denying sequined flapper costume couldn't hide the hourglass shape. One of her long, bare, white-as-cotton arms draped around the neck of a fellow whose high cuffed slacks, eager eyes, and cowlick notified Tom he was a tourist.

Tom approached his sister expecting to be greeted by her on-the-town scent, as if she'd bathed in gardenia water. But as she turned and exclaimed, "Phooey," he caught a whiff of grenadine, Florence's remedy for the acrid taste of Top Hat gin.

The tourist stiffened and opened wide his mouth as if to object to Tom's cutting in. But after his eyes met his rival's, he turned to chewing on his lip and stuffing his hands into his woolen coat pockets.

Florence cocked her head and reached for her brother's shoulder. "Aw, Tommy, I'm just getting started. It's early."

"Yeah." He grasped the hand, lifted it off his shoulder, and pulled her to his side. "A few years too early."

She went along without a fuss, but smiled or winked at every man along the way. On the sidewalk, she stopped to pluck a Chesterfield out of her beaded purse and torch it with one of the new lighter gadgets that would've cost Tom most of a day's wages.

She strode ahead of him. He let her go, but quickened his step to keep within a few yards. Even in her fury, she walked in the way that made her hips sway and roll and made Tom regret he hadn't moved the two of them out of the city long ago.

Just last week, one of the boys brought to rehearsal an article from *Collier's*. Los Angeles, the writer proclaimed, offered more than just sunshine and surf. It also led the nation in suicides, embezzlements, bank robberies, drug addicts, drunks, and murdered or murderous celebrities. Rex, the piano man, suggested a slogan the developers and boosters might use. "Come to the Promised Land, a dandy place to die."

At the cottage, Florence used her key and stomped inside then threw the door back at him. He caught it, went in and locked the door while she kicked off her high-heeled pumps and turned on him, her blue eyes gone fiery green. "What in the devil do you want with me, Tom? I'm a big girl, can't you see?" She wiggled and posed to prove it. "I've got my own mind and my own ways and you're not my daddy." Then she hollered, "Damn you, damn you, damn you."

The sight made Tom queasy. He thought, it's Milly inside her, and caught hold of her shoulders.

She punched him in the belly. He pushed her to arm's length and held on while she flailed and kicked at his shins with such abandon she would've fallen if he hadn't caught her by one of the thin straps looped over her bare shoulders. The strap tore.

She stopped still. As he let her go, she back-stepped, then collapsed onto the sofa. "My dress," she moaned, staring at her brother with bulging eyes, as if he were a brute who'd attacked her. Then her hands flew to cover her face.

She wept, and Tom stood wanting to hold her but judging she wouldn't allow it. For a minute, the weight of raising Florence nearly brought him to his knees. He knew nothing about what a parent should do with a girl too smart, too pretty, and too wild at heart.

Maybe, if he found her a daytime job, if she finished high school at nights like he had, that would keep her out of the speakeasies. Maybe he'd led her astray by giving her too much freedom.

As her weeping faded, she brought her hands from her face to her lap.

"Babe," Tom said, soft as he could manage, "damn me all you want, I'm not going to stand by and let you swill gin and go cheek-to-cheek with every rube that can raise a quarter."

"That so?"

"It is."

"Then I guess you'll be giving up the band, coming home nights to play Chinese checkers with me."

"First, how about we talk things over?"

"Nothing to talk about, Tom. I'm me. You're you. You don't like living with Milly, you go it on your own. I don't like what you want for me. So I do things my way."

"What do I want for you, Florence?"

"You want me to be a wallflower that cooks now and then, and cleans up after herself, anyway. A kid that looks to her big brother for all the answers. About right?"

He could think of no good answer, and she had him doubting his own motives. "Maybe I should call Milly," he said. "Tell her to come and get you."

Florence appeared to shudder. She crossed her arms over her breasts. Then she cocked her head and stared while shaping a coquettish smile. "You won't send me to Milly."

"You sound mighty sure."

"I'm sure," she said. "You love me too much."

Chapter Seven

Tom meant to wake up in darkness, but he miscalculated. The sky was beginning to gray when he hopped onto the streetcar at Wilshire and Vermont.

The car was at least half full. Aside from a couple up front whom Tom counted as lost souls, probably insomniacs, the riders were laborers. Brown cleaning women, Japanese gardeners, white and Mexican men of the building trades. When Tom was a kid, morning and evening riders wore ties, suits, and shirts crisp from the cleaners.

He arrived at Echo Park before the sun topped Angelino Heights. The park looked imbedded in a salty mist that so far held back the daylight.

Since lanterns above the temple entrances were on, meaning they burned all night, he couldn't imagine the killers parking near the tree. They wouldn't have parked on Glendale Boulevard with its streetlamps. Which meant they must've dragged Frank from the unlit narrow road at the foot of Angelino Heights. That stormy night, anyone who saw would've been a resident of one of the cottages low on the hillside, or looking from Angelus Temple.

From the sidewalk of Glendale Boulevard, Tom rounded the temple, peering through glass doors into the foyer, then darting glances he hoped looked innocent at the parsonage windows and balconies. As he began to cross the path that ran between the temple and the Bible school, he encountered a fellow wearing overalls and carrying a lunch pail. He put on a friendly expression. "Morning."

The fellow made a weary attempt at a smile. He didn't look much older than Tom, though rimless spectacles, handlebar mustache, and a decided paunch aged him.

"You work for Sister?"

"Yep."

"Night shift, huh?"

"Custodian, after service till six a.m., provided I get the place spotless by then."

"Work Sunday nights, do you?"

"Listen, Bub, I don't catch the six-twenty, I'm liable to fall asleep on the bench. Adios."

"Mind if I tag along?"

"Suit yourself."

Tom kept abreast of the custodian's long strides, wishing he'd taken lessons from Leo on tricks to use when interrogating. "A week ago Monday, during the deluge, did you see a fellow hanging from the big oak?"

Without breaking stride, the man said, "Hanging, you say?"

"By a rope around his neck."

"That's a hell of a question."

"Got an answer?"

"Ask me something doesn't sound like it came from a guy smoking loco weed, you'll get your answer."

"Try this. A week ago Monday, did you see any cops in the park right around dawn?"

"Didn't see a soul. Then again, I don't go looking for trouble. And rain like that might please the ducks. But me, I care to go swimming, I go to the beach."

A streetcar bell clanged. The man gave Tom a steady look. He was either on the square or an accomplished liar. He tipped his flat cap and set out jogging toward Glendale Boulevard.

Tom crossed the street and walked into the park. He hadn't gone twenty steps toward Angelino Heights when something zinged past the right side of his head, loud enough so it set his ear buzzing. It thunked into the hanging tree.

He dropped to his belly, crawled to a nearby shrub, and peered around the edge. When he spotted something blue halfway up Angelino Heights and moving higher, he bolted from cover and dashed forty yards to the wide trunk of a willow. Since no more shots had sounded, he only stopped for a breath. Then he sprinted out of the park, across the road, and ducked behind a delivery wagon parked at the base of the hill.

A strip of vacant lots zigzagged up the slope. Pepper trees, elms, and a pile of rubbish offered him cover. The higher he climbed, the less his hope of catching the shooter. But on a wide ledge, as he passed the remains of an outhouse, he noticed something through a crack in the wall. An ankle and black boot.

As a fullback he'd learned to cram fear into his belly and not let it out until the whistle blew. So he tested that skill, and whirled himself around the wall.

A well-freckled boy, about ten years, with buzzed reddish hair, squatted there, gaping up at him. A small lever-action rifle lay at his side. His hand rested on the stock. Tom kicked the gun away at the same time he lunged and grabbed the collar of the work shirt that must've belonged to the kid's big brother. He lifted the boy to eye level. "Were you shooting at me?"

"Cripes no," the boy yelped. "I wouldn't shoot at nobody. Only at rabbits. Maybe a crow now and then."

Tom used his free hand to point down the hill. "Which of those houses do you live in?"

"Hey, Mister, don't go snitch on me."

"Why shouldn't I?"

"See, a cop put me up to it. Let me down, I'll tell you."

Tom obliged.

The boy said, "I was after a jackrabbit when this big guy, taller than you even, he comes out of nowhere, scares the piss out of me."

"Uniform?" Tom asked.

"Nope. But he shows me this badge. Then he says, 'See that fat tree? When I give you the nod, take a shot. You hit it, I let you be. You miss, I'm running you in.' I say, 'What the hell you want me to shoot an old tree for?' He says, 'To put a fright in a bum who's been stalking around the temple, giving a headache to Sister.' I say, 'Why don't you go pinch him?' He says, 'Shut up, here he comes, now's your chance.'"

Since Leo had clued him to the danger from cops, Tom bought the story. He wondered if the cop hoped the shot would go astray and rid the city of a problem.

"This tall fella have a squint eye?"

The boy shrugged.

Tom pointed to his chin. "A scar right here?"

"Couldn't tell you."

"He wear a homburg?"

"You got that right."

"Here's our deal," Tom said. "Either I'm coming back to find and whop you before I snitch to your folks, or you do me a favor." He jotted the Villegas phone number on his note pad, ripped off the sheet and passed it to the kid. He nodded toward the hillside lane. "Go to every house, ask if anybody saw a man hanging from that tree." He pointed. "Or if they saw cops in the park around dawn. Would've been early morning during the hard rain. Somebody says yes, make sure they call this number, leave a message for Tom Hickey."

"That your name, Hickey?"

"What of it?"

"Nothing," the boy muttered. "I'm with you."

Chapter Eight

Tom felt crooked for stealing work hours to run errands that, on top of being personal business, put him behind schedule on his route. He promised himself only to stop for a minute at Emma Gordon's, long enough to say he'd missed her all these years and ask if they could meet around suppertime. Or to leave a note to that effect.

Ho Ling had told him where to find her. On East Seventh Street. The neighborhood featured burnt orange lawns, wilting trees, and parched houses, as if a fire had only singed while passing through. Tom thought he smelled a dairy, though he didn't spot any cows.

Emma's address lay between a truck farm, where cabbage and winter greens and plump tomatoes flourished, and what looked like a junkyard conceived by a mad or whimsical artist. Stacks of tires rose into a pyramid, and several cars stood half-planted with their noses in the air.

Now that the mist had blown away, the hottest day in weeks was upon them. With a cloudless sky, the sun at its zenith, folks walking or tending their gardens moved like sloths. Most of them shaded their eyes.

He spotted Emma on the porch of a place that could've been two shacks jammed together to form an ell. Beside the house was the boarded-over, crumbling foundation of a larger structure.

Emma sat with legs parted, elbows on her knees, using a folded section of newspaper to fan her glistening face.

She stared, her mouth crinkled and her eyes full-rounded, as if studying something that puzzled her. The sight of a delivery truck stopping in front of her house didn't alter her expression. Neither did the strange white man hopping out of the truck and striding toward her. Maybe she couldn't see well enough to notice details. Or maybe she'd seen so much, nothing surprised her any more than the next thing.

Tom stopped at the foot of her porch. "Miz Gordon," he said. "I'm Tom Hickey."

Now her eyes shut, her mouth fell wide open and something between a whoop and a wheeze issued out of her. She dropped the newspaper, heaved to her feet and clapped. "Lord, this most surely *is* my Tommy."

He climbed the two steps, wrapped her in his arms, and held on until she said, "Now boy, don't you be squeezing the life out of me."

In her presence, Tom noticed changes in the muscles of his shoulders and neck, their tautness giving way. He felt himself breathing deeper, like folks who climb out of the car after a Sunday drive into the country. Being with Emma felt like coming to a home he'd never known but always longed for.

For a half hour or more, Tom listened to stories about how Robert, her late husband, lost his job as a stevedore when the war ended, and how the killer flu the doughboys brought home convinced them Texas was safer. Besides, they had a son down in Paris, who carried on about how the town was pretty as its namesake and friendly to colored folks. But she found it neither pretty nor friendly, and when Robert died, their son moved to Chicago for decent wages, and took her grandbabies with him. Then she chose to come back west, be near her sister and what dear friends hadn't yet passed.

They talked in the kitchen, while Emma squeezed lemons into a pitcher, hacked chips off the block in the icebox, and added the water and sugar.

Back on the porch, Tom confessed his abduction of Florence from Milly.

Emma said, "Wooee, you some nervy boy."

"Our mama was acting crazy."

"Your mama got a troubled soul, Tommy. Yes she does."

"Say, Miz Gordon, I'll bet you remember Frank Gaines."

Her soft face petrified. "Why you ask?"

He wouldn't make himself use the word lynched. "Did you know Frank got murdered, a week ago Monday?"

Folks as good as Emma shouldn't bother trying to lie, Tom thought. The way she shook her head, she might've been watching a pendulum. Then her eyes shot venom at Tom's. "Who done it, boy?" she demanded.

Tom shrugged and accepted a portion of disgrace, just for being white. "I'm looking into it."

"Why you lookin' in? You police?"

He told her about Oz, the broadside, and the cover up. All of which he supposed she already knew. He didn't mention Leo.

While they let a silent minute pass, Emma rocked sideways. Maybe she was praying. Tom imagined soon she might break into a chorus of supplication in words that sounded like Chinese or Swahili.

He asked, "Want to tell me all you know about Frank?"

"Yes, I surely do."

From the way she talked, she might not have seen Brother Gaines since the old days on Azusa Street. She portrayed Frank as Tom remembered him, always the gentleman, the one who could take the unruly outside without breaking their spirits and, after some prayer, send them on their way feeling delivered. Brother Gaines, she recalled, always had a dollar to pass along to them who needed one.

"Brother Gaines and Brother Seymour, twins they could be. Brother Seymour, you don't s'pose they murdered him too?"

William Seymour was the pastor who founded the Azusa Street mission, and the visionary of the worldwide movement it inspired. Tom had read of his death, three or four years ago. Reported as heart failure. "They?"

"Same as killed Brother Gaines, boy." Her head wagged as if from a spasm. "Thing is, Brother Seymour, he be inviting everybody in, like Jesus his self, Tommy, he don't pay any mind what color. Like the good Lord, he say, come unto me and I am goin' give you my spirit. Jesus say that. And Brother Seymour, just like Jesus. God surely blessed that man, Tommy, the work of his hands, because that man didn't hate nobody but loved us all."

"Frank was that good?"

"Like they was twins."

"Who'd kill somebody like that?"

"Many folks have troubled souls, Tommy."

Tom nodded and moved the Stetson from his lap to the porch rail. "You've seen Frank since you got back from Texas?"

"No sir, I have not."

"Hear any mention of him?"

"Just he took up with a white gal came around to the mission. Name of Harriet." She chewed at a hangnail and sifted through her memory. "A married lady, I do believe."

Tom wanted to sit all day and evening with Emma, watch the sunset and working folks on their way home, find some memories or stories they could laugh together about. But if he didn't hustle back to his route this minute, he couldn't make his deliveries, drop off the truck, and arrive on time for rehearsal.

As he stood and donned his hat, he noticed Emma deep in thought. "Something else? About Frank?"

"Now Tommy." She spoke hardly louder than a whisper. "This be gossip. Ladies telling tales. You hear?"

"Yes, ma'am."

"Lady say Frank got himself mixed up with some of those bootleggers."

"Which lady?"

Emma lied again. "I surely don't recall."

Chapter Nine

The band used to feature twenty musicians before Gary McClellan, the leader, ran off with Adelita, the singer. Tom convinced eleven to stay. He renamed the band "Ernestine's Boys." Banjo, string bass, and drums in rhythm. Piano, five piece horn section, himself on clarinet, and Ernestine of the mighty pipes.

For giving the singer top billing, the jokers among them accused him of having eyes for Ernestine. Oz, being Ernestine's man, didn't care for the joke. He kept aloof, on the lookout for evidence. So Tom decided, if Oz showed up late or tooted some notes that soured the arrangement, he'd better go easy on the nagging. Or Oz might see Tom's words as a move to knock him down a peg, a play to make points with Ernestine.

Tonight, Tom's ambitions were small. A few numbers had given them fits. "Yes Sir, That's My Baby" wouldn't wrap around the jerky rhythm Omar on banjo wanted to give it. And the horn section couldn't agree on harmony.

McClellan had left Tom most of the band's arrangements. Boys in the band provided others. But he needed to adapt every arrangement to his personnel. Which often kept him awake long into the night.

He tried to turn his mind to the music. But Frank Gaines haunted him, as did the fact that he'd run so late on the route some afternoon customers bawled him out. At his last stop, Merlin's Grocery in Burbank, he got told if he wanted to keep the account, be back with a fresh cut side of beef first thing tomorrow. To cap the reproach, Merlin failed to hand over the usual sandwich Tom counted on as his Wednesday supper.

Before he attempted to rustle the boys into making like an orchestra, he rapped his baton on the wall until they paused their chatter. "That broadside Oz passed around last time, about the lynching. Anybody knew Frank, what he was up to, who had it in for him, any old thing like that, let's hear it."

Besides Oz and Ernestine, only Samuel, first trombone, was colored. Samuel gave him a look Tom supposed meant whatever he knew or didn't, he didn't mean to tell any white man. The others turned back to gabbing and fussing.

Tom shooed them into place. They were halfway through the first rough cut of "Yes Sir, That's My Baby" when Oz and Ernestine strolled in.

Tom continued mouthing and muttering the lyric while the band completed the run-through and the singer stood beside her man while he unpacked his gear. When they joined in, Tom asked the horns to try backing the vocal with the melody line, on the chorus. After one middling attempt, he passed the baton to Rex, the pianist, and asked him to take over. He motioned for Oz to join him, away from the others.

Oz came, hands out, palms up, his face asking, What in the world? "Don't talk to me, boss. It's the Mick can't carry a tune."

"Sounded swell," Tom said. "What's the latest on Frank Gaines?"

"Latest, you say? Latest is, we all waiting for the next one of us to swing. That's all. Latest," he sneered. "What, you expecting Bill Pickett goin' ride in and lasso the Grand Dragon?" Pickett was a colored Hollywood cowboy and rodeo star. "Say, whose side you s'pose Tom Mix be on?"

"You know for a fact it was the Klan?" Tom asked.

"I don't know but what I read. Same as you. Who you think?"

"I want to talk to the guy who wrote about it. You know the publisher?"

Tom winced at the sudden recognition that his asking for the publisher might prompt Oz to suspect him of ties to the Klan, who might reward whoever handed over the journalist crusader. But Oz looked simply curious. "What you want to know him for?"

"Frank and I go way back," Tom said. "He was the fellow bouncing me on his knee while the congregation howled to the Lord, down at the mission on Azusa Street."

Oz shook his head and a grin broke out. "You been a holy roller."

"Been," Tom said.

Oz looked over at Ernestine and waved, probably to clue her not to fret about a clash between her man and the bandleader. "I don't know about this publisher. But I know somebody might know."

After rehearsal and a streetcar ride, Tom jogged the two blocks from Wilshire Boulevard to Cactus Court. He ran past the jumping cholla. The reunion with Emma had charged him with optimism. On his own, without Leo's help, he might gather enough truth to persuade a certain USC politics prof and football fan to introduce him to some assistant district attorney like Joseph Ryan. The young turn who had set out to bring Sister Aimee to her knees. Ryan might risk his neck and career to break the silence and win a cache of political spoils.

No lights shone in the cottage. Tom opened the door and called for Florence. No answer. He went to her room and peeked in. Her bed was made, and the quilt pulled tight. Her school uniform lay in a heap. No mess in the kitchen. He surmised she'd come home and left in a hurry, before dark.

He locked the cottage and strode up the path and along the sidewalks of Virgil Street, Vermont Avenue, and Third Street to the Top Hat. Mister Hines might've been waiting for him, the way he spotted Tom from a distance and wagged his creaky head. As Tom neared, he said, "She already gone."

"When'd she leave?"

"An hour, maybe two."

"Anybody with her."

"Yessir. She gone off with a Mexican fella." He pointed east.

"You know him?"

"Can't say I do."

Tom imagined he knew where to find her, a quarter mile up and across Third, in a juice joint alongside which goings on at the Top Hat were a temperance league social.

As far as Tom knew, the joint didn't have a name. The storefront was a magazine and cigar stand. The speakeasy was deeper into the building, behind wall or two. To reach the action, folks came around back, up the alley, and entered from the loading dock.

Tom knew how the establishment operated. Earl, his first trombonist, made book for Charlie Crawford's mob, which ran the joint's games.

The doorkeeper looked like a German foot soldier who'd lost his pride along with the war. He squatted on the dock in front of the loading doors, yards away from the speakeasy entrance.

Tom approached and mentioned Earl. The fellow stood, shuffled to the door, rapped twice then gave a soft kick. The door slid open. Smoke billowed out.

As soon as Tom stepped inside, a portly bar maid in a flouncey blouse and knickers approached. She shouted to make herself heard over the bawdy laughter, curses, and disputes. "What are you drinking, lover boy?" Meaning did he take his gin straight or with tonic water.

He yelled, "Nothing tonight. Tonight I'm looking for my little sister."

He was about to describe Florence when the bar maid pointed with her chin. "Only one here got your looks, darling. But she ain't so little."

Now that his eyes had adjusted, he saw Florence's blond curls and curvy torso in a glittering dress with bangles at the hem and a silver belt tight around her tiny waist. She was in the third standing row that encircled a roped-off square, which would've better served cockfights or dog fights but tonight featured a pair of wiry colored boxers. They danced around the ring, glaring at each other while flexing their arms and shoulders and kneading the air with bare hands. Shifty characters snaked through the crowd, collecting bets.

Florence hung on the arm of a hatless fellow with thick, oily hair and cheeks either sunburnt or rouged. Mister Hines had called him Mexican. When Tom reached his sister, she had her lips close to the man's ear. Tom attempted to eavesdrop but couldn't hear over the racket. From behind, he placed his hands on the sides of her waist. She whirled in his direction just far enough to recognize and hiss at him. Still she let go of the Mexican. Tom pulled her to his side and guided her to the door. The Mexican followed.

Out on the dock, the Mexican cracked his knuckles, though he looked nothing like a scrapper. His shirt and trousers were tight as a toreador's. "You," he said, and stuttered with indignation, "You think I gonna let you go filching my doll."

"Yep." Tom kept his eye on the guy's hands, in case of a shiv.

Florence said, "Don't let the big lunk scare you off, Carlos. There's always mañana, no?"

Proud Carlos swelled, rolled his shoulders, and braved a half step toward Tom. "Who you are?"

"I'm the guy who knows how to get you deported," Tom said.

The Mexican retreated. "Why you say I am no citizen?"

"One reason, citizens know you can do five years for even holding hands with jailbait."

"That so?"

The man attempted to redeem a portion of dignity with a disdainful scowl while he eased himself off the dock, before he vanished down the alley.

"One of these days, tough guy," Florence said, "you're gonna meet your match."

She stumbled on the steps, broke a heel as she landed in the alley, plucked off both glittery shoes and slung them over a fence. Then, while she used her long legs to stride ahead of her brother, a half dozen times she turned far enough to glare at him and holler.

"I've had it, Tom."

And, "That's the last straw."

He paid her little mind, furious as he was on account of her behavior standing between him and the chance to devote his precious little free time to investigating the Frank Gaines murder. After she ran dodging traffic across Third Street, accompanied by angry horns and wolf whistles, Tom caught up, grabbed her wrist, and wouldn't allow her to wrench away. He flagged a taxi.

A jitney pulled to the curb. Tom delivered Florence into the back seat and shut the door. Then he leaned on the open front window ledge and asked the driver to see his sister home and walk her to the door. The driver held out his palm. Tom rummaged through his pockets and billfold and came out with $2.50. Every cent he had, until Friday. As he gave it up, he made a point of studying the driver's face.

The cabby said, "It's jake, boss. I got a decent wife and three babies mean everything to me."

Tom watched the cab pull away before he entered the Top Hat. At the foot of the stairs, he asked Abe to go fetch Max.

The little man hustled up the stairs and disappeared into the speakeasy. A minute passed, then he poked his tall hat and his head out and waved to Tom.

The upstairs combo was jumping and swaying to "Sweet Georgia Brown." Abe held Tom by the arm, escorted him around the dancers and into a closet-sized room between the front windows and the bar.

Tom hadn't met Max Van Dam, though folks said he owned half the neighborhood. He sat behind a glossy cherry wood desk, a cigar stub between his ruby lips. The pearl buttons of his cowboy shirt glimmered. "Pull up a chair." He rasped a smoky laugh, no doubt because he occupied the room's only chair.

When Tom tried to introduce himself, the man waved him off. "Hey, I don't miss a Trojan game. What do you need, Tom?"

"Some answers is all."

"You want to give me the questions?"

"Frank Gaines, a colored fellow, got hanged from a tree in Echo Park."

"Yeah?"

"Rumors have got him working for bootleggers."

"And you're saying I associate with bootleggers. Smoke?"

Tom shook his head. "Any truth to the rumors?"

"What's your angle?"

"Frank did me plenty of favors, that's all. Look, Mister Van Dam, I'm not asking much here. Only for a clue whether I'm snooping in the right direction."

Out of nowhere, Max produced a match. He reached down and scratched it on something then lit the stub. "What's in it for me?"

"I've still got pals on the team. Say a halfback turns his ankle, steps on a nail, say I deliver the news and you adjust your bets accordingly, should you be a betting man."

Max reached across the desk for an ashtray and flicked his stub. "I place a bet now and then. Look here, Tom, about this colored chum of yours, you appear smart enough to put together, if Two Gun Davis don't want the news getting out, he don't want you snooping."

"Stands to reason."

"Maybe you read, a couple of Davis' bulls chopped down Sid Fitch, a rum runner, and three of his boys. In an alley over by Broadway and Figueroa."

"I got told about it."

"S'pose the coppers want rid of a bootlegger they can't get the goods on."

"They lynch him and hush it up?" Tom asked.

"Who'd put it past them? Not me."

"Where's the hush up get them?"

"Keep it in mind," Van Dam grumbled, as if he didn't like being stumped. "Give me a few days, come on back."

Tom thanked the man, hustled out of the office, past the dancers, down the stairs and outside. In hopes of catching Florence before she slipped out again, he loped all the way home.

He found her waiting in the parlor, wearing slacks, perched on the edge of a wooden chair flanked by an army duffel bag she had packed so full it looked bloated. Beside it lay a small leather case he bought her for a weekend in San Francisco, the only vacation he'd managed to afford since they ran from Milly.

He turned the other wooden chair to face hers and sat close enough so he could reach her if he decided to. "Leaving?"

"Think you can stop me?"

"No. Look, Sis, I believe you've got my intentions all wrong. I'm not anybody's jailer. Matter of fact, I've been thinking, we ought to pal around. I mean, soon as we get home from work, where I go, you go."

"Yeah? What's so delightful about where you go?"

"Well, tomorrow I figure we ought to catch Sister Aimee. I hear she puts on a show Buffalo Bill couldn't top."

Florence allowed a smile. "Did you hear about her bringing a camel on stage, testing whether it could squeeze through the eye of a needle? She's a cut up."

Tom chuckled, while his sister turned sober. "Tommy, you know darn well, we go there, we're liable to run into Mama."

"Suppose we do," he said, "it could mean livelier action than either of those dives you seem to favor."

"More blood and guts, anyway." She gave him a mischievous grin.

"Day after tomorrow," Tom said, "the band's in Santa Monica, booked at a swanky new beach club."

"Casa Del Mar?"

"You bet. Come along, I give you a tambourine and a share of the kitty."

"Casa Del Mar," she said. "Place like that's full of swells. Suppose I walk out of there with Fairbanks?"

"Miss Pickford'll chase you down and neuter the both of you."

"Okay, so much for Fairbanks. Suppose I fancy a nasty old oil man, maybe a Sinclair or Doheny, ask him to be my sugar daddy?"

Tom reached for her hands but she drew them back. He said, "Then I do to him like Pickford did to you and Fairbanks in the previous scenario."

She laughed from deep in her belly, then grabbed his waiting hand and pinched it with her sharp, crimson nails.

Chapter Ten

On Thursday, before he loaded the morning's orders and the block of dry ice into the box on the rear of the Alamo Meat truck, Tom went inside past the butchers already hacking and the sides of beef hanging from meat hooks, and into the offices. The secretary and bookkeeper had yet to arrive. The door to Mister Woods' office stood open.

Sam Woods was granddad old, barrel shaped, tall in torso and short-legged. His face at rest was rose-hued. When angry he turned crimson. Over five years now, he had treated Tom well, rewarding him with ever better jobs. Tom supposed the old man felt an affinity to him through Charlie Hickey. Like Charlie, Sam Woods apprenticed in the meat business as a Texas cowboy. All over the walls hung framed photographs of horses and rodeos.

He folded and laid down the *Times*, invited Tom to sit, and leaned back to listen, hands behind his thick neck. "How's the kid?" He meant Florence.

"Something of a hellion," Tom admitted.

"How old?"

"Seventeen next month."

"If she's like my offspring, the worst is yet to come."

"Boss," Tom said, "I've got to tell you, something's come up has me making a stop now and then on the route."

"So I reckoned, from the complaints."

"Complaints?"

"Don't take it hard, son. Only a couple. Go on, about this something?"

Tom pondered a moment and decided to trust the boss, at least half way. "An old pal of mine got killed. I'm helping locate folks who might afford clues to the murder."

"I see. And this pal got murdered is?"

"Colored fellow, used to keep me out of harm's way when Milly brought us to Azusa Street and went off carousing with the Holy Spirit."

Sam Woods leaned forward, palms down on the desk. "Fella's name was?"

"Frank Gaines," Tom said, and noticed the flush of the old man's cheeks and forehead. "You heard about him?"

"Where'd you say this murder happened?"

"Here in Los Angeles."

"That so? How'd I miss reading about it, when I go through the *Times* each day?"

"Didn't show up in the news," Tom said. "I got wind of it from a broadside I picked up."

Mister Woods shifted his jaw back and forth, a trick Bud Gallagher contended the old man picked up from cows. "Who puts out this broadside?"

"Beats me."

"Why believe it, then?"

"Good point," Tom said, although had he cared to argue, he might've asked the boss why he believed Harry Chandler's *Times*.

"Best left to the police."

The boss' narrowed eyes warned Tom to reveal no more. He said, "I ought to get on the road. What I meant to tell you, I'm going to buy any gas I use up, work early and late to make up any time. You can count on me, no more complaints."

The man's jaw still shifted, and his eyes remained narrowed. "I'm counting on it."

"One more thing, I'd like to take Florence to a hash house tonight. If you could authorize a draw against my paycheck, just a few dollars, we'd be grateful."

Woods reached for a pen and scrap of paper and scribbled on it. As he handed it across the desk, he said, "Give it to Ruby. And mark my words, this town's got three first-class dailies with dozens of reporters looking for a scoop, none of them likely to pass up a murder. This colored fella, he's gone for a holiday. I expect right about now he's sitting on the bank of a stream, bare feet dangling in the water. Now, who'd you say you're helping out, rounding up clues for?"

Tom attempted to make his answer sound congenial. "He wouldn't want me to say."

"Well, that's no business of mine. On the other hand, fact is, you're a talented youngster, with a football, and that instrument you play, so I hear. But you're no policeman."

"Yes sir. I certainly am not." He heard a chair roll in the lobby behind him. "Ruby came in. Thank you, sir."

Tom went to the front office, gave Ruby the note, took the five dollars and hustled around the building to load his truck. After he'd loaded, he sat in the cab for some minutes reviewing thoughts that rose during the talk with Sam Woods.

One, the task he'd accepted was madness. He could imagine no answer that excluded the *Times*, the *Examiner*, or the LAPD from the cast of conspirators.

In a modern history class he'd learned that William Randolph Hearst had instigated, and Harry Chandler championed, the Spanish American War. Without their prodding, Roosevelt wouldn't have launched it.

The police had their tommy-guns. The news tycoons had the power and voice. Tom had nothing and nobody. He might as well be a recruit in the army of some banana republic who was trying to single-handedly orchestrate a coup.

Chapter Eleven

All morning, he stewed about Mister Woods. At first, he couldn't quite decipher why the meeting turned his stomach queasy, but soon enough he reasoned it out. The only men he'd ever looked to as substitutes for Charlie Hickey were Frank Gaines, Leo Weiss, Mister Woods, and Bud Gallagher. Now Frank was gone. Two of the others, when he asked for help, instead tried to unnerve him. Leaving only Bud.

If he needed to choose between hunting Frank's murderer and selling meat, Tom would be out of a job. Which meant broke. He could find work, but none that would pay enough to keep Florence in school, or earn her respect, without which he'd never persuade her to give up playing vamp.

He decided to make only one extra stop that day.

In place of a lunch break, he drove downtown. From Pico, he followed the roads less blocked, but still found the need to swerve, jump on the brakes, and inch his truck between double-parked wagons and terrified Nebraskans who'd never gained the bravado daily traffic taught. As he inched past a cart, the way the horse whinnied and bucked, Tom feared he'd scraped the poor beast's foot.

From Figueroa, he swung left onto Sixth then cut up Olive, which he followed past Pershing Square, where he sometimes enjoyed meandering among the folks clustered around the bronze cavalryman. He imagined they came to the square to seek the elusive promise by sampling the rants of raw food worshipers, advocates of universal nudity, prophets declaring the drift of the southland toward its destiny as a Pacific Island, and boosters offering shares in oil property or residential lots along some projected auto or rail artery for ten or twelve dollars a month.

He turned on Fourth then on Broadway because he held fond memories of his trips, researching for a term paper, through the Bradbury Building. With admiration, he recalled its sky-lit central court, cage elevators surrounded by grillwork, and floral patterned wrought iron once displayed at the Chicago World's Fair.

His destination was the Hall of Records at Broadway and Temple. On his first trip around the block he noticed a police truck discharging escorted prisoners in front of the courthouse. Next trip around, the police were pulling away, leaving a space for Tom.

Beyond the lawn with its bushes cut to spell "Court House," he climbed the steps and entered the Hall of Records. Such a bedlam of noise filled the main corridor, he wished the architect had studied acoustics at USC under Professor Korngold. He passed lines of heavy-footed builders carrying plans, shopkeepers grousing about license fees, and cooing mothers, some of whom cradled their infants as if they feared an official would snatch them away.

When he found a door lettered "Archives," he went in.

Tom enjoyed the smell of old paper, in libraries, bookstores, and in the Archives lobby. He stood in front of the counter savoring while he asked himself how someone in the know would begin a search for death certificates, marriage licenses, deeds, or whatever might give him something about Frank Gaines.

He glanced at the counter and noticed the clerk staring. A redhead with a china white face, arms adorned with a few delicate and well-placed freckles, and a smile that implied she knew the way to paradise.

She said, "I'm here to help, and I'm plenty good at it."

Tom wondered how much longer he would need to renounce women for the sake of Florence and music.

"What'll it be?" she asked.

"For starters, how about telling me what I'm able to see."

"Depends." She allowed a long moment, probably in case he cared to imagine what her cooperation might depend upon. "What are you? Police? Lawyer? Or just some good looking stiff passing the time?"

Tom knew he didn't lie well. Besides, he hadn't thought of a story any better than the truth. "A pal of mine got murdered."

"Sorry." She lowered her eyes. "That's a tough one."

"Yes ma'am."

She leaned forward, made her silky voice softer, and beckoned him with a red tipped finger. "Tell me more."

Tom rested his elbows on the counter. "If I do, you'll help me out?"

She looked both ways and over his shoulder. Then she whispered, "See, some of us *are* civil servants, play by the rules. The rest of us, it's only an act."

"Lucky for me."

"Righteo."

Tom saw no need to mention the lynching or cover-up. "The morning of Monday, October fifteenth, Franklin Gaines was found dead in Echo Park. Anything I can turn up might help."

She reached under the counter for an "Out to Lunch" placard and placed it on the counter. "Follow me, comrade."

While Tom followed, he commanded his eyes to avoid her swaying hips. His eyes wouldn't obey. Her sunny yellow skirt was cotton yet it clung to every wondrous swell, contraction, and ripple.

The archives were windowless. The overhead bulbs gave off no more light than candles would. The hallway was hardly wider than his shoulders, the rooms off it small and crowded with dusty shelves and file cabinets. Tom sneezed. The redhead blessed him.

"If I came in here without a guide," he said, "I might never find my way out."

"It's a puzzle. They might not find us for days." She gave him a wink. "How would you like that?"

Tom felt a fever rising. "You'd consider a rain check?"

"Well, I like a guy sticks to business. You talk to his neighbors yet?"

"I don't know where he lived."

She entered a room and peered down a row of files, pulled one open, rooted through it. "Doesn't own any real property. He married?"

"Could be. We lost touch some time ago."

He followed her back to the hall and two rooms deeper into the labyrinth. Again she peered and rooted then turned and shook her head. "Never married, not in Los Angeles anyway. When'd you say he turned up dead?"

"Monday, ten days ago."

"He could've got filed by now." She led him down the hall to a room with a plaque above the doorway. "The Dead." Like a story a mousy girl who tailed him around USC gave him to read.

"Anybody named Colleen work here?"

"Nope," she said without looking up from the file drawer. Tom stood admiring the nape of her neck below the bobbed hair.

"He's probably in transit," she said. "I'll do some snooping. You got a telephone."

The winsome smile made him wish he'd attended to Florence's pleading and leased a telephone. "You can call Fairfax 1972, ask for Leo. He'll know where to find me."

"Fairfax 1972. Got it." She batted her eyes and swished past him into the hall.

In the lobby, a half dozen folks waited in line at her counter. Tom thanked her. They shook hands and traded names. She was Madeline. She winked goodbye.

"Madeline," Tom said, "you've got quite an arsenal."

"Why thank you, Tom." Her emerald eyes twinkled. "A girl likes to feel appreciated."

Tom walked outside with spirits boosted, though he had no right to, as he'd learned nothing. Then he glanced across Temple Street.

A couple yards from the Broadway corner, a man leaned against the construction barricade, gazing over the other pedestrians. Though the man wore his homburg pulled low, Tom recognized the temple usher, the driver of a tan Nash. Maybe the guy who bullied the kid into shooting.

Tom broke into a sprint that concluded after he saw the bus. He threw head and shoulders back, and used a double straight-arm to keep from plowing into the vehicle, which belonged to the police.

Chapter Twelve

After parking his meat truck in the Alamo lot and swabbing out the icebox, Tom hustled through the butcher shop. He was on his way to the gents' until Bud Gallagher called, "Tom," and waved him over.

Usually, when they met in the shop, Gallagher tossed him a new gag line or a hunk of entrails Tom needed to catch or suffer the consequences. Today Bud wore a face as grim as his bloody apron.

"Make it quick," Tom said. "I've got to iron my shoelaces."

"Get on with it then, and meet me out back."

Tom used the gents', scrubbed away the day's grit and gore, then weaved around the butcher counters, dodging bloody splatters and hoping Bud would offer a clue or tip about the investigation. He supposed the boss had consulted Gallagher about his pursuit of the murderer.

Bud was waiting beside his Chevrolet coupe parked against the high chain fence beyond which a lineup of trucks crept toward the produce market. He said, "I hear you're playing Sherlock." He sat on the running board.

Tom nodded and joined him. The car tipped their way, as they were big men. They sat close, to hear over the trucks' roars and rattles.

"Thing is," Bud said, "you're getting a swelled head if you think you're such a scrapper you can take on what the police aren't willing to."

Tom, impatient with getting reminded how incapable he was, allowed his voice a note of disrespect. "What would you have me do, Bud?"

"For one, ask yourself what are the chances your old pal didn't have it coming."

Tom's scowl changed Gallagher's tune. "Okay, say he didn't have it coming. Say you get a line on the killer. Now what? You mean to call in the police, the same folks who already didn't give a damn?"

Tom shook his head, wishing he believed the police didn't give a damn.

"Then what?" Bud demanded. "You planning to fix him on your own?"

Tom said, "I find him, I'll come ask your opinion. Meantime, I'm looking for answers, not criticism."

Gallagher stood and loomed like the Phantom of the Opera in a movie Florence insisted her brother come to the Egyptian for. "I got one more piece of criticism. When a friend's looking out for you, you don't spit in his eye. Now get up off my car."

Tom obliged. "Question?"

"Yeah."

"Do you know something I don't?"

"If I do, it's not for you to know."

Gallagher hopped into his Chevrolet, fired it up and drove off. Tom stood and watched, ruefully deciding if he couldn't trust Gallagher, Mister Woods, or Leo, he would make a point of trusting nobody.

As he rounded the building toward the vendors and Japanese chatter on San Julian Street, he asked himself whether Woods and Bud were holding back answers, like he believed. Or maybe a guy with a lively imagination made a bum investigator.

By the time Florence dressed, then changed at her brother's insistence, and primped until her hair not only featured a perfect flip just above her shoulders but also had gotten even wavier than Tom's, they missed the six p.m. streetcar.

Ten minutes later, the next one arrived. They crammed themselves on board. Then Florence said, "Tommy, what do you think Milly will do? About us showing up at her church, I mean."

"They've got about twenty of these services a week. Odds of her being there tonight are slender."

"Odds of her finding out we came are damned good."

A woman with a prim and doughy face gave Florence a "shame on you" look. Florence leaned her way and opened her mouth. Tom cupped his hand over it.

They reached the Temple in time to get seated in the second balcony. The moment they sat, Florence began to squirm. Tom wondered if, no matter that she could sit entranced through a Sister Aimee radio broadcast, actual churchgoing conjured more visions of Milly than his sister could abide.

Tonight featured a choir of forty or so in scarlet robes, and a full orchestra of whose expertise Tom heartily approved. As the orchestra struck up the opening phrase of the third piece, Tom caught the melody right away.

It wasn't a number he expected out of Sister Aimee. But she came sweeping down the ramp in a dark blue caped uniform. She wore a Civil War cap and carried a Union flag on a short pole. She waved it above her while she took the solo on "Battle Hymn of the Republic."

Tom knew most of the words, but a verse he didn't recall both tripped and intrigued him.

> "I have read a fiery gospel
> writ in burnished rows of steel.
> 'As you deal with my conviverous soul
> with you my grace shall deal.'
> Let the hero born of woman
> crush the serpent with his heel.'
> His truth is marching on."

Tom was a reader who possessed a well-stocked vocabulary, but it didn't include "conviverous." He reached for the pocket note pad and pen he'd carried since becoming an investigator. As he finished jotting the word, Florence leaned over and whispered she needed to powder her nose.

He let her go.

Sister Aimee claimed she had recently prayed for a revived spirit and been answered by an astonishing vision of the coming rapture and of the heavenly choir and orchestra of angels descending to accompany the saints in their journey home.

Tom got distracted watching for Florence to return. Then he heard the preacher exclaim, "The Lord put His hand to His mouth and gave a shout, and every angel struck his harp of gold and sounded upon the silver trumpets. For years, artists have sought the lost chord. But, oh, surely never was a chord of such wondrous, melodious beauty as this."

Tom began to fret and think he should've followed Florence and waited outside the powder room. He scanned the aisles on the ground floor, then decided to go find the wayward girl before she enchanted some yokel having a smoke out front. He imagined her persuading the fellow salvation could wait until his billfold got thinner, and meanwhile, they should go out dancing.

He tiptoed and pardoned his way to the aisle, found his way to the side-by-side lavatories, and waited a few minutes before a gal dressed as if for a barn dance approached. He asked, if she found a blonde wearing beige and a cocked sailor cap in the ladies' room, tell her to make it snappy. Then he waited until the gal came out and reported no Florence.

Outside, all he encountered were latecomers and a few lost souls peeping and listening through the open doorways.

Soon the congregation began to file out. Tom wandered from one exit to the next. When he saw a shiny outfit, the color Florence had settled on after her big brother nixed the slinkier purple one, he fixed on it. The dish inside the outfit wasn't Florence. But she held his attention long enough so that when he turned and commenced wandering, he nearly stepped on the boots of the bouncer.

The man squinted his eye under its swollen brow. He began to gnaw on something.

"Well now," Tom said, "shall we talk here or go across the street?"

The bouncer spoke from the side of his mouth, without wasting breath, like a ventriloquist working his dummy. "What's to talk about?"

"How about why you tailed me in a Nash, loitered across the street from the Hall of Records and beat it when I spotted you, and why you bluffed a kid into firing a shot my way. Or we could skip all that and go right to you coming clean on the lynching." He pointed across the street at the hanging tree.

The man rocked back and forth, heel to toe. "You're talking crazy," he said.

"Hey, let's go over by the tree, jog your memory."

The bouncer eyed him head to toe, probably looking for his weakness. "That's the way you want it."

As they stepped off the curb, Tom saw Leo striding toward them, rounding the temple from the Glendale Boulevard side. He stopped and waited. As Leo neared, Tom saw he had Florence in tow.

He didn't notice the bouncer leave. But he was gone.

Tonight, Leo looked sober and on the alert. When he reached Tom, he let go of Florence and squared off. "What's with bringing a kid along when you go out looking for trouble?"

Florence tapped Leo's arm. "Trouble? We're at a church for Christ sake."

Tom moved to her side. "Shhh." To Leo he said, "You just happen by? Or did you come to get converted?"

"Maybe I'm watching your back," Leo said.

"Yeah, well then you saw the mug I was chatting with, right?"
"Yeah."

"So who is he? Why'd he beat it when you showed?"

Leo shook his head and put his arm around Florence's shoulders. "She's going with me, Tom. Are you coming?"

"Hold on," Florence said. "I'm going to stand here and scream bloody murder unless one of you jokers lets me in on the secret."

"Fair enough," Tom said, his eyes fixed on Leo's. "I'm helping the cops solve a murder."

After Leo glanced around and scratched his chin, he nodded. "Tom'll tell you all he's allowed to, once we're in the car."

Chapter Thirteen

Tom often took his Friday lunch break on a bench near the entrance to the new Central Library. He ate while gazing up at the pyramid tower with suns on either side, and at the severed hand holding the Light of Learning torch. The bold design of the place made him dream of a windfall so he could return to college and finish the architecture degree.

After a cheese or meatloaf sandwich and an apple, he always entered the wondrous building and checked out books. History, biography, novels. Or something Florence requested or he hoped might pique her interest, maybe keep her home some evenings.

Today, he hustled through the rotunda with its glossy chessboard floors, passed beneath the solar system chandelier, and rode the elevator to the spacious reference room. The high ceiling crossed by heavy beams and the mahogany tables, each with a lamp of its own, made him feel as if he'd earned a scholarship to the university of his dreams.

He found a table devoted to dictionaries. He sat and picked up a Webster's, turned to the C pages and searched for "conviverous." No citation. An Oxford proved no more useful. Three others also failed him. He might've spent all afternoon, there were that many dictionaries. Besides, he wanted to scan every newspaper of the past few weeks for clues about why the *Times* and *Examiner*, meaning Hearst and Chandler, would conspire on a cover up. From what he knew about those tycoons, he'd have been less surprised if one had shot the other in a duel.

But he was due to deliver a tub of ground round to El Cholo café. Anyway, he'd studied Latin at Hollywood High School and at USC. It didn't take all of that to decipher a meaning for "converous." He translated the word to mean "inclined to live in harmony with all." In the context of the Civil War anthem, it meant welcoming and respecting all races. So the lines, "as you deal with my converous soul with you my grace shall deal," warned that God's grace got meted out to those who fought for the good of all, and got withheld from those who kept their brothers enslaved.

Which accorded with a Sister Aimee story he'd read, about a service during which dozens of Klansmen trooped in. Sister watched until they were seated. Then she announced that God had just given her a story to tell, and she gently related a tale about an old negro who passed by a church from which glorious music streamed. The old fellow walked in, stood in the rear, and soon found himself ushered back outside. He sat on a step in dejection. A stranger came and sat beside him. "Don't feel sad, my brother," the stranger said. "I too have been trying to get into that church, for many, many years."

Of course, from her description of the stranger, everyone knew he was Christ. So the Klansmen rose and filed out of the temple.

Not long afterward, several men in work clothes arrived and seated themselves in pews the Klansmen had vacated. And the next morning, hoods and sheets were found littering Echo Park.

As Tom re-stacked the dictionaries, he wondered about the visitors who hadn't shed their hoods that evening, and how Sister might've turned the Klan from fans into enemies.

He determined to make the preacher's acquaintance, and judge for himself if her heart was as big as she let on. Maybe he'd learn whether, while her passionate contralto belted "Battle Hymn of the Republic," she was sending a clue about the lynching. Or a message to the murderer.

Chapter Fourteen

A booking in the Colonnade Ballroom at Casa del Mar in Santa Monica made Tom feel like a celebrity. With its ocean view balconies, Venetian chandeliers, and dance floor waxed to a glittery sheen, the club only catered to the city's high and mighty. As Tom informed his sister, anybody might come strolling in. Chaplin, Pickford, Keaton, even Hearst. Though Tom was no fan of big shots, he wouldn't have felt any prouder if they'd gotten a call to play Roseland.

He couldn't recall Florence ever looking quite so wide-eyed and enchanted. The hours spent on her hair and makeup somehow caused the powders, oils, and paints to vanish. They only served to highlight her lusciousness. Tom had let her wear a snug item of blue velvet, sleeveless and cut to exhibit shoulders and too much chest, and hemmed above the knees with tassels. She had created and stitched a head wrap out of a swatch from her dress where she lifted the hem. A triangle, pleated and starched, waved out on one side, like a flag. Not one of the debs in attendance caught men's eyes like she did.

Archie the drummer asked Tom if he and Florence had the same mother. Rex the pianist said, "She got the looks, you got the what?"

"The hair," Tom said. "Mine's wavy, hers is straight as a straw, before the curlers."

Oz and Ernestine came strutting in through the lobby, probably against house protocol. Tom smiled at their moxie, even while a few of the swells shot indignant glances his way.

Oz split off from his gal and came directly to Tom, rummaging in his pocket. "You going keep this a righteous secret, between you and me and nobody. You hear?"

"I sure do," Tom said.

"Nobody. Not Ernestine. Not that sweet baby you try and make all us believe be your sister." The note he'd pulled out of his pocket he held at his side.

Tom vowed, "Nobody." Then Oz slipped him the note.

It read, "Sugar Hill Barber Shop. Ask for Socrates." Tom felt a rush of exuberance. Finding the broadside publisher would lead him somewhere, at least.

He returned to the stage and suffered the usual anxieties. Half the horn section slinked in at the last minute, straightened their shirts, kicked sand off their shoes, and snickered as though to boast they'd been down on the beach sharing a flask.

He'd built the evening's repertoire around numbers whose melodies everybody heard at the movies. He waved his baton and kept one eye on his sister. Through "Rockaway Baby" and "Ain't We Got Fun," she glided around the ballroom like a trout circling a feast of lures and flies. By the fourth number, "It Had to Be You," she'd let herself get hooked.

The fellow was younger than most of the crowd, though twice Florence's age. From his hair, sandy colored and shiny, Tom suspected he dropped by the barbershop every morning for a trim and scalp rub. He sported a Fairbanks mustache, a boater's tan, a Gabardine suit, and patent leather shoes. He danced like a prince and floated Tom's sister around the floor through "Just Because You're You," and "The World is Waiting for the Sunrise." Whenever he cut her loose for a shimmy, Tom got tempted to leap off the bandstand and throw his coat around her.

With the last verse of "It's Up to You," she appeared to hang limp in the fellow's arms. Tom called an early break.

Even so, even while the couple turned and watched Tom's approach, the fellow's arms stayed looped around her shoulders.

Tom caught a glimpse of three men in black and white coming in from the ocean view balcony. He supposed they were waiters, and that they would fan out to serve club members and guests the tonic and soda waters they could fortify with the Scotch and Cuban rum they'd smuggled in.

He didn't suspect foul play until, when he was a few steps short of Florence and her Romeo, he felt sharp pressure on the small of his back.

A reedy voice said, "Need a word with you, Hickey."

The men stayed behind where he couldn't see even by crooking his head around. The blade kept jabbing his back. While somebody's hands steered him toward the balcony exit, he expected at least a couple musicians to notice and come running. Nobody came.

A few steps outside the French doors, stairs led off the balcony to a wide sandy beach. As they started down, two of the men came alongside and grabbed his arms. The guy on his right had a jutting chin and gray streak in his hair. Tom didn't recognize him. The one squeezing his left arm kept his face angled away. All Tom could note of him were a bull neck, a peculiarly small ear, and glossy black hair.

At the base of the stairs, two guys in all black stood waiting.

Tom lunged ahead and to his right, hoping to dive over the rail, but the graying guy held on and got plowed into the rail, which cracked and gave out. The two of them pitched over the edge and caromed off a stone wall before they hit the beach. Tom scrambled to find his footing. One knee buckled. Then the two guys in black appeared, between him and the open beach.

One of them looked bigger and tougher by half than any team's lineman. The other held a pistol. His arm was cocked, the gun barrel up, alongside his shoulder.

The big one threw a punch at Tom's head. He ducked, but an uppercut caved his belly. And something harder than a fist whopped him in the left temple. He folded.

A half dozen feet took shots at his ribs, kidney, and neck. But Tom's eyes never shifted off the pistol.

Chapter Fifteen

Tom knew his sister's scream. It came accompanied by clacks and clomps on the wooden stairs. The men in black and the ones dressed as waiters fled, kicking up flurries of sand.

Florence took charge. She sent somebody to alert the musicians then stooped, helped Tom to his knees, softly demanded to know what hurt, and petted his cheek and hair.

When some of the boys came running, she took Rex the pianist aside. Knowing Rex had stood in for Tom before, she asked him to lead the band and explain to whomever cared that a sudden, severe stomach pain had sent her brother to the hospital. Probably a result of his football career.

Her dancing partner, who called himself Pablo, proved strong enough to keep Tom upright and serve as a crutch all the way up the path that led from the beach to the sidewalk. He delivered Tom into a car like none he'd entered since he moonlighted as a bell hop at the Ambassador and a valet sidekick of his took him for a spin. The upholstery reminded Tom of a certain USC coed, especially the flesh of her neck, beneath her silky hair.

Florence sat in back where she could cradle her brother's tender and throbbing head. Once they got settled, she explained she had thought Tom followed the men to the balcony to talk business. She said Pablo insisted he and Florence tag along, because he wanted to meet her brother before the music called him back, let him know he was on the up and up. "See, Tommy," she said. "We better thank Pablo, on account of he probably saved your life. Who were those monkeys, anyway?"

"Beats me," Tom mumbled.

"No bushwah," she said. "Don't make me nag it out of you."

"Give me a chance to think."

Pablo sped through Beverly Hills on Wilshire, Tom knew because he glimpsed the dome of the new cinema with its mosque-like dome. The fellow, had Tom been an objective observer, would've passed any gentleman test. He obeyed Tom's command to forget hospitals and doctors and just take him home. He spoke softly, called Tom "Sir." He helped Tom up the path, into the cottage, all the way to his bed, following Florence's directions. Then he wished Tom and his sister well, and without so much as inviting her to step outside for a smooch, said goodbye and made a swift exit.

"Who is that guy?" Tom asked.

"An oil man. He's got plenty of shares in few gushers out by Long Beach."

"Don't they all."

"Sure, only Pablo's got the automobile to prove it."

She peeled off Tom's bloody shirt and trousers, then ran for a bowl of soapy water. She soaked and patted his wounds and used her sharp nails to pluck grains of sand from them. Though he ordered her to quit fussing, she ran to the Villegas' cottage, returned with a bottle of Mercurochrome, blotched him with it, and shushed him whenever he bothered to complain.

Once she desisted and tucked him in, Tom said, "I don't like your Pablo knowing where we live."

"Crying out loud, Tommy," she said, "look on the sunny side. Don't you think it was worth getting whipped to take a ride in a Rolls Silver Ghost?"

"I didn't get whipped."

"You look whipped to me."

"Whipped is when you lose a fight. I just got started."

"Got started?"

"Round one," he mumbled while massaging his jaw.

"If I go borrow a Bible, are you willing to swear you don't know why they came and jumped you?"

"Go get it," he said.

"You got some shady business on the side? Say pedaling Mary Jane to the nightclub crowd? Or how about the murder you're helping Leo on? That it?"

"Thanks for babying me, kiddo," Tom said.

She sat on the bed, used the washcloth to daub an ooze of blood from his brow. Then she picked up his hand and kissed the palm. "Tommy?"

"Yeah?"

"One of those guys that went running off. I think I saw him last night, taking in the Sister Aimee show."

Chapter Sixteen

Next morning on the streetcar, Tom eased the pains by telling himself he'd gotten at least this bruised and aching from the 1924 USC vs. Stanford game. But the walk from the Wilshire stop to Leo's convinced him football was a rather gentle sport. The walk sapped his last trickle of power. Instead of staggering to the door, he lowered himself onto the steps. He reached for a fallen pine cone, tossed it over his shoulder at the door, then slumped and waited.

Leo came out while straightening his trousers. Shirtless except for his union suit, he joined Tom on the steps.

Tom glanced over. "Who looks worse, you or me?"

"You."

"Your eyes are worse. At least I got some sleep."

"How's a guy supposed to sleep when he's worried about a pal who's in way over his head?"

"I presume you mean me."

"Who did it?"

"Did what?"

"Took you down to the beach and stomped on you."

"I intend to find out. How about I start with you telling me who got word to you?"

"A cop who rats on his sources isn't worth much."

"Yeah, sure. And this source didn't say who the tough guys are, or who they belong to?"

"Coffee?"

"If you lace it with something besides sugar."

Tom rubbed various parts, avoided others, wondered how deep the deepest of his bruises went, and if some miracle had kept bones from breaking. He imagined numerous bones had cracked and would splinter with his next exertion.

Leo returned and handed him a tall mug. He sipped, then gulped, and sighed with the heat coursing through him. "It's not gin."

"Canadian whiskey," Leo said.

"A bribe, or something you boys confiscated?"

Leo ignored the crack. "Ready to give up?"

"I don't give up."

"You ever read about the gold rush?"

Tom glared. "What?"

"*Desperado*, Joaquin Murieta. Heard of him?"

"So what if I have?"

"The guy that took him down, hacked off his head, pickled it, sold it for a side show. A bounty hunter named Harry Love. Heard of him?"

"Has this saga got a moral?"

"A detective I know says he's Harry's great grandson. Tall fellow, squints, wears a homburg, drives a Nash."

"Whew," Tom said, and clutched the step beside him while some dizziness passed. "Now we're getting somewhere."

"Name's Fenton Love."

"Chief Davis put him onto me?"

"That I can't tell you."

"Can't or won't?"

"What I can tell you, Fenton's mean." Leo grimaced then scowled, as if a he'd gotten hit in a sore spot. He turned away, plodded to the kitchen, and returned with a refilled mug. "Suppose they get to Florence?"

A charge of fury surged up from Tom's belly and radiated all through him. He pushed to his feet, paced up the walkway to the sidewalk and back, then stopped and leaned over Leo.

"Pass the word, to Fenton Love and who all else needs to hear, anybody does my sister wrong, they're going to need to kill me. So they might as well skip over Florence and get on with it."

Leo watched Tom while he fished a pack of Lucky Strikes and matches out of his pocket, tapped a cigarette out of the pack, and lit up. "Wouldn't stop Fenton."

"So," Tom said, trying not to snarl, "looks to me like you're going to have to choose one team or the other."

"And do what?"

"Talk," Tom snapped. "You know plenty. You sent Vi home to mama. Something's eating you, making you sit up all night. I say it's the lynching."

"Then let me set you straight," Leo said. "I don't *know* a damned thing about any lynching or any cover up, but I've got ideas. That's all. And I didn't send Vi anywhere. She left to make a point. You want to hear it?"

"Sure."

"She doesn't like me drinking."

"And why the drinking?"

"Because I'm a cop. Cops do things nobody ought to have to. Now, I came as clean as I'm going to. You tell me, what is it about this Frank Gaines that makes him worth dying over?"

In Tom's condition, thinking didn't come easy, though finishing his coffee helped. "Suppose some Jew hater knocked you off. I should leave it to the law?"

"Makes sense, doesn't it, when they've got the weapons and jails and all?"

"Sure, and they drop the ball, then what? See, when a kid's got no father, and some fellow steps in and treats him like he counts as much as anybody does, the kid owes that fellow a debt of gratitude deeper than he'd owe his own father."

"The kid owes nothing," Leo said. "If the fellow did it to get paid back, he's a bum."

"Even so, he did it. And he didn't owe the kid a blessed thing."

"Tom, suppose you follow this murder into hell and come out alive and you know beyond a doubt which creep or mob of them lynched Frank Gaines. You aim to kill him? Or them?"

Tom said, "What would you do?"

The way Leo crushed his half-smoked Lucky on the step, he could've been declaring war. "If I knew that, maybe I wouldn't be drinking."

"Huh? I don't make the connection."

"So forget it," Leo said as he turned toward the bedrooms.

Chapter Seventeen

Leo drove Tom to Alamo Meat, where he used the office telephone and promised customers to deliver tomorrow. Or, if they didn't open Sundays, then before eight a.m. on Monday. The arrangements freed time he meant to use hunting down the broadside publisher.

To avoid butchers' questions about his looks, he exited through the Alamo façade in front and rounded the building to his truck. All morning, he drove, lugged meat, and endured the repeated indignity of lying about the welts, scabbing cuts, and bruises, most of which Florence had painted red.

Back at Alamo Meat, he rounded the building, avoided the butchers, and escaped unseen by anyone except Ruby the bookkeeper. Crossing Eleventh, while he dodged a truck from the Imperial Valley, one from the San Joaquin missed by inches sending him to oblivion, perdition, or paradise.

He took the red line down Central to Jefferson, all the way summoning the willpower, football trained, to replace the smidgen of strength he'd possessed before he spent it on the meat route. But his first step off the car proved the summons had failed. His knee buckled and landed him in the gutter. He climbed to the sidewalk and limped past a tobacco shop, a second hand store, and a vendor of oranges and shoelaces to the address on the note Oz had given him.

Sugar Hill Barber Shop was a three-chair establishment that still featured the mahogany bar and swivel stools from its days as a saloon. Before Tom crossed the threshold, a grinning barber cheered, "Sweet Lord, you going let me get my hands on that wavy yellow hair?"

"Depends," Tom said.

The barber's grin vanished. "Oh do it?"

"Depends if you're going to send a word to Socrates."

The barber's supple face went cold and hawkish, as if Tom had come to sell him scissors that never dulled, or a miracle tonic. Tom said, "I want to give him a story."

After a minute of studying as though he could read minds, the barber turned to the bar and called, "Get on out here, rascal."

A boy crept from behind the bar, his hands full of marbles. "Scooter," the barber said, "you go fetch Socrates."

"Where he at?"

"Just you find him. The man going give you a nickel."

The boy crammed marbles into his pockets and approached Tom, palm up. Tom gave him a dime. The boy ran out.

"Sit down, young man," the barber said. "I can make you look like Barrymore. Shave too?"

"I've got my own razor."

The barber chuckled and covered him in a sheet. Even before the first snip, spectators appeared. They formed a crowd in the doorway and watched as if they suspected the barber might cut more than just hair. Tom wondered how many of them knew about Frank Gaines.

The boy came in and returned to his lair behind the bar. Tom watched a long-necked fellow who'd joined the rear of the crowd. His skin was dark and rough, nappy hair parted in the middle, which made ridges along both sides. He wore rimless glasses and a suit coat over a lacy shirt. As he didn't appear to be aiming for anonymity, Tom supposed he wasn't the anonymous publisher.

The barber held out a mirror for Tom's approval. When Tom had dismounted from the chair, given the barber a quarter, and gone to perch on a bar stool, the long-necked fellow came and joined him.

"I don't pay for stories," the man said. His voice, wistful and unhurried, reminded Tom of a balladeer's.

"Fair enough. My story isn't worth a thing, except to me. It started on Azusa Street, almost twenty years ago. Care to hear it, Socrates?"

The publisher rested both arms on the bar behind him, ready to listen, as was the barber, leaning on the arm of the nearest chair.

The publisher kept a stoic expression while Tom tried to recall to life the mission and the little boy who witnessed the "saints" heave, thrash, and make eerie harmonies out of howls, pleas, and incantations in a bedlam of sounds they called tongues.

Tom's story gave a clear message. While the "saints" considered Christ their savior, his personal savior was Frank Gaines.

The publisher held up a hand. "Brother, you want justice for Frank. That what it is?"

Tom nodded. "But it's taking too long to get to first base. One problem, I don't believe your story about the gentleman out for a stroll. That particular morning, the newsboys called it a deluge."

Socrates smiled. The telephone on the wall gave a startling clang, which called the barber away from his post.

"Who brought you the story?" Tom asked.

"I'll stand on what I wrote."

"Give me something else then. An amigo of Frank's, his family, where he worked, went to church, drank, or whatever he did."

The publisher reached into his coat for a steno pad. He scribbled, tore off a sheet, folded it into fourths, and handed it over. "Go to his house, talk to his neighbors. Ask and keep asking till the truth comes, you hear?" His eyes fixed on Tom's and gave his words the weight of advice about how to live. "You find the answer, come to Socrates." He handed Tom the steno pad. "Put down your name and where I can find you."

Tom obliged. He and the publisher shook hands. On the way out, he saluted the barber.

"Get ready, young man," the barber said. "Gals can't help it, they be grabbing at your hair."

Tom would've gone directly to the Frank Gaines address, except he felt the need to check on his sister, whom he imagined cruising in a Rolls Royce Silver Ghost.

By the time he arrived at his court, walking upright or straight was out of the question. He weaved along the path hoping the stab of cholla needles might effect a cure quacks in Chinatown charge for. But the cholla let him pass unpunctured. Maybe it was conscious, like Milly used to say plants were. Maybe it pitied him.

He staggered into the cottage and found Florence showing off a new slinky dress to Bud Gallagher. On the edge of the couch, hands on his lap, Bud wore the sober face with which a prudent older fellow should assess seventeen-year-old beauties.

Tom sat in the wooden chair. Gallagher said, "You look worse than Flo let on. Are you going to live?"

"You bring me news? Or flowers?"

Gallagher turned to the girl. "Honey, you want to get out of earshot for a while, I'd be pleased."

"Aw, Bud, I get a rise of raw jokes. I'm a big girl, aren't I?"

Tom pointed the way to her bedroom. "Try on something down to the ankles."

Florence huffed and sashayed into her room. Bud waited for the door to click shut. Then he leaned toward Tom. "I've been thinking. And judging by what you ran into last night, I wish I had started thinking sooner."

"Just give it to me, Bud."

"It's about Mister Woods."

"Yeah?"

"Well, it's nothing I'd want to get around. Only for your ears." He glanced toward Florence's bedroom and lowered his voice. "Mister Woods may very well belong to the Klan."

"God, no."

"Now, it may be talk, and no more. But look here, Sam's an old cowboy, brought up poor, could've heard so much hate, it got into his blood. Tom, I'd bet the bank he didn't have a thing to do with lynching Frank Gaines. But, life being what it is, I would advise, watch what you do and say around that man."

Chapter Eighteen

Tom got a promise from Florence. She would stay home that evening if he did. She made a stew, boiled the beef and vegetables soft on account of his sore jaw. She fed him while he reclined on the couch, shifting this way and that to give each pain a moment's relief. Afterward, she helped him into bed and tucked him in, then ran next door and borrowed a handful of aspirin from Tomasina Ornelas, who used the stuff for her rheumatism. Florence brought her brother pills and water, and pulled a chair up next to his bed.

"You're going to tell me a bedtime story?" Tom asked.

"Depends."

"Uh oh."

"You're going to tell me all the secrets?" she coaxed.

"Can't."

"Okay, maybe not all, but you can let go some of them."

Tom sought for a morsel to give her, something that would placate without putting in danger a girl apt to talk before thinking and prone to trust too easily. "Tomorrow we're going to church," he said. "When we find the guy you recognized, I'll get some answers."

"And you'll cut me in?"

"On what?"

"Answers. Promise?"

"Yeah. Now scram, let me sleep. And, you hear anything funny, anybody coming up the walk, you wake me up. And get my old Louisville Slugger out of the closet and set it by the door."

Tom fell asleep counting his wounds. In the morning, he rolled out of bed onto the floor, crawled to the bedroom door and used the knob to pull himself up.

He roused his sister, limped to the kitchen, brewed coffee and cooked oatmeal. Florence came out in a modest sage green dress with pleats and shoulder puffs, her hair pulled back into a bun. "What do you think of my disguise?"

"Gorgeous. Are you going to lay off the makeup?"

"But Pablo might be there."

In response to Tom's glare, she said, "It's not like we've got a date. But you never can tell who's going to the Sister Aimee show. Am I right?"

Tom imagined himself explaining to Pablo the several reasons why he'd best go shopping for a grown-up doll.

On the trolley Tom and Florence overheard a report that today's production would be so spectacular, Sister would repeat the same message afternoon and evening, adding new features to each performance, for the folks who cared to attend more than once.

They meandered through the crowds around the entrances, searching for the guy she saw on the beach. When they entered the sanctuary, they stopped and gaped at Eden.

The stage was a tropical paradise. A stream ran through a jungle of vines and potted rubber and carob trees adorned with orchids, lilies, and violets. The stream's source was a trickling waterfall.

"Looks like Milly's back yard," Florence said.

Tom agreed, and viewed the scene with a vague foreboding. He supposed Sister Aimee had reasoned that because the alleged human population of Eden was small, a fifty-voice human choir would look out of place. So each singer wore a smallish pair of angel wings.

On a thick branch of the tallest rubber tree, at the edge of the stage and hovering over the choir, sat a green bird the size of a champion tomcat, its head tilted upward at a dignified angle. It was cinched to the tree by a cord Tom had to squint to see.

"A macaw, right?" he asked his sister.

Florence whispered, "When do the naked people come out?"

Then Sister Aimee glided down the ramp, in a gown of shimmering green. Her arms swept out in circles, as if she were throwing kisses. With classical grace she seated herself at the piano, raised her hands high then lowered them to the keyboard.

As she led off with a minor chord, the bird interrupted.

Sister Aimee turned and gawked as if astonished the creature could talk, never mind what she'd thought she heard him say. Likewise, every choir member turned to watch the bird.

The macaw rotated his head, took them all in, then repeated his commentary. "Aw, go to hell," he squawked.

For some moments, aside from tortured sighs and muffled giggles, a deep silence reigned. When Sister broke from shock or a dramatic pause, she flew to her feet, tiptoed toward the green pagan, lifted her hands, and cooed, "My dear fellow, haven't you heard the good news?"

"Aw, go to hell," the bird replied.

Sister rushed back to the piano and cued the choir to "The Old Rugged Cross," a number they apparently hadn't arranged. Half of them stood mute, the rest sang the lyric with no attempt at harmony.

After the song, Sister leaped from her bench, strode toward the bird, and demanded, "What do you think of that?"

The bird squawked, "Aw, go to hell."

"Oh, you are a brazen and cold-hearted sinner," Sister declared with a mighty passion. The bird glanced here and there, lifted a wing, and used a claw to scratch underneath.

Sister stood with hands on her hips while she informed the bird of the blessings Adam and Eve enjoyed, "until vanity like yours, sir, tore asunder the precious mantle of innocence that had clothed them. Oh," she cried, "what a striking type you are of our fore-parents who stole and ate the fruit of the forbidden tree. No doubt the old serpent has whispered in your ear, 'Eat thereof. Ye shall not surely die.' You believed that old liar. You ate and then, guilty and sinful, you sought to hide yourself behind the trees of deception.

"But just as surely as Adam and Eve heard the footfalls of Almighty God, just as surely as God called out, 'Adam, where art thou,' just as surely as He discovered, condemned, and punished their sin, just so surely shall His divine law seek and overtake you, oh proud green sinner." Sister's arms shot heavenward.

The bird squawked, "Aw, go to hell."

Sister reached out as though inviting the wretch into her arms. "Oh, hear your deserving fate. Plunged into the blackness of the darkest dungeon, your chains clanking on the dank flagstones as you writhe in the anguished throes of remorse, you shall cry aloud, 'Oh, bitter chains of justice. Is there no escape from thee?' And the voice of relentless law shall echo, 'An eye for an eye, a tooth for a tooth. You who would send your brethren to hell, are to hell assigned.'"

The horror on faces Tom noted as he glanced around told him more than a few believed the preacher's accusations were meant for them as well as the obstinate bird.

Sister glided backward to the piano. Eyes on the macaw, she played and sang as though to him alone. The choir and congregation joined in. As if their corporate voices might win the green sinner's soul, they sang,

What can wash away my sin?
Nothing but the blood of Jesus.

The final verse and refrain, they sang a capella, because Sister had leapt to her feet and dashed to stand beneath the rubber tree.

"Come forth," she pleaded. "You are free. Another has died in your place, one named Jesus has borne your cross and paid the price of your redemption. Come forth, come forth."

Sister visibly trembled while she turned and faced the congregation, arms wide as if to embrace them all. "Come forth, oh trembling souls, why sit longer in the valley of the shadow of death? The door is open, the chains are broken. Come forth. Come forth."

She wheeled toward the bird, her arms stretched like those of a pass receiver desperate to make the catch.

For once, the bird kept its peace.

Sister Aimee swung around toward the congregation. "The Spirit calls, 'Come forth, the sunlight of God's love and mercy awaits you.' Will you turn just now to Calvary, and gaze into the face of your Savior?"

Folks began making their way to the aisles and toward the front. A winged fellow slipped out of the choir and seated himself at the piano. Accompanied by hundreds, Sister sang,

> Jesus paid it all.
> All to him I owe.
> Sin has left a crimson stain,
> he washed it white as snow.

"Aw, go to hell," the bird squawked.

Tom and Florence followed a stream of folks toward the nearest exit, Florence in the lead. As they reached the sidewalk, she stood on tiptoes and craned her neck. A squeal issued out of her. She grabbed her brother's arm. "There he is. See, brown coat, black hair, gray trousers, shorter than the rest of them."

Tom hustled off, pardoning his way through a mob of chattering tourists.

The man stood lighting a cigarette and glancing around. When he spotted Tom, the cigarette dropped. He wedged between the other men and bolted across the street into the park.

Tom, though no speedster, was plenty fast for his size. He dashed past the hanging tree. The man kept tossing glances over his shoulder. He ran a path between the lake and Glendale Boulevard, through a game of catch, a klatch of aged fishermen, and a party of waddling mallards.

Tom threw a tackle, waist high. The man splatted face first on the muddy ground. He groped for a pocket of his baggy trousers. Tom grabbed the arm, wrenched it up and backward.

The man yelped, "Hey, whatsa matter, you crazy?"

Tom stared at the tiny right ear, which made the man as one of the Casa del Mar thugs. Tom lifted and marched him to a nearby eucalyptus, spun him around, and slammed his backside into the trunk.

"Who killed Frank Gaines?"

"Lemme go."

Tom threw a backhand. The man's head smacked the tree trunk. "Who killed Frank Gaines?" Tom shouted.

The man thrashed, trying to break the grip on his arm. "How should I know?"

When Tom heard Florence call his name, he supposed she had enlisted help. He didn't stop to question, until two strong-men caught hold of his elbows, tugged them backward, and cuffed him.

Chapter Nineteen

Tom estimated his cell was on about the tenth floor of the Hall of Justice. Through the open but barred window he smelled what he guessed was pork frying in lard. Some out of work fellow peddling tacos to the gang of spectators ogling the steel frame for the new City Hall across the street.

The cell, about the size of his cottage living room, provided a cold floor and one bench. Most of the dozen occupants had resided there since various hours of Saturday night. Compared to this place, Tom thought, a team locker room smelled like chrysanthemums. He judged from the pools and splatters on the floor and cinderblock walls that several, at least, had drunk too much of the wrong stuff.

They were a glum but inquisitive crowd. When he'd asked the fellow beside him if he knew Frank Gaines, the eight colored men on the floor or propped against the walls responded with questions, looks of keen interest, or suspicion,

The fellow he asked said, "No sir." They all claimed, one way or the other, the dead man meant nothing to them. But they knew about the lynching, having read the *Forum* or otherwise heard.

One man assured Tom the police lynched Frank. "Why else they be covering up?" he demanded. Two of them blamed bootleggers, about whom they admitted insider knowledge, though neither obliged when he asked for a name. The rest agreed with Socrates, it was nobody except the Klan.

"S'pose it been the Klan," the accuser of the lawmen argued. "A goodly number of those police go home and skin off the blue suit, put on the white one."

Tom asked every question and tried every angle he could dream up to squeeze his cellmates for clues or insights. Then he heard Leo's growl from the hallway.

As the jailer who accompanied Leo unlocked the door and held it for Tom, one of the fellows he was leaving behind begged the jailer to call his mother. Another gripped his belly and groaned from an ailment he hadn't suffered a moment before.

Leo and Tom walked out and reached the elevator without a single formality. On the way down, Leo said, "Tia Consuelo's?"

Outside, the sun appeared to sink into Temple Street. "Wasn't coming for me risky?" Tom asked.

Leo shrugged, but Tom knew bravado when he saw it. Beyond placing Leo's career in jeopardy, he might've landed the good man in mortal danger. "Florence get home okay?"

"Vi's keeping company with Florence. You've got a live one there, Tom."

"What'd you do to get Vi back?"

"Made promises."

When Leo didn't look his way, Tom knew better than to ask what promises. "I'll take my sister off your hands."

"Vi has her at the picture show. *The Volga Boatman*. Seen it?"

"Movies are for dreamers," Tom said, as he watched a redhead who waved at a passing taxi. She reminded him of the Hall of Records clerk. He sighed.

As Leo nosed his Packard to the curb in front of Tia Consuelo's, he said, "I could go for a beer."

"Don't tell me," Tom said. "Tell our congressman."

"I don't see any reason to bother with Senator Shortridge. I'll go straight to the top. Tell Mister Hearst."

Leo led the way inside and past a life size statue of Pancho Villa to the last vacant booth. "Why Hearst?" Tom asked, then sat and waited for an answer. But if Leo had mentioned Hearst for a reason, he didn't mean to give any more than a clue.

So Tom devoted some minutes to pondering and found a pinch of solace. Even though he felt no closer to solving the murder, at least he knew three of the collaborators in the cover up, without whose agreement the hush couldn't succeed. Tomorrow, he vowed, he'd get to Hearst, or Harry Chandler, or Two Gun Davis.

The waitress stood up from deep in a cushioned booth and waddled over, pad and pencil at ready. She nodded and raised her right eyebrow.

"How hot are the tamales?" Leo asked.

She shrugged and raised the left eyebrow.

"Give him tamales," Tom said. "I just need a taco."

"On me."

"Make it three tacos." Tom waited for privacy, then leaned across the table. "Who's the mug?"

"The fella you tackled?"

Tom didn't feel obliged to answer what was clearly no more than a stall.

"Aw, what's the use, you'll find out. Name's Boles. Theodore Boles. Goes by Teddy."

"Where's he fit?"

"In the alleged murder?"

"Sure."

"He doesn't."

Tom rapped on the table. "Hey, bailing me out put you in the thick of this mess. Now don't you go soft."

Leo scowled. "Easy, boy."

Tom raised a hand in peace. "Talk behind bars is, a goodly number of the force are KKK."

Leo turned to look out the window. The sky had gone gray. A pack of wolves stood at the corner preening, twirling their key chains, scouting for prey of the Florence variety.

"Back to this Teddy Boles," Tom said. "You say he doesn't figure in the murder. So why'd he bring his pals to the Casa Del Mar?"

"You don't want to know."

"I damn sure do."

Leo reached into his breast pocket for a Lucky Strike. He lit up, blew a couple smoke rings. "I don't know a thing about Teddy Boles. I checked him out. No record. No warrants. Works for the city as an electrician. You want I should say where to go if you won't take my word?"

"Yeah."

"To your mother."

The waitress arrived while Tom sat gaping. After she threw down the plates and retired, Leo said, "He's Milly's man."

Tom's stomach swelled and churned so he couldn't even finish one taco. Leo helped him with the other two.

Off Wilshire, while gasoline poured into the Packard, pumped by an attendant dressed like a cross between an admiral and a soda jerk, Tom stared over a vacant lot toward Westlake Park, a place one could always spot dramatic scenes unfolding. But this evening, so strongly had the Milly connection shaken him, all he noticed was a mob of folks clustered beneath an Iowa banner refusing to let dark close their reunion.

As they pulled out of the station, Leo said, "I could pay Milly a visit."

"Let me sleep on it."

Tom meant to talk this business over with Florence before he chose a path. If Milly would send a gang of roughnecks after him, she might send another crew to snatch her daughter. She might do anything.

In Cactus Court, Tom failed to mind his steps and brushed too close to a cholla. A barb nailed him, pinned his trousers to his ankle. With that, he hoped he'd experienced the day's finale. But a note on flowered paper hung by a tack on his cottage door. In round script much like a sample from evidence leaked by the Grand Jury and copied and printed in the *Times*, the note read, "Dear Tom Hickey, please come for a brief visit with me at nine a.m., in the parsonage, which you'll find next door to Angelus Temple. Come to the front. Emma will show you upstairs. With anticipation and respect, Aimee Semple McPherson."

Chapter Twenty

Early morning sun was a pleasure Tom relished. Given time between rising and work, he brewed coffee and often carried it outside and around the side of his house to a patch of dirt with a eucalyptus stump sawed off at stool level.

He was on his way outside when he barely missed stepping on a copy of the *Forum*. He picked it up, continued on to the stump, and read it while drinking his coffee. The date was yesterday. Following the headline, BEWARE, the text read:

```
We darker folk are by nature a gentle
people, content to live and let live, as a
rule willing to suffer a lifetime of insult
and hardship rather than respond to the
voice of our baser natures when that voice
advocates violence. The grievous history
of our people in this land, as well as our
patience enduring trials no human should be
called to endure, is common knowledge.
    Even the dreamers among us, who upon
arriving in this young and vital city,
allowed ourselves to believe we had crossed
the Jordan and reached the promised land,
now find ourselves mired in gloom, fear,
and confusion. The despair that took root
on Monday, October 11, with the murder of
an innocent who harbored ill-will toward
none, has since been magnified by the con-
tinued silence of the Times, the Examiner,
```

the *Express* and the *Herald*. Either none of
these institutions possess the courage to
report the truth, or all have conspired, for
reasons beyond our comprehension, to deceive
the same public that pays their salaries,
enriches their owners, and relies upon their
integrity.

How then can this reporter, though he
remains dedicated to the ideal of peace and
brotherhood, condemn the desire of a certain
element of the darker community in their
efforts to organize and prepare for battle,
as the enemy has organized into a fraternity
of demonic principles and blatant symbolism
that flaunts those principles?

A free press must accept the duty to warn,
and on occasion to prophesy, as well as to
report. What follows is this reporters studied assessment of our moment in history:

Perhaps if Mister Hearst or Chandler will
break the silence, publish the truth, and
thereby cause justice to be duly adminis-
tered, by doing so they will prevent the
bloodbath that otherwise may occur once a
certain element of the darker community
concludes that, for the sake of us all and
our loved ones, they must drive a certain
white element out of the city and back to
whatever the place, be it Georgia or hell,
whence they came.

A half hour later, Tom slapped the broadside on the desk of
Mister Woods. The boss didn't reach for it, but sat as though
immovable except for the hand that opened a side drawer of
his desk.

Tom said, "I suppose it's none of my business, but I'm asking
you to tell me anyway. Do you belong to the Ku Klux Klan?"

The boss' hand remained on the rim of the open drawer
where, according to shop rumor, he kept an ancient Colt
Peacemaker, a relic of his years as a Texas cowboy. His face and
his tone could've served as a poster for a film about gunfighters.

"As you say," he replied in gunfighter tone, "my associations are none of your damned business."

Tom leaned both hands on the desk. "Frank Gaines is my business," he said, his voice easily hard and resolute as Woods'. "Because I appear to be the only real friend he's got." He slapped the *Forum*. "And, as you'll see when you read, some folks want to use his murder to justify something he would never have condoned."

"Why are you here?"

"I want you to tell me if the Klan killed Frank. That's all. If you can give me your word they didn't, I'll believe you. But if you won't give your word, I'll believe in my heart they killed him. And I'll act accordingly, even if it means a race war."

Woods closed the drawer and lay both hands atop the desk. "Tom, I'll pardon your behavior and consider your request. But hear this. If I learn anything about a lynching, I'll be the one to decide if and when you should know."

"Sure," Tom said. "Just keep in mind, history's full of tragic characters who waited too long."

Woods lifted a fountain pen and tapped it on the back of his other hand.

"Meantime," Tom said, "I'm not working for anybody who won't deny being an accomplice to murder. You can get one of the butchers to drive my route, and send Bud or somebody for me when you've got an answer ready."

The boss said nothing. His eyes never wandered from staring at Tom's.

Tom nodded, turned, and walked out to the lobby. Then he noticed Mister Woods behind him, plucking bills out of his wallet. He handed Tom a twenty.

"In case you think you can buy me," Tom said, "no deal."

The boss' face darkened to such deep purple, Tom worried the insult might've killed the old fellow.

But his voice came strong and sure. "Call it severance pay."

Chapter Twenty-one

Wedged between Angelus Temple and the Bible college, the parsonage was a concrete gray two-story of somewhat Italian design, with a rounded front and a dozen arches only a few feet apart, each with a glass door and small balcony.

A woman Tom knew from the newspapers stepped out to the balcony directly above the front door. Emma Shaffer, who on May 18 accompanied Sister to Ocean Park, watched her run into the surf, and after an hour reported her disappearance. With mouse brown hair pinned tight, wearing a formless housedress, she gazed around like a vigilant sentry. As plain and impervious as Sister was comely and magnetic, she looked straight at Tom without giving any sign she saw him. Then she made a quick turn and ducked inside.

Tom approached the porch and waited, hat in hand. The front door opened a crack. He heard women talking in hushed voices. When the door opened, Emma Shaffer studied his face, appeared to find it unpleasant, and said "Follow me" in a voice she could've used to host an execution. He walked a few steps behind, across a dark wood foyer, up the half-circular staircase, and into a small sitting room. He smelled lavender.

As Sister Aimee rose to greet him, a flicker of light refracted off her wide-set hazel eyes. She wore a lacy emerald-green dressing gown. Her thick auburn hair was tied up into a spiral with a bun at its peak. Her long, pianist's hand gripped his more firmly than was common with women. "Thank you, Tom, for coming," she said, in a voice both melodious and hoarse.

She guided him to a padded bamboo chair, held the back of it until he sat, then perched on the edge of a Queen Anne loveseat that faced him, close enough so they might've touched fingers if they both reached out.

"I know your mother," she said.

"We heard she came here, but I haven't seen her. Not yet."

"Do you want to?"

"No."

"So she told me."

"Do we need to talk about Milly?" Tom asked.

Sister Aimee smiled her understanding. "Milly was always so generous. She gave me hundreds of flowers in glorious bouquets, and many exquisite dresses she made. Telling her she had to leave us truly pained me."

"You kicked her out of the church?"

"You're surprised?"

Tom shrugged and supposed if he hoped to earn the Sister's trust, he needed to confide a little. "It wouldn't be the first time she got expelled."

"Oh?"

"Pastor Seymour kicked her out of Azusa Street. Or so Frank Gaines told me." He fixed his eyes on the Sister's. "Frank said the pastor came to believe Milly got filled by a spirit that wasn't so Holy."

Sister Aimee gave no hint that the lynched man's name registered. "Well, though we certainly try not to harness the Spirit, neither do we encourage its manifestations during services. We hold many smaller prayer meetings for that purpose. I can't recall your mother attending those. No, I asked Milly to leave us because she, in my judgment, became too attached to the temple, and to me. You see, she knew quite well our purpose is to sanctify the brethren and send them out into the world. I asked her to leave for her own spiritual good."

"I'll bet she loved you for that."

Now she gave him a conspirator's smile. "Milly knows everything about flowers and gardening." Her eyes zeroed as if to imply some deeper meaning.

"Did you know Frank Gaines?" he asked.

"I don't. Didn't."

Tom fetched from his pocket his copy of the *Forum* with the lynching story, unfolded and handed it to her, then watched her read. After she returned the broadside to him, she lowered her eyes and might've sent off a prayer.

When she looked up, he saw why reporters at the Grand Jury hearing expressed their amazement at her composure even while accusations flew her way. No doubt she had feelings. Maybe deep ones. But she didn't waste time on them.

"May I call you Tom?"

"You bet."

"And you may call me Aimee. Now, let us presume for the sake of argument this Socrates' account is true. It's quite possible a motive of the murderers for hanging the poor dear man in our park was to turn a city of precious, impressionable souls away from the gospel. Do you see, Tom, it could well be the same villains who are out to convince the people I'm a liar and a seductress."

"Could be," Tom said. "Would you care to provide me with the most likely villains' names?"

"It's not my place to accuse." She appeared to enter a place of rapture in which she looked Florence's age, and far more guileless. "Villains may be the wrong label. Among them may be those who feel betrayed by me because of the lies about my abduction. Some, feeling betrayed by the Lord who allowed them to believe in me, may have turned to Satan."

Her cadence and angelic pose were casting a spell. To break it, Tom assumed the offensive. "Thing is, we've got two crimes, the murder and the cover up. I'm betting you know something about the cover up."

"Please don't *you* accuse me."

Her eyes appeared to retreat as if from a blow, and her rosey lips quivered. Tom said, "I mean, who do you *think* is behind the cover up?"

She sighed as though from the weight of his question. "If one of my staff were to ask a favor of the police to thwart Satan's scheme, I could hardly blame him. They are desperate to protect me. They know I'm under more pressure than any woman should be asked to bear. Every day, during this vicious inquest." She turned to glance at a clock in the corner. "Oh horror. I must leave soon, to go there once again. Tom, every day come more slanderous claims contending that I was not kidnapped but was involved in a tryst. They treat me like a vain charlatan." She lifted both hands and pressed them to her cheeks. As if an awful fear had just dawned, she said, "Tom, you don't believe them, do you?"

From instinct, he shook his head. "But my opinion shouldn't count. I haven't paid much attention."

"Oh, you are a rare one. I believed every citizen of the world was reading the lies. They are lies, of the devil, I assure you." She moved to the edge of her loveseat and spent moments gazing as though admiring his features. "Suppose you weigh the evidence and consider me guilty."

"Okay."

"Tom, would you make me a promise?"

He understood how Sampson got hoodwinked by Delilah. To stifle the answer she wanted to hear took all his will. "Depends."

"Of course. Tom, I want you to promise me you will never blame the Lord for the transgressions of his servants."

"That's a tough one."

"Yes, it is. But think. All of us are human, we all contend with a legion of passions. Perhaps those of us who give our lives to the Lord do so because our hearts recognize we haven't, on our own, the power to restrain those passions."

While she spoke, her right hand drifted and hovered above a vase and bouquet of white roses on the table beside the loveseat. She turned toward the flowers and fingered some petals. Then she said, "You must go visit your mother." She glanced at the clock and motioned toward it.

Tom stood and reached for her hand. "Thanks."

She gave his fingers a warm squeeze. "I trust we'll meet again."

He nodded and turned to leave but stopped in the doorway. "The little I know about the kidnapping and all, here's why I believe you. See, if I read you correctly, the two fellows who died looking for your body in the waves, if you had them on your conscience, you couldn't live another day without coming clean."

Her grim stare so gripped his heart, he wondered if the devil might've armed him with that last remark.

Then she said, "You're a good man, Tom."

Which left him to walk out feeling as if this preacher, only two years younger than his mother, had captured some part of him.

Emma Shaffer appeared out of nowhere, led him down the stairs, and showed him out. As the door closed behind him, he remembered something he'd meant to tell Sister Aimee. He crossed the street, sat on the first bench, and jotted on his notepad, "Fenton Love, one of your ushers, a tall fellow with a deep scar on the middle of his chin, and a squinty eye, has been tailing me. He's LAPD, and one of the meanest, I hear."

He returned to the parsonage and knocked. Emma Shaffer opened the door. Tom handed her the folded note and asked her to deliver it. Without asking, she unfolded and read it.

Chapter Twenty-two

Tom had often driven his meat truck past the Azusa Street mission. He might've stopped to go in and remember, except he imagined the happy times would get swamped by memories of cringing in corners, deserted and mute from terror.

But today he remembered the blessings. The guardian angel voice of Frank Gaines. The women, Emma Gordon and others, who wrapped him in the comfort of their arms and against their dark bosoms. Jennie Seymour was one of them.

When Tom rapped on the mission door, she came and opened it, holding a broom. A dignified woman with smooth russet skin, generous eyes, and a mouth that, even while she studied him, formed a modest smile.

"I'm Tom," he said. "Milly Hickey's son."

She leaned the broom against the a wall. "Tommy." She reached for his right hand and cupped it while she beamed as though his growing into a big handsome fellow was another miracle. When she let go, she said, "Do come in, please."

Inside, he recalled the music, and how the eerie harmony of a hundred voices in dozens of keys and languages sent his terror fleeing, and how passersby heard and entered, their mouths agape.

Jennie Seymour showed him to a slat-backed wooden chair. "Tea?"

"Yes please."

"Sugar?"

"Okay."

At a corner table, she poured water from a pan on a hot plate into a cup and lowered a tea bag into the water. "Tommy, you know my William passed away?"

"I heard. I should've come and offered condolences. From what I remember, he was a great man."

"Yes. Powerful. Gentle. Not of this world." She delivered the tea and sat beside him. "Are you right with the Lord, Tommy?"

He thought of telling a white lie, mentioning his attendance at Angelus Temple without admitting his reasons weren't all that spiritual. But Jennie Seymour didn't deserve any lies. He shrugged and said, "I came here to ask about Frank Gaines."

She looked away, gave him a profile. "Is it true?"

"I believe so."

"And was it the Ku Klux Klan, as folks are saying?"

"I hope to find out." He explained that he was investigating, and why. He told her his belief that the cover up couldn't have succeeded without Hearst, Chandler, and Police Chief Davis knowing and at least approving.

She agreed. Then she looked him in the eye. "Tommy, do you know the Holy Spirit will never come in his full power and beauty until the brethren of every color and stripe seek him together in selfless love and true equality?"

"Yes ma'am. Anything you can tell me about Frank?"

She stood, served tea, then sat and stared at the cup in her hands. "I heard, though I do not recall the source, that Brother Gaines was a stevedore. In San Pedro, or was it Long Beach? This was some years ago. He didn't come to the mission regularly, not since the early days. Once or twice a year, I reckon, he came for a meeting, but he never stayed after. He was a quiet man."

"I remember."

"Much like my William, he kept his own council, and bridled his tongue. In William's opinion, Brother Gaines had not felt right in our company since he began living out of wedlock with the young woman. Oh, what was her name? Harriet.

William spoke with them at length, when Brother Gaines and Sister Harriet began keeping company. William was not one to preach the dangers of adultery but neither would he withhold his counsel from those who fell prey. Tommy, her being a white lady, could that be a reason for the murder?"

"Miz Seymour, I'm sure you know more about people than I do."

"I've known many people," she said. "You'll need to excuse me for a short time, while I use the telephone."

She stood and crossed the room, went behind the altar, to a staircase Tom remembered. He shuddered at the vision that came. Milly climbing to the room where the pastor and helpers took those who screamed or wept too loudly, or thrashed in seductive or other dangerous ways. To blur the vision, he listened to the Sister's muted voice from the upper room, and made a rough count of the hours he could've saved over the past few days if he had agreed to Florence's pleas and ordered telephone service.

When she returned, she asked, "Tommy, is your mother right with the Lord?"

He wondered if whomever she had phoned inquired about Milly. "As far as I know, she's never been quite right with anybody."

"Should we pray for her? And for you? And, wasn't there a little one."

"Florence."

"Can I pray right now?"

Tom accepted the offer, though an old terror had already begun to rise. As she moved her chair closer to his, he felt blitzed by a squad of demons. She grasped both his hands. Though she barely squeezed, he tensed to keep from recoiling, as if she had caught hold with fiery pincers.

She began by praising God for his grace and mercy to sinners like them, fervently requested the coming of his kingdom and torrents of the latter rain. She pled for forgiveness of all debts and transgressions on the part of Milly and her children, and for the Holy Spirit to call them ever closer. For a long while, she fell silent. Then she commenced to quake and sing in soft, ghostly tones and long circular phrases, in a strange, tender language. He let himself shiver, chilled all over and through except where she held him with her burning hands.

Chapter Twenty-three

Tom rode south along Central, past Sugar Hill Barber Shop, past a hobo camp alongside a creek shaded by cottonwoods, houses painted gaily in the Mexican style, and small factories with big incinerators pouring black smoke. Even before he hopped off, he caught the scent of Mud Town Barbeque, to which he'd delivered tons of ribs.

The closer he came to the place, the more he lamented having skipped lunch. Inside, he asked Moze, a waiter and part-owner, for directions to Frank's address. Moze obliged, noticed Tom licking his lips, ordered him to wait, and fetched a sack of ribs.

Tom was still gnawing when he reached Frank's block, in a gone-to-seed tract the developer no doubt billed as craftsman bungalows, though they lacked any evidence of craft. Judging from the way some of them leaned, earthquakes had abused them.

In place of sidewalks, weedy dirt paths separated the street from the front yards. Some yards were grass. Others were adorned with succulents, rock gardens or patches of winter vegetables. From a distance, Frank's house appeared among the tidiest on the block, though the knee-high lawn had begun to go brown. Tom didn't notice the broken window off the porch until he approached the steps.

He climbed, and knocked on the door, out of courtesy and habit, though he doubted anybody lived there now. After a minute, he tried the doorknob.

Inside, he balanced on two-by-four beams above a crawl space littered with trousers, dresses, underwear, cans, broken bottles and dishes. Whatever looters hadn't bothered to salvage.

They had spared one parlor wall. A painting of bright garden flowers hung surrounded by photos. One photo showed a crowd of people, brown and white, outside the Azusa Street mission. Another was a framed photo-portrait of Frank Gaines, with the wide and hearty smile Tom remembered, and a lovely, pale brunette. Frank held her close to his side. Though bosomy, she looked frail.

Tom crossed the room, teetering on a beam. He plucked the photo off the wall and tucked it under his arm. Then he hopped beam-to-beam, reached the kitchen and peeked in. The floor was intact and tiled, strewn with litter. Cleaner where the ice box and stove used to be.

Tom guessed the house wasn't a rental. A landlord would likely have found a new tenant or boarded the place. Madeline, the city clerk and redheaded charmer, hadn't found any deed in Franks' name. Maybe, Tom thought, the pale woman owned it. Harriet. His next task was to find her. For a start, he needed her last name.

He left the place to ghosts and looters. The neighboring house he picked to start his queries was a challenge to reach. He inched his way through a maze of tangled weeds, a rusty bicycle frame and wheels, the remains of what might've been a sled, a bottomless bucket, and a decapitated baby doll. As he neared the house, the front door flew open. A small boy in socks and drooping underpants charged out, followed by a taller, shirtless boy who waved a broom and yelled death threats.

The boys raced past and circled the yard, yelping and tripping. Tom proceeded to the doorway. "Hello in there?"

A gang of tinier boys dashed to the door, stopped just inside, and stood gawking at him.

"Mom around?" Tom asked.

She peered out of a back room, then crossed the parlor dodging piles of clothes and bedding. "What, Mister?" Like her sons, she was bone thin and blond enough to pass for albino. She pointed to the framed photo under Tom's arm. "Been helping yourself?"

"Got a minute?" Tom asked.

With a raised fist and a bark, she chased the boys out of her way. She stepped outside, crossed the porch and sat on a step. She patted the wood beside her, meaning Tom should sit there, and pulled a sack of tobacco and Juicy Jay's rolling papers from a pocket of her housedress.

"You the law? Insurance? What?"

"You know who killed him?"

"You kidding?" She blew smoke. "Could've been most anybody. Colored and a white gal's trouble enough. When she drops dead, folks go talking."

"Dead."

"Yes sir, only some months back. And she ain't no older than me." The woman glanced over at Tom, probably itching for a compliment. When he didn't comply, she said, "Folks say the Klan killed him, they don't know from nothing. My cousin's Klan, he tells me that bunch don't do half what the gossips have them doing. He says they just aim to keep the developers from ruining the country."

"Tell me about Harriet?"

"Never done nothing to cross me. She had, I might could call her a hussy, the way just the sight of her got my so-called husband lathered. Mister, I'd suspect he might've killed Frank, on account of what the gossips saying, as how Frank been the one killed Harriet. Only my man's up in Montana. He lays track for the Union Pacific. Keeps him gone, leaving all these little devils to me alone. Jesse," she called, "you mash my broom, I'll whoop you with it. You get over here."

The boys plodded over. The woman said, "Tell the gentleman about Miz Harriet."

The taller boy said, "We done found her out back in the flowers. She was blue."

When the boys ran off, he asked, "She go by Gaines or another name?"

"Gaines, sure," the woman said. "She got another?"

Tom shrugged and said goodbye.

From a neighboring porch, a graybeard colored man watched Tom as though awaiting his turn. He wore a porter's cap, and sat tall on the high end of a sagging sofa, sharpening a kitchen knife with a whetstone. "Here about Frank?" he bellowed as Tom approached.

"Yes sir," Tom called out. He stopped at the foot of the porch steps.

"You family? Harriet side?"

"No sir." Tom wagged his head and raised his voice. "Frank ever talk about Azusa Street?"

"Many's the time."

"That's where I knew him."

"You a holy roller?"

"My mother. Any police been around since Frank got killed?"

"Police," the man snorted. "What you think?"

"I expect they haven't. That's why I'm here."

The man sharpened his blade with added force and resolve. "Well sir, you go tell whosoever you please, Harry Chandler the man killed Frank."

Tom must've looked dumbfounded as the old fellow said, "No, no, not with his own soft hands. His union busters, they do his bidding. And you can tell whosoever you report to, tell him Lincoln Peters, he the man say so."

While Tom used a minute to consider how Hearst might fit into a union busting plot, the man tested his knife on the hair of his forearm.

Tom said, "Mister Peters, did you see something that proves what you're telling me?"

The man laid his knife and whetstone on the sofa arm. "Son, Frank a union man, much as anybody can be in General Otis and Mister Chandler's town."

"The way I heard, Frank was a stevedore."

"No sir, he were not. A welder. Worked on oil rigs and ships, down in Chandler's yard. Till the strike. He spoke out. Speak out, they kill you. You going to see Mister Chandler?"

"Yes sir," Tom said, and meant it as a promise.

"You tell him, he got the spine, he need to come talk to Peters."

"I'll do that."

Tom thanked the man and crossed the street. A woman was plucking tomatoes from vines staked and rising as high as Tom's shoulders. When she sensed him, she turned and yipped with surprise. She wore a *reboso* that covered all but the head of a tawny baby with bulging ebony eyes.

In high school Spanish, Tom explained he was looking for clues about the Frank Gaines murder, and told her why. The woman wrapped her baby tighter. Then she spoke. He asked her to repeat, more slowly.

Pausing between each word, she told him Frank was a *caballero* who always overpaid for tomatoes. And she described a Chevrolet she'd seen parked across the street from the gentleman's house, just as dark fell, on a stormy night two weeks ago.

"*Domingo?*" Tom asked.

"*Si, Domingo,*" she said with assurance.

He asked if she saw the driver or any passengers. No people, she said, only the car, before the rain and darkness sent her inside.

With a frown and a furtive glance behind her, she returned to pinching leaves off her tomato plants. Tom was thanking her when he noticed a tan Nash parked just far enough up the street so he couldn't read the license. He started walking that way. Before he'd made ten steps, the Nash pulled out and drove off.

Tom returned to the woman. "A Chevrolet? *Por seguro?*"

"*Pues si,*" the woman said. "Chevrolet. *Negro.* Shiny."

Chapter Twenty-four

Violet Weiss and six-year-old Una wore matching yellow sundresses that rustled in the Santa Ana breeze Tom was enjoying until Vi's expression altered his mood. He'd known her eighteen years, and never before seen her impersonate an ogre.

She and Una showed Florence and Tom across the backyard past the fishpond to the redwood bench under the magnolia. The bench featured a bouquet centerpiece. Tulips and daisies surrounded a single white rose. Vi loved flowers. That mutual passion had kept her friendly to Milly even after Tom's mother called her a snoop.

Tom gazed over the flowerbeds at the edge of the Weiss property into the yard he remembered as a magical place, with flowers so high and abundant, he often ran and hid there, amidst rows of plump boysenberries whose vines jabbed and scraped long red lines in his skin.

Leo came out with a pitcher of lemonade and a flask. Violet scowled. On her round and soft face, any sour expression usually looked like a comic pantomime. Not tonight. She seated Tom and Florence and poured their lemonade, then wheeled and marched to the house without excusing herself.

"Vi get some bad news?" Tom asked.

"Yeah," Leo said, "when she married me." He lifted his flask in evidence. "You see her coming with a weapon, don't ask, just run, follow me." He tipped the flask into Tom's tumbler. To Florence, he said, "Sorry gal. You're not legal."

"Legal?" Florence said. "Maybe I should turn you in."

Tom let them chat about Florence's school and the last time she had a bowl of Violet's chili. Then Leo said, "Take a big gulp, Tom. Honey, don't listen. This is man talk."

Florence made a pfft sound and inserted a finger into one ear.

"Chief of Detectives knows every step you've made this past week," Leo said. "Knows all about the *Forum*, Frank Gaines."

"He admit Frank got lynched?"

"Naw. In his book, Gaines was fomenting a strike at the Long Beach shipyards. Says somebody must've ran Frank out of town. That's the kind of game Harry Chandler plays, he says. Chandler's a Lutheran, finds murder distasteful. And then he says, 'Weiss, you're a policeman, and as such you don't go helping a civilian investigate a murder that's nothing but a tale dreamed up by some negro thinks he's a Greek philosopher.' He says your Socrates heard Frank Gaines got run out of town and saw an opportunity to arouse the coloreds, increase his circulation. He puts on a smile, and says, 'Leo, don't believe whatever you see in print. Hearst is backing the progressives, worming his way back into politics. Chandler, he's all development along with his California Club cronies. And this Socrates, he's a mouthpiece for the Bolsheviks.

"Next, he says I'll need to go up to the Owens Valley and work with the local sheriffs, where a fellow reported the latest plot to sabotage the aqueduct. I ask, isn't that a job for the feds. He says they need the help of a real cop, and we need somebody to look out for the city's interests, and I should tell Vi I'll be gone about a week. He wants my report next Wednesday."

He leveled his gaze on Tom. "Next Wednesday, see?" He raised his eyebrows.

"What am I missing?" Tom asked.

Florence raised her hand. "The election. Tuesday. Don't you get it, Tommy. They're sending Leo out of town until the day after."

"Family's got one informed citizen. See, I ask if all this keeping tabs on you, and shipping me off, came out of his fertile mind, or from Davis himself. He points straight up."

"Meaning who? Hearst? Chandler?"

"Kent Parrot."

Every USC ballplayer and fan knew plenty about Kent Parrot, a hard-hitter some years back. These days, Boss Parrot not only ran the Harbor Commission, but called the plays for the Police Department and coached Mayor Cryer on the ins and outs of the politics racket. The last Tom heard, a couple of Parrot's intimates were gambling hall tycoon Charlie Crawford and bootlegger Tony Cornero.

Una ran across the yard and begged Florence to climb the magnolia to her tree house, a platform about eight feet up. While Tom watched them shimmy up the knotted rope, a connection knocked him lightheaded.

Sister Aimee preached to a parrot. Nobody with any sense would attribute the work of a mind as keen and crafty as the Sister's to coincidence.

Leo said, "Let me in on it."

Tom recounted the parrot sermon. Because Una was close above them, a word got slightly revised. "I'd bet my life savings Sister Aimee was sending a message."

"His life savings is way less than a nickel," Florence called from the tree house.

Leo asked, "Message to who?"

Florence started down the rope. "Let's go ask her. I want to meet that dame."

Una followed. As she touched ground, she grabbed Florence's hand. "My cornbread's going to burn. Mama let me make the cornbread."

While the girls were gone, Tom used the privacy. He pulled out the latest *Forum* about the coming attack on the Klan. He passed it to Leo and watched him read. Leo shook his head, handed the broadside back, and reached for his flask.

"What do you figure," Tom asked. "How many of your cops belong to the Klan?"

Leo growled, "You think they report to me? Hey, if I went out looking for Klansmen, one first place I'd stop would be Angelus Temple."

Tom said, "You'd come up empty."

"Oh, would I? Could be we're again running into your failure to keep up with the news. It's common knowledge that the Klan made some deal to protect the little huckster."

Tom felt his face bristle, and heard his voice rise. "What I hear, no matter they're fans of hers, she's none of theirs. They show up at the temple, she puts them in her place."

"Sure, I heard that story. Could all be for show. Tom, has the pretty little humbug artist got her claws into you?"

Only because Tom saw Vi and Una marching his way, he managed to keep from replying with fighting words, and going home hungry.

Chapter Twenty-five

Una delivered plates and spoons. Vi set a crock of chili and a bowl of salad on the table, and marched back to the house. Una ran after her and soon returned with cornbread and butter. Vi didn't return. Noticing the look Florence gave him, Leo said, "Chili gives her gas."

Tom and Florence feasted. Afterward, when Una had finished nibbling her corn bread, Leo said, "Dolly, go help mom."

Una grabbed Florence by the wrist and tugged until she gave in. Once the men were alone, Tom said, "I got Frank's address in Mud Town. Rode down there and talked to a couple of neighbors. One said rumors were flying that Frank killed his woman, and her being white, any true blue white boy might've done it. Another blamed Harry Chandler."

"Let's hope they're wrong."

"Why's that?"

"Harry's a devil. Looks like mama's boy, acts like a deacon. But you don't own the city of angels unless you've got a tolerance for murder. If Chandler lynched your man, I fear you won't last the week."

"Do Chandler's union busters drive Chevrolets?" He reported the neighbor's sighting of a Chevrolet that stormy Sunday.

"Bootleggers go for Chevrolets," Leo said.

Tom finished his lemonade, poured a refill, and pointed to Leo's flask. "Emma Gordon heard talk about Frank peddling booze."

"There we go," Leo said. "Frank pulled a fast one, they gave him what he had coming and figured if they're going to bump off the guy, they might as well double down, send your little preacher up the river."

"Frame Sister Aimee for a murder. Who's going to buy that?"

"Even so, what's it take to send her supporters packing? And without that judge chum of hers and the rest cutting deals in city hall, she goes down on the fraud charges. Then half the city's churchgoers step out on a bender, to dull their grief. The other half go on a bender celebrating. Both ways, the bootleggers make like Midas."

"Suspect one," Tom said, "union busters. Two, bootleggers. Three, some creep thinks he's Galahad and wants to blame Frank for Harriet's dying."

"Good. And, if your man Socrates is on the level, we had best choose one of those thousands of suspects as the killer, and deliver the guy to certain concerned citizens. Or else a bloodbath ensues. How many days have we got?"

"A few, let's hope."

Leo picked up his flask, gave it a shake, and grumbled as he heaved himself off the bench and plodded toward the house.

Before he returned, Florence came out alone. She sat next to her brother and put a hand on his knee. "Tommy, I've been thinking."

"I thought you were making pudding."

"Which doesn't require my whole brain. See, I figure you need my help. Now listen. I'll skip school a few days. Tell the Egyptians I'm sick. I won't even go to the Top Hat. You and me and Leo, we'll be a team."

Tom said, "You know the rule. Skip school, I take every one of those flapper outfits you've worked for, borrowed, stolen, or sweet talked some chump out of, and give them to Miss Elva's boarding house and finishing school."

"Phooey." She made a pout and lifted her hand from his knee. "You're all talk."

"How about that pudding?"

As she practiced her sashay crossing the lawn, she passed Leo on his way out. He allowed himself a double-take before continuing to the picnic bench. "Think she knows what that move of hers can do to a man?"

"Let's get back to business."

Leo doctored their lemonade. Tom said, "Try this. Say the killer's a cop on the take, and his bootleggers are getting nervous about the Klan siding with the temperance crowd, which includes Sister Aimee. And the killer cop is holding something over Davis, or over Parrot and the City Hall gang."

"Maybe he cuts a deal with Hearst," Leo said. "Or with Chandler. But if you can tell me one previous instance when those two agreed on anything, I'll give you my Packard."

"Suppose one of the tycoons is holding a card the other doesn't want him to play."

"What card?"

Tom sat wracking his brain while Una ran back and forth delivering tapioca pudding heaped with whipped cream and Florence brought and lit a kerosene lantern. All through dessert, he groped and came up with nothing. Tomorrow, he promised himself, he'd go to the library and read every local newspaper of the last month or so.

Una fell asleep with her head on Florence's lap. Florence, sitting close to Leo, looped an arm around his and watched her brother with a look that kept switching between a bestowal of respect and a glare.

"Back to the murder," Tom said. "Suspect five. Some disenchanted fanatic. Or a zealot of some other brand."

Leo said, "A loony the Reverend Robert Shuler's campaign against the little swindler heated to the boiling point."

"What's your gripe with Aimee?" Tom snapped.

"Aimee, is it?"

Tom scowled.

"She's a crook."

Florence gazed up at Leo with an impish smile. "You wouldn't be one of those thinks us girls ought to stick to making chili and changing diapers?"

Leo snorted.

"You want to look into the death of Frank's woman?" Tom asked. "Harriet. Nobody I've talked to knows her last name. Unless you're leaving right away for Owens Valley."

"Why should I go to Owens Valley? Mulholland can go to Owens Valley, do his own dirty work."

Florence said, "I'll bet Sister Aimee knows everything that goes on in this town."

"What makes you think she's so smart?" Leo asked.

"Well, if she isn't so smart, how's she know who's the biggest liar in Los Angeles."

"Who says she does?"

"There's a handbill going around," Tom said. "She's going to preach on the topic."

"On Tuesday, November second," Florence said. "I can hardly wait."

"Election day. Day before I'm due home from the Sierra." Leo made a face Tom interpreted to mean, there's the key to this whole ugly business.

Vi came out and called Tom to the phone.

All the caller said was "Hi there" before Tom recognized the sultry voice. Madeline, the heartthrob city clerk. "I get a coffee break at 9:30," she said. "Tomorrow, I'm going to bring my friend. He cleans up after the coroners. We're going to talk about Frank Gaines. Want to join us?"

Tom would've accepted if Madeline and her friend were going to talk about Parchesi. "Uncle Sam's Automat," Madeline said. "Coffee's on me, this once."

Though Tom and Florence promised they'd be happy riding the coach home, Leo insisted on driving. But Vi blocked the door and told her husband, "The way you've been drinking, before you go off on a drive, get yourself into the men's room."

"Men's room you call it," Leo grumbled, "with all those doilies?"

Vi waited until the bathroom door shut, then she studied Florence and must've decided the girl was old or wise enough to acknowledge the ways of the world. She laid a hand on each of them and pulled them closer. "Leo had a pal, way back before prohibition, used to meet and play billiards, go surf fishing, do whatever men do. You might've read about Sid Fitch?"

"The bootlegger," Florence said. "A shootout with the cops. A few weeks ago. That Sid Fitch?"

"You might call it a shootout," Vi said. "Leo calls it a massacre. It got him back drinking. Now the booze won't let go."

Chapter Twenty-six

On the way home, along Wilshire, Tom tried to imagine how Leo must feel about his pal getting tommy-gunned by his fellow detectives. Florence tapped her brother's leg and pointed past Leo at the vast and stately Ambassador Hotel. "Who's going to take me to the Coconut Grove, you or Pablo?"

"Next payday," Tom said. "Say, Leo, I let Sister Aimee know this Fenton Love usher of hers was a cop who'd been shadowing me."

"That makes two reasons you both are going to swear not to get caught out alone after dark."

"And the other reason?" Tom asked.

"Teddy Boles beats up on you. Then you thrash Teddy. Whose turn is it?"

"Who's Teddy Boles?" Florence demanded. "Okay, I get it. He's the guy you jumped. Right, Tommy?"

Tom nodded. Nobody spoke during the last mile.

In the cottage, Tom knew sleep was a long shot, with theories and questions competing for his mind, and with Florence staring daggers he supposed wouldn't relent until he came clean or tossed her some distraction.

When he flopped into the padded armchair, she scooted a wooden chair up close and sat with crossed arms like an indomitable schoolteacher.

"Teddy Boles is Milly's fellow," he said.

She unfolded her arms and slapped her bare knees. "Oh Lord. You don't suppose Mama put him up to it?"

"What do you think?"

"Why, though?"

Tom shrugged.

"God, Tommy, what makes her so loco?"

"You tell me."

"The way I remember, it's like some devil gets into her. Remember the tar pits?"

"Sure." Tom remembered so well, his palms went clammy. "And the time, out in the garden, she was talking with another gal, and next thing you know she's stabbing a pitchfork into the ground and shouting about Pastor William Seymour. Kept calling him a liar, ranting at the other gal, that one who dressed like a gypsy."

"Always wore two or three big flowers in her hair."

"That's the one. Must've been a sidekick of Milly's in that bunch, what'd they call it? Something about Eden. Anyway, it's coming back to me, Milly telling this gal how every time she got the spirit, Pastor Seymour went and doused the flame, making her hold her peace. Or if she didn't simmer down, leading her upstairs and praying against the spirit that'd caught her, saying it wasn't from God but was some demon. And the gypsy gal, I remember her ordering Milly to stay way from the holy rollers."

Florence had moved her hands to her lap. Her shoulders sagged forward, knees pressed together as if she had transformed from a willful scamp into a timid and confused little girl. "Tommy, do you believe in the devil?"

"Let's just say I'm not ruling much of anything out."

"How about us?"

"Us?"

"You and me. If some devil got into Milly, could be we're next?"

Tom wasn't about to tell her he worried along those lines whenever he chased her down in a speakeasy or watched a tantrum of hers. Sometimes he caught himself worrying for no good reason, only that she stayed way too long in front of a mirror fussing with her face or hair. Or when she came home from work in the harem girl outfit.

He stood and lay a hand on her shoulder. "Not a chance, Sis. We're going to be just fine."

Chapter Twenty-seven

Next morning, concerns about Pablo, Leo's warnings, and an ominous feeling persuaded Tom to accompany his sister on the La Brea streetcar to Hollywood High. Florence rewarded his brotherly diligence by deserting him to sit with the closest boy, whom her proximity clearly flustered.

On the way home, he tried to plan his day as well as he could when any one meeting might clue him to something new and urgent. He jotted: Madeline. Milly. Sister Aimee. Hearst. Harry Chandler. Max Van Dam. Fenton Love. LIBRARY.

After a stop at home to shower and shave, when he left Cactus Court he peered at the cars up and down the street, a habit he'd fallen into this past week. He noticed what might've been a police car parked behind the delivery truck from Miller's Dairy and would've investigated, but a beef with Fenton Love might keep him from the meeting with the redhead and her associate. He walked to the Vermont streetcar stop. While waiting there, he saw a police car make the turn off Vermont onto Wilshire and pull over a block ahead in front of the newsstand. On the ride, as they passed the cruiser, the driver sat with his head turned away. Not Love, Tom believed, but a uniform cop with a fatter head. Until the cruiser fell out of Tom's sight, it remained at the curb. Which meant nothing. Anyone tailing a streetcar wouldn't need to hurry.

Downtown, along the blocks to Uncle Sam's Automat, the only police he saw were cuffing a gal who looked at first glance like Florence in one of her speakeasy getups.

The eatery was dimly lit and smelled as piquant as Vi's chili. Madeline and a short man shared a booth in the dimmest back corner. The man sat facing the back wall, leaning across the table as if it was the only thing standing between him and the redhead's charms.

Madeline stood and offered a smile that raised her brows and flashed her dark green eyes. The fellow remained seated. She slid into the booth and patted the cushion beside her. "Coffee's like mud," she said, "but it puts a kick in your step. On me."

The fellow grimaced. Tom supposed she hadn't offered to buy his coffee. He was a pale fellow with thick rimless spectacles and pursed lips. "Tom," Madeline said, "meet George, hygienist to the dear departed, without whom the morgue would smell like a morgue."

Tom put out his hand. George complied and squeezed Tom's hand as if he hoped to crush it. A whiskered fellow in a cook's cap brought coffee. Tom reached into his pocket, found a quarter, and slid it like a puck to the redhead, which seemed to pacify George. At least the set of his jaw slackened.

"We've got to run before too long," Madeline said, "what with the mayor and his public counting on us." She turned toward George and whispered, "Tell him what you know about Frank Gaines."

The man crooked his head around and leaned as far toward Tom as the table allowed. "You say this fellow was lynched?"

"What do you say?"

"Well, yes, his neck was broken and scarred, potentially from rope burns. Now, though I watch and learn, I'm not a trained examiner. Still, I can assure you, your friend was stabbed. Thrice. In the midsection and higher. In the left chamber of the heart."

Tom devoted some moments to quieting his pulse. "Before he hanged?"

"I see no reason anyone would stab a hanged man."

"How long before the hanging?"

"As I told you, I'm no expert."

"How about I ask the coroner?"

"At best, he would tell you we have no record of the man." George reached for his pocket watch, and stared at it as though counting seconds.

"And at worst?" Tom asked.

"I leave that to your imagination," George said as he slid out of the booth.

Tom stood, waited for Madeline to go ahead, and followed them. On the sidewalk, he said, "Frank had a lady friend, common law wife you might call her. Died around July or August this year. Name of Harriet. Come up with any details, dinner's on me."

Madeline said, "Would you be sore if I make up a detail or two?"

Chapter Twenty-eight

Inspired by Madeline and the news George delivered, Tom double-timed, weaving along the crowded sidewalks of Grand Avenue and Fifth Street. Without stopping to study the library's Egyptian spire or reread etched inscriptions about the glory of books, he bounded up the entrance steps, up the staircase to the second floor, and into the periodicals room.

He came out of the stacks with a pile of recent *Times* and *Examiner* issues. He looked for headlines that addressed next Tuesday's election and tried to avoid distractions such as "Bathing Beauties Take Wax Baths to Bleach Themselves for the Latest Evening Gowns," and "Skyscraper Four Miles High Possible."

Since Republican progressives had ousted Governor Richardson in the primary, his conservative and corporate backers including Harry Chandler had nobody to promote. The only other viable candidates were Democrat Wardell and Socialist Upton Sinclair. Hearst's *Examiner* stood behind the Republican progressive C.C. Young, whose victory seemed assured. Nothing in the governor's race appeared liable to motivate the cover up.

The *Times* favored incumbent Senator Shortridge against the Democrat John B. Elliot. The *Examiner* reprinted a poem by Ambrose Bierce, whose stories Tom had begun reading after he learned that Bierce disappeared not long after Charlie Hickey vanished. About Shortridge the orator, Bierce wrote:

Like a worn mother he attempts in vain
To still the unruly crier of his brain:
The more he rocks the cradle of his chin
The more uproarious grows the brat within.

Otherwise, the race didn't seem to attract a mite of passion in either Chandler's or Hearst's newspaper.

On state, county and city propositions, the *Times* and *Examiner* generally agreed, although Chandler's stand was decidedly less fervid than Hearst's on the bond for a University of California campus in Westwood. A half dozen bond propositions regarded solutions to city traffic issues, local and suburban roads, and state highways. The *Examiner* and *Times* both lobbied in favor of them all.

When Tom returned to the stacks to exchange his pile of news for another, he spotted a whole shelf dedicated to the *Forum*. He wondered if Socrates' was the world's most prolific essayist, until he discovered multiple copies of each issue. Donated, he supposed.

He selected issues dedicated to Harry Chandler, William Randolph Hearst, the Klan, and Sister McPherson. Back at his table, Tom had company. A fellow turned from a book just long enough to shoot Tom a savage glare. He wasn't one of the disheveled crazies. Rather, his hair was slick with pomade, he wore pressed tweeds and a bow tie.

Tom sat and chose the Sister Aimee issue.

The Forum, September 20, 1926

For the people, by Socrates:
   This reporter must acknowledge he does not
stand with Sister McPherson on all issues.
When she rails against Mister Darwin's theories, I have to smile. She's a wise one,
who knows you don't build a legion of devotees by advocating a doctrine that, if you
accept it, will make you revisit all you've
ever learned. We who survived the Great War,
and the influenza plague that called away

our loved ones, need comfort, not science.
Broach science after we're comforted. For
now, heal us.

As a fellow scribbler, I admire her poetic
sense. Even while tending toward the flowery
and archaic, it rises above the ordinary
through its consistent vigor and frequent
brilliance.

The Reverend Robert Shuler deems our
Sister a charlatan, a P.T. Barnum who stages
melodramas with costumes and facades that
put the faith to shame. He calls her an
entertainer who takes her cues from the
devil. He condemns her for owning a fine automobile, dressing like a queen, and traveling
in luxury, without noting what she gives.

Temple sisters stitch baby clothes for
poor mothers. Brothers find jobs for men
released from prison. Her commissary pro-
vides food, clothing, and rent money for the
needy, regardless of race or religion. The
prayer tower with its switchboard ministers
advises and consoles parents, embattled hus-
bands and wives, and those brought to their
knees by opium or liquor.

For seven years, with her children in
tow, Sister traveled the land, sleeping in
her automobile, preaching glad tidings to
the poor, the ailing rich, the colored, the
foreign. By all accounts, she has been the
conduit for healing thousands of the lame,
the blind, the deathly ill. Mothers who
cannot shoulder the burden of another child
send her their babies. Since her arrival in
Los Angeles, Sister has served as profound
evidence that our wives and daughters can
exhibit strength, wisdom, and courage far
beyond what we may have believed. For this
valiant woman of exuberant good will, I say
to the Reverend Shuler, step aside. Our
Sister, who preaches recovery of innocence
to prostitutes, moderation to nightclub
revelers, and sacrifice to the favored, earns

from both saint and sinner respect and regard
for the same reason she won the hearts of
Klansmen, Gypsies, and the prize-fight crowd:
because she does not judge them.

How, I ask, can we look upon her current troubles without recognizing the grand
irony, that she who is loath to judge is
being judged by us all.

The man in tweeds had jumped up and rushed away after another savage glance. As he'd left books on the table, Tom leaned over and read the titles. One was a historical study of California earthquakes, the other a primer on explosives.

A wall clock informed him time was in short supply. After folding and pocketing several *Forum* issues, he left the library on heavy feet and with a fluttering heart. Because his next chore would take him to Milly.

Chapter Twenty-nine

Tom stopped by home for a sandwich and to stall. For the first time since Oz brought him news about the lynching, he wondered if he should give up. But he couldn't hope to live in peace as such a coward he wouldn't face his own mother.

He was slathering butter on a roll when the front door rattled. He opened it to find Mister Hines from the Top Hat staring up at him.

"Good day, Mister Tom."

"And to you."

"You see, Mister Max he ask can you stop by the club tonight. He come in about nine o'clock."

"Sure will," Tom said. "Stay for a sandwich."

"No sir, but thank you kindly." Mr. Hines tipped his derby and scooted off.

The walk, bus, and streetcar rides, Tom wasted on the futile attempt to calm himself by planning for the showdown. But he couldn't imagine what to say to the woman who bore him, smothered him with what she fancied as love, and found ingenious ways to terrorize him and Florence. The woman who took her children at least monthly on walks around the La Brea tar pits and convinced them that, should they defy her, she would heave them into the pits where they'd spend eternity with the ghosts of ancient beasts. Because she had born them, she claimed, she held forever the legal and moral right to end their wicked lives.

Her current home was near the corner of Apex and Fargo, in a boxy clapboard duplex of wartime construction, and with a castle turret more recently tacked on. A lookout tower, Tom thought. From up there with binoculars she could spy on Angelus Temple.

As always, Milly had transformed simple and spare to exotic. Bougainvillea grew high on the east wall and rounded the corner to frame a front window. Tall lilies and gladiolas spanned the front except for the small porch, which was enclosed by an arch of trellises woven with vines of emerald leaves and bright blue flowers like tiny trumpets.

He would've preferred a blitz straight into the toughest line Coach Rockne could field to knocking on Milly's door. He glanced down at his shirt that quivered with the pounding of his heart, and rapped on the door frame.

He expected her to react with a scream. But she simply yanked the door open, stared for a couple seconds, turned without a word, and strode back to her occupation, which was sewing.

She worked on one of the new electric machines that resided in a wooden cabinet. He wondered if she still made costumes and offstage outfits for Mary Pickford, whom she used to both idolize and passionately envy, even before the star married Douglas Fairbanks. Milly sat as her son remembered, with statuesque posture, her long neck bending slightly forward. Her golden hair was curled up in a topknot somewhat like Sister Aimee's, only of lighter, finer hair.

Baskets of ferns and vines hung from the ceiling above Milly's head.

"You've come to apologize," she said.

"Mind if I sit?"

Though she didn't answer, he believed he saw a shrug. He sat on a loveseat with arms of carved mahogany, which he remembered, and newer stitched magenta upholstery. He noticed the familiar odor of moist soil. On every surface, potted succulents, herbs, or flowering plants grew.

"Florence is well, I presume," she said.

He wanted to ask why in hell she'd presume anything of the sort. Instead he chewed his lip until he could mouth the words with which he'd decided to lead, before Milly could stun and confuse him with accusations. "Your man," he said, "Teddy Boles. Why'd he come after me?"

"Well, Tom," she said, her voice measured and calm, "I suppose it's the only way he knew to pay you back for what you've done to me, how you've broken my heart."

"Uh huh, I could possibly buy that if he hadn't come with a gang that included a shooter."

She kept sewing, didn't glance his way. "Then I'm a liar?"

He wanted to demand, and what word could describe you any better? But that would bring the interview to a close, with him ducking and running from whatever she chose to throw. "Teddy live here?"

He noticed a move of her throat as if she'd choked on a sob.

"You want me to leave," he said, "just tell me when and where I can meet with Teddy."

Her arm flew to her face. A ghostlike wail burst out of her. She wailed and wept for a minute or so. Tom didn't budge but sat and suffered the familiar gut-wrenching helplessness until she wiped her eyes with a sleeve and wheeled on him. "Teddy's gone," she bellowed.

"Gone where."

"Packed his belongings and ran away. From you."

"Where'd he go?"

"Why would he tell me, when he knew very well you'd come and beat his whereabouts out of me?" She sprang to her feet. "I suppose I'll never see him again. He skipped town at the first sign of trouble. Just like your evil father."

The smooth and graceful lines of her face had warped. She'd become a harpy. The pale skin she pampered with a movie queen's ration of herbs and ointments glowed like a block of ice in summer sun. He expected a barrage of potted plants, scissors, or stuff more lethal, or an assault with her flailing fists and torrents of garbled speech from the Azusa Street days. But she threw nothing, yelled nothing, only attacked him with the eyes of a tigress fighting for her life.

"Teddy's an electrician, I hear. For the city. Where's he work?"

"Leave me alone," she commanded.

"Give me a friend of his. I can track him down anyway, bring him back if that's what you want."

"I won't let you hurt Teddy. I know you. A violent and hateful man. Like your father."

Tom tried not to snarl. "You're lying again."

"Oh am I? For God's sake, he beat me mercilessly, don't you remember?"

While Tom shook his head, she turned and dashed to an easy chair quilted in daisies, threw herself face first into its cushions and sobbed.

Tom could think of nothing to do.

On his way to the door, the brilliance of a sequined scarlet evening gown caught his eye. It hung on a rack in the hallway to the back rooms. Pinned to its collar was a tag with the name Marion in bold capital letters.

Chapter Thirty

Tom walked uphill, then down, not quite sure of his destination. All that mattered was, each step put him farther from Milly. Even after he began to sense a tail, minutes passed before he stopped and looked around.

He leaned against a power pole and reminded himself that lying came as naturally as breathing to Milly, that Charlie Hickey was a kind and gentle fellow. For at least the thousandth time, he wondered why would a good man run off and leave his kids behind with a savage woman.

He set out across a small park beside a Victorian structure labeled by a sign as "Aunt O'Dell's Room and Board for Young Ladies." Two ancient fellows sat on a bench ogling a voluptuous pair who frolicked with badminton rackets and a birdie. Before Tom approached the men, he rolled his neck and worked his jaw back and forth to relax his expression, which he supposed could pass for the grim reaper's.

"Sirs?"

One of the men grudgingly turned his way. "Need something?"

"I believe there's a city maintenance office in the neighborhood."

"Yep."

"How about pointing me there?"

The old fellow hitched a thumb over his shoulder and turned back to the badminton game.

Tom plodded across the park. While circling around a football game of three man teams, he allowed a moment to dream of running a play. But he knew better than to let himself lament or long too deeply for a life he could only have by sending Florence into the world on her own, which he wouldn't consider.

The city maintenance station was a dirt lot, a gang of trucks, and a shed, on Glendale about a half mile past Angelus Temple. He entered and found a portly man napping, leaned back in the swivel chair behind his cluttered desk. Tom stood a minute shuffling his feet, hoping the man would rouse. Then he opened the door and slammed it.

The man startled, quaked, and muttered something. Tom guessed it might've been, What do you need?

"I'm looking for Teddy Boles. Electrician. You've got a roster?"

"That I do, only you ain't getting a look at it." The man showed him a bulldog face.

Tom stared back and decided the offer of a bribe, at least what he could pay, would only rile the fellow. "How about you look up Theodore Boles, tell him to come see me." He leaned over the desk, helped himself to a note pad and pencil, and jotted his name and address. "Tell him I said we're square, and I've got something important he needs to know." He gave the man a look he figured might befit a loan shark's collector.

As he stepped outside, he noticed Fenton Love. Leaning against a light pole. Tom would've bolted across the street, except the eastbound streetcar came rattling. In the time the three cars took to pass, Love vanished.

Tom walked to the next stop and waited for the westbound. On the ride, between Vermont and Normandie, he noticed a banner draped between windows of an apartment building. It advertised a new film, Marion Davies in *Beverly of Graustark*. The image, Tom had seen before, on the cover *Theatre Magazine*. Florence had brought it home to prove Mister Hearst's lover could be Milly's younger twin.

"Marion," he said, in a pitch that earned him curious looks from fellow travelers.

The scarlet evening gown had clued him that Milly sewed for a Marion, with an "o." Which connected Hearst and Milly. What that meant, he couldn't guess. He thought of racing back to her place. But she would only lie. And a sudden fear struck him. Milly might already be on her way to avenge herself against Tom by stealing her daughter.

From the bus stop at Vermont and Third Street, he ran home. He heard Florence's radio and flopped on the sofa in relief.

She came out and looked him over. "Teddy Boles whip you again?"

"Teddy skipped town, according to Milly."

She dropped to her knees and clutched his wrist. "You saw her?"

"In the flesh."

"What'd she say?"

"That Teddy came to pay me back for what we did to her by running off."

"Five years later."

"Some people are slow to anger."

"Not Milly."

"I meant Teddy. Now the bum's gone off, she said, on account of I attacked him. And good thing he did, since I'm a wicked and violent monster."

Florence's hand rose and muffled a nervous laugh. "Did she say anything about me?"

"Said I ruined her life when I snatched you away."

"Aw, Tom."

"Hurts?"

"Not me, it doesn't. You?" She was patting his hand when the front door rattled.

Tom sprang up, led her to the kitchen, and told her to stay put. He went to the door and flung it open.

"How's tricks?" Bud Gallagher asked.

"So so."

"Well, I came to ruin your day. Mister Woods wants to see you, right now."

"He give a reason."

"Says there's a fellow you need to meet. Sounds fishy to me. You want, I can tell him you're at the opera."

Florence had strolled out to join them. Tom said, "Sis, you'll wait right here? Please?"

"Can't I go?"

"You wanted to help, so sit down and read." He fetched the *Forum* copies he'd taken from the library. "When you get these read, borrow the *Times* and *Examiner* from Señor Villegas. When I get home, tell me what all's at stake in next week's election."

"Sure."

"Promise?"

"Unless an emergency comes around."

"Define emergency."

"Look it up," she said.

Chapter Thirty-one

Sam Woods drove a Cadillac Brougham touring car. From Alamo Meat, he followed Central to Firestone and took the boulevard east to El Camino Real.

Sunk into the leather seats, Tom watched packing plants give way to groves of olives and oranges then vast fields of cabbage and cantaloupes bordered by smaller Japanese farms, each with its own produce stand.

Mister Woods wasn't talking. Roaring down the road and honking at the slightest annoyance appeared to require all of his powers. He hadn't mentioned their destination. If he meant to rattle Tom with ominous suspense, the gimmick failed. After the visit to Milly, Tom supposed he wouldn't rattle if the Ku Klux Klan tied him to a cross and brought out the matches.

His meat route didn't extend this far south. A couple of years had passed since he'd ventured into Orange County. He'd heard about the tracts, but hadn't imagined the extent of them. Whole villages of square stucco, low roofed, hardly bigger than sheds. Countless variations on the hacienda, from miniature to grand and showy as the mansions around Westlake Park. Along wide streets that featured a citrus tree every twenty yards or so, signs and banners implied that even yokels could own an eighth-acre of paradise. Between the tracts lay more groves of oranges and grapefruit. Then came fields of broccoli, a legion of Mexican workers trudging home, and another tract.

A few city blocks beyond the "Welcome to Anaheim" sign, the Cadillac turned, then rolled along an avenue bordered in avocado trees, and pulled to the curb across the street from the town plaza.

"I go in first," Mister Woods said.

Tom climbed out and rounded the car, stretching and watching the schoolgirls and boys. They strolled Mexican style, boys clockwise, girls counter, and circled the plaza while they eyed each other and exchanged remarks and snickers.

"Tom," Mister Woods beckoned from the doorway to a storefront with its display window covered in thick white paint. Inside were rows of white wooden chairs facing a lectern and a long table behind which a ruddy man of forty or so looked intent on calculating, jotting on a tablet.

Mister Woods showed Tom to a seat across the table. The ruddy man greeted him with a smile. He had big teeth, sharp blue eyes, and a shiny bald dome fringed in black. His shoulders were peculiarly narrow, his hands large and meaty. He gave Tom's hand a firm and cordial shake. "We've heard plenty about you."

"That so?"

"Why'd you give up football?"

"I grew up," Tom said.

Mister Woods added, "The choice was between playing football and taking good care of his little sister."

"Orphans, are you?"

"More or less. Are you some kind of dragon?"

The man chuckled. "You bet I am. And I hear you're involved in activities besides peddling Sam's choice meat and raising a frisky girl."

"I keep busy."

"And you've got into your mind a notion that one of our Klaverns has gone in for lynching."

"Suppose I do."

"Son," the man said, "I'm well aware that in other regions, our brethren have acted with excessive zeal against those whose actions and heritage they mistrust. But here, in what many regard as the promised land, our aim is simply opposing those bent on profiting by the destruction of the culture our forefathers established. I'm referring to the developers, the bootleggers, the oil profiteers, the financiers who hold no reverence for God, community, or tradition, whose greed excludes all other values."

He gave Tom an earnest smile and waited.

"Good," Tom said.

From under the tablet, which was covered with algebraic formulas, the dragon pulled a sheet of heavy paper. He held it up as though in position of honor and read aloud, in a voice that rose to a sermon's pitch, "Whereas Sister Aimee Semple McPherson has proven her God-fearing and obedient nature by healing the sick and the lame, advocating the old time gospel, we Knights of the Invisible Empire do pledge to revere her and call her our Sister. As we have bestowed this honor, we solemnly vow to protect our Sister from all harm, and to defend her wherever and whenever danger or unrighteousness threaten. We admonish our brethren everywhere to forever hold true to this vow. Denver, Colorado, 1919."

Toward the end of his proclamation, the door had opened and three men dressed in overalls entered and stopped just inside. Now the dragon signaled and the men withdrew.

The dragon sighed and turned a solemn gaze on Tom. "Son, not only did we have no hand in this lynching your negro muckraker claims as a fact, but we doubt such a regrettable act occurred. In addition, we're not about to let you, the Jew cop, or anybody else, discredit Sister Aimee."

Tom noted that the mention of Leo could mean the Klan maintained sources amongst the police. "Based on your reverence for Sister, maybe you engineered the cover up?"

"Tom, what do you think of Sister Aimee?"

"She's a pip."

"Do you wish her well or ill?"

"Whatever she deserves."

"Well, keep in mind the inquest into her disappearance and realize that broadcasting stories about this lynching you allege too place might drive the final nail into her coffin. Think, son. Do you want to see Sister in prison?"

Chapter Thirty-two

As the Brougham turned onto El Camino Real, Mister Woods said, "Smart fellow, don't you think?"

"Pal of yours?"

"A friend of the family."

Tom fixed a stare on the boss' profile. "Tell me, are you a Klansman?"

The car lurched and sped faster. "If I say no, will you come back to work?"

"Maybe."

"Then we're done talking."

From there to the city, Woods ran stop signs and passed every vehicle, including a policeman, as if a license to speed came with each Cadillac.

Tom asked to get dropped at the Top Hat Ballroom. When the boss delivered him to the curb out front of the speakeasy, the valet tipped his cap. He stood ogling the Cadillac as it roared away.

Mister Hines showed Tom from the entry to the stairs. Little Abe accompanied him up the stairs and ushered him across the dance floor. Tom looked for Florence, though he didn't suppose this dive was slick Pablo's style.

Dancers crowded the bar. The four-piece combo was on break. The drummer, who'd sat in with groups in which Tom had moonlighted, played a roll on his snare.

Max stood in the doorway to his office. "What do you drink, Tom?"

"The best you've got."

Max laughed and sent Little Abe after Canadian whiskey. He led Tom into the office, kicked the door shut, sat on the desk and invited Tom to do the same.

Tom declined. "You've got something for me?"

"Ain't you going to ask how's business?"

"How's business?"

"To get ahead in this world, a guy needs manners."

"Thanks for the reminder."

"Frank Gaines, either nobody knows him or nobody's talking. But I got something better. See, a colored boy comes to a Dragna associate and inquires about hiring a few tommy-gunners. Says he'd pay them well to drop in on a KKK meeting and blast away."

A knock sounded. The door eased open, the combo led into "Limehouse Blues," and Little Abe handed Tom his drink then backed out and shut the door.

"They make a deal?"

"No deal," Max said. "The associate, he put it to the boss. The boss says tell the colored boy to get lost. Hell, if they made a deal, I wouldn't be telling you. Thing is, Dragna's not the only fellow knows where to go for tommy-gunners."

Tom nodded and drank from his whiskey.

"Stick around," Max said, "A little dancing would do you good. No telling what might come of it. Know what I mean?"

"Only I've got a little sister to find." Tom hopped off the desk and set his glass on it. He thanked Max, shook his hand, then hustled down the stairs and out. He jogged all the way to Cactus Court and walked a fast clip past the cholla.

Florence was gone. He found her room littered with dresses and slips, the usual scene she left behind when skipping out. The only time he'd asked why she didn't cover her tracks, she said, "Come on, Tommy. If I didn't hurry, you might show up and catch me."

He moved a chair to the best angle for keeping one eye on the window that overlooked the path, giving him a view of an avocado stump, an ancient well, and the street. Then he sat down with his *Forum* collection and read using the available eye.

April 6, 1926
For the people:
    Harry Chandler, you ask:
    To expose Chandler's nature, one can begin with his forbear, the man who elevated young Harry from a delivery boy to son-in-law and heir. About that man, General Otis, founder of our city's most circulated, if least trustworthy newspaper, I cannot choose better words than our Senator Hiram Johnson, who knew the man all too well and wrote, "There he sits in senile dementia, with gangrened heart and rotting brain, grimacing at every reform, chattering impotently at all things that are decent, violently gibbering, going down to the grave in snarling infamy. Disgraceful, depraved, corrupt, crooked, and putrescent is the General, a man who turned his wrath against whosoever dared to organize in the quest for a wage sufficient to feed and clothe their children."
    Over the decade since Harry Chandler assumed control of our city's most influential news source, the heir has shown such a dearth of humanity, compassion, and integrity in reporting the truth, the late General would be exceedingly proud.
    Of a limit to Chandler's ravenous hunger for property, power, and influence, no evidence exists. Not only has he acquired more land than most emperors claim, but in league with conspirators from Sacramento and Washington, he drained the Owens Valley of the water upon which its farms once flourished, simply to raise the value of his holdings, and he aims to repeat the scourge upon all communities in California, Arizona, and

Mexico that depend upon the Rio Colorado.
    Lord Acton spoke the truth: "Power tends
to corrupt, and absolute power corrupts abso-
lutely. Great men are almost always bad men."
    As evidence, I present Harry Chandler.

When Tom heard a scrape from outside, looked up, and spotted his sister, she was weaving a little more than required by her normal swishy walk. He dashed outside just in time to glimpse an automobile a king's chauffeur might drive, gliding away from the curb.

As Florence wobbled close, she gave him a loopy grin. "Good evening, Tommy."

"Evening's gone. It's night."

"Oh dear." She slipped past him.

He sat on the sofa waiting while Florence used the toilet and changed. When she leaned out of her bedroom door and called, "G'night, Tommy," he raised his hand and beckoned, in a manner that meant business.

She came and sat beside him. "Got news for me? Or you want to know about the elections?"

"What've you got?"

"Nothing different than what you'd think. Them that favor the builders and boosters, the *Times* can't praise enough. The *Examiner* newshounds, they're after the wise crack and looking for reasons to quibble. But real controversy, not on your life. For that you go to the Little Blue Books."

While Tom sat marveling at her fluency, she gave him a peck on the cheek and stood.

"Whoa," he said.

"Yes, brother dear."

"Tell me about Romeo's cars."

"Romeo was Italian. Pablo's Spanish. Descended from nobility."

"He's got a Rolls and a what?"

"A Leyland."

"Where'd you go?"

"Just a little dinner by candlelight, then a dance or two, and straight home. Are you worried about my honor, Tommy?"

"What's Pablo's angle?

"He thinks I'm a dream."

"His angle?"

"He's looking for films to invest in."

"And he wants to make you a star?"

"No." Her brow furled and lips pursed, the expression that came when she was pondering whatever troubled or puzzled her. "Not so far. But he's awfully interested in you. I thought at first he wanted to use your orchestra in a movie. But tonight, he asked what you've learned about the lynching. And I said, 'How do you know about the lynching?' He sort of blushed and mumbled that a pal of his knows most everything."

Chapter Thirty-three

Tom fried eggs and potatoes for breakfast. He called Florence, then ate while she roused herself. Before he left, he kissed her cheek, which was no part of their routine.

Around seven a.m. every bus bench was occupied by laborers. The Chinese sat together, as did the Mexicans. Negroes and whites mingled. Some of each color didn't look pleased. Tom spotted neither lost souls nor crazies. Among workers, they were rare.

He caught Leo still in his pajamas. Vi was busy dressing Una for school. Over coffee, Leo said, "Yesterday, I call in sick, leave a message for the captain, tell him send some other stooge to Owens Valley. I go out, Vi gets a call. The man says, 'Tell Leo he ain't sick, what he is, is fired.'"

"Sorry," Tom muttered.

"For what? We run out of money, I'll go work for a bootlegger no less crooked than the law."

"Hush," Vi called from the kitchen.

Tom briefed Leo on last evening with the dragon. "Only surprise is, they're keeping an eye on you. Who do you suppose?"

"Search me."

"How about Davis himself?"

Leo kept his own counsel.

"I'll guess you know Max Van Dam."

"He a confidante of yours?"

"Football gambler. He claims a Jack Dragna associate got approached by a colored fellow in the market for tommy-gunners who'd welcome a fracas with the Klan."

Leo closed his eyes. "Give me orders, would you?"

"Orders?"

"Funny how life goes. Me playing assistant to a pup."

"You could find Teddy Boles and scare the truth out of him. And you could stakeout my place this evening, get a tail on Florence. Something's fishy about Pablo, the dreamboat she thinks saved my neck at the Casa del Mar."

Leo dressed and gave Tom a ride. On Wilshire, as they passed the Talmadge Apartments Tom thought about the day, less than two weeks past, when he parked his meat truck and stood admiring the place. Brocade trim around the top and between the second and third floors and insets of the goddess with hand-maidens turned an otherwise plain building into art. That day, he'd gone into the lobby and inquired about renting, in hopes that the orchestra would soon draw more bookings. Today, he wondered if ever again he'd get to follow any of his dreams.

Leo drove to the east end of Wilshire and through downtown to the Examiner Building, a Moorish fortress. As Tom climbed out of the Packard, Leo said, "Best get your head out of the clouds."

Tom paced back and forth on the sidewalk, watching for police, Fenton Love in particular. When he gave up, he entered through the main arch and crossed a verdant patio. Had he known where to find Hearst's office in the labyrinthine maze, he would've bypassed the checkpoints and gone straight there. Lacking a map or knowledge, he chose to stop at the switchboard. On his way, he noticed a gallery of photographs. Portraits of *Examiner* employees. He inspected a couple dozen of them and recognized no one. But when he reached the end of the second row from the bottom, he said, "Bingo."

Either the guy who appeared to stare back at him or his twin sang in the Angelus Temple choir. Jack Chavez. Reporter. City beat.

A few strides up the shiny-tiled hall, a harried gal ignored him for minutes though he leaned over the switchboard close enough to savor her lilac perfume. When at last she glanced up from stabbing the key ends of phone cords into jacks and yanking others out, he said, "Ring Mister Hearst, would you? Say Tom Hickey needs a few minutes."

"Huh?"

Tom repeated his name. The girl rolled her eyes, made a poof sound, and jabbed a key into a jack. She twirled a lock of her hair and listened. "Tough luck," she said, and returned to yanking and stabbing.

He might've persisted except his next destination promised a more agreeable female.

He hoofed Broadway from Eleventh to Temple Street, cut across the lawn, and entered the Hall of Records. He dodged the builders, architects, petitioners of all sorts lined five or more deep at a dozen counters, and ducked into the quiet of the Archives. Madeline stood behind her counter, reaching over to pat the shoulder of an ancient fellow who looked so grieved he might expire any instant. While Tom was leaning against the wall beside the entry door, she glanced over and winked at him but withheld her comely smile, which might've belittled the old fellow's sorrow. Soon enough she sent the man away with a gentle promise of some clerical duty she'd perform.

As Tom approached, she raised her eyebrows. "You again?"

"I mean to stop by every day."

"Business or pleasure?"

"Take your pick."

"You're the business before pleasure kind, unless I'm all wet."

For an instant, Tom let himself wonder what she would look like all wet. "Any word from George?"

"Sure. He doesn't like you. You're too big, too handsome, too smart."

"He said that?"

"Men don't need to talk. A girl can read their minds."

"Did he give you, or think, anything about Harriet Gaines?"

"Buy me lunch?"

Tom felt a wave of shame. "If you know a place that takes IOUs."

"So happens, I do. Come on back at eleven. Meantime, I'll talk to George." The office door opened, a petitioner entered, and Madeline whispered, "Now scram." She reached out and gave his shoulder a pinch and a shove.

With most of an hour to kill, he walked to a newsstand and spent a portion of his last few dollars on today's issues of the *Times* and the *Examiner*. Then he found a Hall of Records patio bench under a palm and beside a patch of desert rose and agave. He searched the *Examiner* city section for a Jack Chavez byline but found none, though most every section carried the latest on Sister Aimee. Local and national ran disclosures of evidence linking Sister to a Carmel hideaway her radio engineer had rented. Fashion described the outfits found in a trunk said to belong to her. Sports ran photos of Aimee on horseback.

With the rumble and toots of cars and trucks, the clangs of girders from the site of the new City Hall, and Madeline's stealth, he didn't hear her coming until she was beside him, saying, "Wait till you hear what I've got for you."

He folded the *Examiner*. "Yeah?"

"Oh no," she said. "I tell you, you'll run off to play Sherlock and leave me eating lunch all alone."

"What if I promise?"

"How do I know you're a man of your word?"

Tom resigned himself to waiting. They walked side by side while he followed her cues, going down Temple and up a few side streets to a grocery on the corner of Olive and Third. As they entered, the fellow behind the counter said, "Good girl, Maddy, bringing me another customer."

The fellow was her cousin Bruno, a big guy with a smashed nose and a mop of black hair. She said, "Tom's a detective."

Bruno scowled. "As in police?"

"Private."

The scowl darkened. "You work for Burns?"

Tom knew of the Burns detective agency, which Harry Chandler's union busters kept in their pockets. "Not on your life."

Florence added, "Simmer down, Bru. He's one of the good guys."

She led Tom through aisles of canned goods to the meat counter, where she grabbed a salami, then to produce for green apples. Back at the counter, when she told her cousin to add the purchase to her tab, Bruno said, "Your pal ain't paying?"

"So what?"

"Man oughta pay."

"You calling Tom a deadbeat or me a tramp?"

Bruno groaned and turned to other business.

Tom followed Madeline out and around the building's corner to a staircase. As they started up, Bruno appeared and said, "I'll give you twenty minutes up there."

Madeline unlocked the door to her flat, stepped inside, and held the door open for Tom. Her place was a single room about the size of a Cactus Court parlor. A table with a hot plate, a few pans and a stack of dishes, a small ice box, a sink and a toilet stall filled one side. A wardrobe, two wicker chairs, and a Murphy bed she had made but not bothered to lift crowded the other side.

She ordered Tom to sit, went to the table and wielded a butcher knife the size of a machete to hack the salami and apples into chunks. Then she fetched a jar of lemonade from the icebox and filled two brandy glasses. She delivered Tom his lunch and turned the other chair to face him. "What do you think? Could the Biltmore do any better?"

"No ma'am." Tom pointed to the framed sketches on the walls. He'd recognized Paul Whiteman, Bessie Smith, Al Jolson, and Gene Austin. "You draw those?"

"There's a guy uptown I save up and buy them from. Drawing's not my talent."

"What is?"

"I can sing like nobody. You want to hear, Mister Bandleader?"

"You bet."

She stood, placed her lunch on the chair, caught a few breaths and belted a verse of "Yessir, That's My Baby," complete with the swaying hips and come-over-here smile, in an alto as strong as Ernestine's.

While Tom applauded, she curtsied, picked up her lunch and sat. "Now, you ready for the secret?"

Tom nodded.

"Well, George got the lowdown on your Harriet. She went by Gaines, but her actual name was Harriet Boles."

The news struck Tom like a tackle from behind.

"Hey, you look like Dempsey socked you below the belt."

"I'll live," Tom muttered.

"Husband's one Theodore Boles. What's it mean?"

"Give me a minute." Tom rubbed his temples, then sat up tall and looked her in the eye.

She said, "And George got more than that. Anytime you're ready?"

"Go on."

"Want to guess what she died of?" She frowned. "Naw, don't bother. You wouldn't guess in a million years. I never even knew the stuff was poison."

"What stuff?"

"Belladona. Purple nightshade. The only thing George couldn't get out of anybody is what made the cops so sure it was suicide."

Chapter Thirty-four

They hadn't eaten half of what Madeline prepared when Tom's Elgin clued him time was up. "Let's get you out of here."

"Aw, Bruno's all bark."

"Got a sack?" Tom asked.

She packed the apple slices and salami. He meant to walk her back to work, but she asked where his next stop would be. When he mentioned the library, she insisted on walking him there.

She let him carry the sack. With her arm looped into the crook of his, she now and then nudged a reminder to hold the sack open and let her grab a slice of salami. After each bite, she licked her lips, which gave Tom the shivers.

On the bench he frequented, with its view of the library pyramid tower and "Light of Learning" torch, he nibbled an apple wedge and asked himself once again what Frank Gaines' woman being the legal wife of Teddy Boles should tell him. About Frank. And about Milly.

Madeline took a gentle hold on his wrist and rotated until she could read his watch. "Last thing I'd want is to interrupt this exhilarating chat we're having, but duty calls."

"Sorry."

"Or, I could stay while you tell me what's the story on Teddy Boles?"

Any talk about Teddy Boles would lead to Milly, about whom he wasn't ready to talk. Besides, he'd vowed to tell nobody anything beyond what he needed to. And nobody included redheaded beauties with silky legs and moist cherry lips. On the other hand, she was helping and for all he knew might've risked her job. He said, "Boles and some pals of his jumped me, roughed me up."

"What for?"

"He didn't say."

"Did you ask?"

"It slipped my mind at the time."

She stood waiting, in a cocked-hip pose with a knowing smile, as though she believed if he gazed at her long enough, he'd break and come clean. After a minute or so, she shrugged. "Keep the salami."

He watched her walk away, with a swivel like Florence's only subtler. A few other men stopped and joined him, until a glance from Tom sent them on their way. Once she turned the corner, he entered the library, passed through the rotunda and beneath the solar system chandelier, and caught the elevator. In the reference room, he waited his turn to inquire of the librarian, a silver-haired gal with a child's faultless posture. Her mouth looked toothless when closed, but Tom caught a glimpse of shiny white teeth when he asked for a lead to the facts about belladonna. Not a smile. More of a grimace. She requested his name, scribbled on a pad, pointed to the nearest of the mahogany tables, and invited him to sit.

She rushed off, holding Tom's name, and vanished behind rows of stacks. He wondered if she might return with police, or whatever a library called a bouncer.

Ever since the news about Harriet Boles, he'd felt as if all but his brain's simplest aptitudes had departed. Which made him the last man on earth worthy to investigate a murder, challenge the high and mighty, and find the truth that might stop a gang of concerned citizens from delivering a massacre.

The librarian returned alone, balancing a pile of books, magazines, and leaflets that reached from her waist to her ribs. Tom met her and offered to relieve her of the pile. She curtly declined, brought them to his table, and sorted them into three stacks. Books. Magazines. Pamphlets.

First he tackled the pamphlets and learned the deadly secret of mistletoe berries, and discovered that he might've died a hundred times in the back yards Milly populated with such killers as hyacinth, narcissus, daffodil bulbs, buttercups, and wisteria. On nightshade, belladonna, he found plenty. Every part of the plant and its flowers, especially the unripened berry, was deadly as hemlock. When eaten, used as an extract, or drunk in a potion, belladonna seized the digestive and nervous systems, inflicting torture that concluded in death.

He turned to the window and sat gazing at the wintry branches of an elm and a sky streaked in brown and tried to imagine a Harriet Boles who loathed herself enough to add torture to her suicide. He tried to convince himself he'd misjudged Frank Gaines so fundamentally that Frank could've killed his woman in such a way.

Neither effort succeeded.

He returned to the pamphlets and shuffled through a half dozen without discovering anything beyond what he'd already learned. Then he came upon a tract from the Eden Now Society. One of the subjects of Milly's peripatetic beliefs.

As Tom recollected, she joined the group a year or so after she left Azusa Street, and attended the society's meetings every Saturday for months, leaving Tom at home to watch after Florence. He remembered she called them the Edenists, sometimes with a smirk he didn't understand on account of his seven-year-old vocabulary. Neither did he know, back then, what they were up to. The pamphlet spelled it out.

Each of the thirty or so plants, fungi, and herbs the tract mentioned lifted the knowledgeable partaker into one condition or another of higher consciousness. Belladona, taken properly as a tincture blended into any of a long list of herbal teas, unlocked the gate to the heavenly kingdom.

Chapter Thirty-five

The Glendale Boulevard line carried Tom, a mob of folks, a few lost souls, and a troop of smiley tourists on their way to a healing service at Angelus Temple.

At the Echo Park stop, he stared from his seat at the hanging tree, then rode on toward the address the Eden Now Society pamphlet gave. A new passenger, groomed like a hobo, stood in front facing the rear, swaying in the aisle and staring at riders until the timid ones flushed or squirmed. He rubbed his hands together as though enraptured by the notion that soon he'd find someone to kill.

Tom missed his stop while watching the fellow. He spotted the Edenist address as the streetcar whizzed past. On the way walking back from the next stop, a sharp pebble stabbed through the worn out sole of his brogans.

The address was next door to a nutburger stand with brown palm fronds scattered atop a corrugated tin roof. The Edenist headquarters doubled as the residence and workplace of a fortune teller who called herself Flora. He might've guessed the name if he hadn't been plagued by visions of Frank swinging from the oak and Harriet kneeling and vomiting her bloody guts, and by questions whose answers he feared. Though he'd learned to accept having a crazy mother, the thought that she might've poisoned somebody left him feeling estranged from everything decent.

Flora was in. She wore a silk blouse with orchids that could've been painted by the same artist who sold Leo his ties. Flowers in shades of red and purple were pleated into the woman's gloss black hair. Her front room was a jungle of hanging ferns, furnished only with a round knotty pine table scarred by cigarette burns and a few mismatched wooden chairs. She seated him, then herself.

"Name's Tom," he said, "I'm hoping to write an article for *Sunset Magazine* on our region's native vegetation. The Eden Now Society seemed a good place to start."

Her look and tone, Tom imagined a follower of Sigmund Freud using. He'd gained some knowledge about those fellows because Milly consulted at least two of them and ranted about their gall charging for quackery.

"Miz Flora," Tom said, "if you'll provide me with a membership list, and your educated guess about who among them I'd best consult for of my article, I'd be grateful and on my way."

Her grin showed off a gold front tooth. "Our membership is strictly confidential."

"Suppose I join?"

"In that case, we might allow limited access."

"Sign me up," Tom said.

She stood, strolled into a back room, swishing her pleated skirts on the way, and returned with a paper and pen. "Twenty dollars."

"For what?"

"Initiation fee."

"Right. Sure. I'll come back tomorrow with the dough. Meantime, I expect you'll let me take a look at the list. I'd really like to get moving on the article."

She gave him the gold-toothed grin.

The last time Tom had assaulted a woman he was younger than five. Milly was screaming at Florence and cursing his father. Tom socked her. Now, when he caught himself wondering if he should lift this gypsy by the throat and hold her aloft until her attitude changed, he decided to leave.

◇◇◇

He stood in his bedroom staring at his Selmer clarinet and Buescher True Tone alto sax, trying to decide which to pawn. With a sigh and promise to fetch it before the claim expired, he picked up the sax.

Auggie's Jewelry and Loan, on Broadway and Seventh across from the Lankershim Hotel, fronted him $26.50. He crammed the ticket and the money into his billfold. He hadn't walked fifty yards before he checked to make sure he hadn't already lost the ticket. Then he tried to convince himself the sax was only a hunk of metal. For now, all that mattered were Frank, Harriet Boles, and Florence.

The streetcar was running behind, and the cause was clear enough each time the coach stopped. The driver couldn't let a skirt enter or exit without showing off his repertoire of wit.

At Flora's place, Tom sacrificed two tens. Trying to send a twinkle from his eye, he said, "How about a few minutes with the membership list, make it easy on us both?"

She pushed the application form across the table.

He filled it in, a lie on every line, and passed it back. "The membership list."

"Limited access," she reminded.

"Meaning?"

"Certain members request anonymity, for reasons of their own." She reached under the table and came up with a thin pamphlet.

He opened the pamphlet. As he scanned the names, he asked, "You have some of these from past years?"

"Why would you want them?"

"It's not just current members know about the region's vegetation, I'd expect."

"Current members will give all you need, I'm sure."

Tom only recognized one name. Pointing to it, he leveled his gaze on the gypsy. "Harriet Boles."

She gave him a woeful smile. "Harriet was one of us, though inactive lately. A pity."

"Huh?"

"Her passing."

"Belladona," Tom said, and waited for a reaction. All he got was a sorry gold-toothed smile.

Chapter Thirty-six

Even halfway between the afternoon healing service and evening's worship and sermon, the sidewalks around Angelus Temple roiled with a wondrous assortment of humans. Brand new Angelenos, aglow with blind faith in the boosters' claims of all life's needs and delights free for the picking, mingled with hostiles carrying signs and banners, who hollered slogans that proclaimed Sister Aimee a swindler. Devotees shouted down the antagonists. Here and there a policeman attempted to mediate. And, alongside one of the uniformed cops, glaring at Tom, stood Detective Fenton Love.

No doubt Sister was back home from the Grand Jury proceeding. Which meant, to wedge himself through the crowd in front of the parsonage door cost Tom several minutes and some of his fullback skills.

Emma Shaffer stood guard at the open door, backed up by two swarthy fellows. She looked even sallower than before. Her drab hair appeared to have sprouted gray over the past few days. Still she stood tall, chin out. "Good day, Mister Hickey."

Tom removed his fedora and held it to his chest as if he meant to pledge allegiance. "Ma'am. I could use a few words with Sister McPherson."

"Not today, sir. We fear Sister is ailing."

Tom might've asked for an appointment, but after what he'd learned today, he knew he couldn't rest without some answers.

He said, "Let me in, please. Give me your ear for one minute, in private." A reporter tried to circle on his right. Tom blocked with an elbow and leg.

Emma Shaffer stepped aside, as did one swarthy fellow behind her. He let Tom pass, then closed the door.

Shaffer said, "Yes?"

"Private," Tom said.

She huffed but wheeled and led him to a small library off the kitchen. Half the shelves were devoted to Sister Aimee's *Bridal Call* magazine. Shaffer shut the door, squared off, and lifted her chin even higher. "Be brief, please."

"Sister probably told you I was investigating the lynching."

"The alleged lynching."

"Either way, it's got some colored folks making plans to go gunning for Ku Klux Klan. And I expect nothing's going to stop them but the truth, which I'm not likely to get without your Sister's help."

"Then I would suggest you return tomorrow."

Tom supposed the woman had resided in hell since the day she accompanied Sister Aimee to Ocean Park Beach. Either she came home believing Sister had drowned, or she'd risked body and soul as a conspirator in the preacher's outrageous con. He said, "You'd let the whole world burn if it meant saving your precious Sister?"

"I would." She averted her eyes and stood still as though allowing a moment to reconsider. "Yes."

"I'll be here bright and early." Tom opened the door, passed the swarthy fellows, went outside and wedged through the gang of reporters throwing queries at him.

As he stepped onto the sidewalk, a hand grabbed the back of his collar and gave it a mighty yank. Tom's guard flew up while he wheeled. He found himself staring at Fenton Love.

"Here's for telling lies about me," Love said, and threw a roundhouse punch.

Football had trained Tom's reflexes. He ducked in time so the punch only glanced off his cheekbone. He could've landed a jab in Love's belly, but the man was a detective with four or five uniformed cops nearby to back him. Tom preferred a beating to another lost night in jail. He backed away with long strides. The detective stalked him.

"What lies?" Tom said.

As Love rushed, the elbow Tom threw up to block caught him square in the mouth. The man didn't wince, grimace, or rage. Instead, he grinned, lifted a hand, and made a beckoning gesture to the fellows in uniform. Then he rushed again, both arms slashing.

The detective was taller, but Tom had longer arms. He sidestepped all but a glancing blow to the shoulder, and threw a right that doubled the man over. An elbow to the back of the neck dropped Love face first on the pavement. He lay for half minute before trying and failing to roll over. By that time, Tom saw the uniformed cops weren't about to detain him. They appeared in no hurry to assist the detective in any way.

Reporters followed Tom all the way to the streetcar, some wanting to hear what he'd learned from Emma Shaffer, others curious to know what Fenton Love held against him. His patience depleted, he turned on one pushy fellow. "You want to tell me why none of you louses wrote a word about the lynching? Give me that story, I'll tell you mine."

All five reporters backed away.

Maybe, Tom thought, as he boarded the streetcar, if he talked things over with the right person, between them they could begin to put in order the awful thoughts cluttering his mind. Intuition or hope, surely not reason, told him Madeline could be the right person.

He arrived at Bruno's Grocery a few minutes after six. He would've rounded the corner and climbed the stairs except Bruno was outside, boxing lettuce from the sidewalk display to take it in for the night.

"Too late, chum," Bruno said. "She's already out on the town. Most nights, she don't come home till late."

Tom walked off shuffling his feet, thinking he ought to kick himself for letting his heart drift away from where it was needed. He wondered what kind of rat would forget that his little sister might already be painted up, dressed in something silky, shoulderless and backless, V-cut in front, hemmed above her pretty knees, and on her way out the door. He double-timed to the bus stop.

Chapter Thirty-seven

As Tom reached his block of Virgil Street, he saw the Packard up ahead on Fourth at the base of the hill. In the moonlit dark, he didn't see a driver inside. He squinted and made out a scratch along the passenger side. The car was Leo's.

He wished he and Leo could talk, but wouldn't risk Florence and her Romeo showing up and spotting them. He walked on home and gained hope for relief from the dread that possessed him, because he saw a light in the cottage.

The relief didn't come. Florence was gone. He looked in the kitchen where they often left notes to each other. He scrambled a few eggs, brewed coffee, sat at the kitchen table, picked at the food, and brooded. He devoted a few minutes to Fenton Love, far more time to Milly.

Then he turned out the kitchen light, moved to the parlor, and sat in the dark. Just maybe, if Florence thought he wasn't home, she might invite Romeo in, or at least let him walk her to the door where Tom could meet him. Not since Coach Gloomy Gus chewed out the team at halftime had Tom felt so willing to thrash an adversary.

His mind kept whirling and refused to pursue any sort of logic. Still he tried to sift through all he'd learned or speculated about the lynching. He groped for evidence that led anywhere other than Teddy Boles.

Long before he expected her, he heard the tap of Florence's Mary Jane shoes with their two-inch heels that called attention by the noise as well as the lift they gave her already notable rear end. The only footsteps were hers.

He sat still, let her use her key. When she entered, flipped on the light and saw him, she jumped back and squealed, "Tommy, you sap. What's the big idea?"

"I'm setting an example," Tom said. "Water and Power's got all the dough they need." He eyed her spangled outfit. "Did you go to church?"

"Wouldn't you like to know. Say, you're so curious, why weren't you out snooping on me? Give up?"

"Busy," Tom said. "I'm afraid giving up's not in my nature."

She sat on edge of the sofa and leaned his way. "You don't look so good."

He wanted to tell her about belladonna, the suicide diagnosis, Flora, and Frank's woman's real name. But within that quagmire were paths he didn't know if he'd ever be willing to lead her down.

"Discouraged?" she asked.

He couldn't deny that, so he nodded.

"I'm here to help, Tommy," she said. "Really. It's a standing offer." She stood and kissed him on the forehead, then continued on to her room.

For some minutes, Tom sat and listened to her barefoot steps, the rustling of her clothes, then her splashing in the bathroom. After she turned off her bedroom light and shut her door, she sang a verse of "Gimmee a Lil' Kiss, Will Ya, Huh?"

A wave of shame caught him and knocked him off balance. Because he saw a woeful truth. Suppose he managed to save Florence from the treacherous world. Still, he lacked the wisdom to save her from herself.

He didn't hear Leo until the knock. He opened the door and put a finger to his lips, hoping they could keep from waking Florence.

Leo sat where Florence had, only he sank deep into the cushion. "Hmm," he said. "Where to start? Teddy Boles?"

"Yeah."

"He flew the coop all right. At least he didn't come to work all this week. You must be scarier than I thought. Next, would you care to hear about my tribulations?"

"Get it over with," Tom said.

"A couple of the boys who've been tailing me walked up and handed me my walking papers. Cause, insubordination. And one of them says, 'You want to talk about it, Chief Davis will see you.'"

Tom made fists and rapped them on his ears. "Go talk to him, then make a beeline for the Owens Valley."

"Hold on. I haven't yet told you what you sent me out to find."

The bedroom door cracked open.

"Sis," Tom said, "If you're listening anyway, get on out here."

Florence appeared wearing a silk teddy Tom had told her to save for her honeymoon. Any other day, or with any other man but Leo, he would've sent her back for a robe.

After Leo greeted her, he watched Tom until he got a nod that meant go ahead and talk.

He only glanced at Florence. "Her fellow drives his swanky auto into the garage at the *Examiner*."

"Hey, what is this?" Florence snapped.

Leo held up a hand, palm in her direction. "A minute later, he walks out and down the street to a vacant lot. He gets into a jalopy. Next stop, his digs. A duplex on Del Valle." He handed Tom a card with an address.

"The louse," Florence said, in a voice so ghastly, Tom shivered. His sister's eyes had darkened and shrunk. Cherry red blotches appeared on her cheeks. "The filthy louse." She glowered at Leo, then at her brother. He wouldn't have bet a nickel on whether the louse in question was him, or Leo, or Pablo. Or men. When she sprang to her feet, he worried she'd find something to hurl at one of them or through a window.

But she ran into her room, slamming the door, and threw herself at the bed. Tom heard the frame collapse. Then she broke into loud sobs. He would've gone in if other such spells hadn't taught him to wait until the noise subsided. For now, she was inconsolable.

"You're going to do what it takes to get back on the force. Am I right?"

"Not on your life."

"Leo, Frank's dead. To you, he was nobody. And if some guys shoot up a Klan meeting, maybe the dragons will wise up and make tracks for Utah. Who knows what'll come of it all? Anyway, what's the odds the two of us can outsmart Hearst and the whole rotten oligarchy?"

"What's eating you, Tom?"

Maybe tomorrow he'd tell Leo about belladonna, Harriet Boles, and Fenton Love. "Not a thing," he mumbled. "Looks like Hearst used Pablo to go through Florence and get the low-down on me."

"Looks like. Question is why?"

Chapter Thirty-eight

He boarded the bus at dawn. The other bus passengers on west-bound Wilshire were gardeners, maids, a few guys so tattooed with black grime, no doubt they were riding to the oil fields.

Tom didn't look toward the tar pits, but he smelled them and grew so disturbed he failed to notice the Fairfax stop. A few blocks along, he jumped off. He walked down San Vicente and along Del Valle, watching for the address on the card Leo gave him.

The duplex was a miniature hacienda. Tom strode to the front door of the east side unit, and knocked hard. The door had a peephole. He stood to the side and knocked again, harder, telling himself he was ready for whatever Pablo might come at him with. If it was a pistol, he would kick the door shut and dive. Otherwise, he'd rush.

The door opened a crack. "Who's there?"

"Tom Hickey."

"Oh. Yeah. Give me a minute." Pablo retreated.

He'd left the door open. Tom shoved it open wider, looked around, and entered a barren parlor. The wall had separated at a corner seam, probably during an earthquake. Two chairs leaned backward against the far wall. A stack of magazines served as the coffee table. On top of another stack a dead aloe repined.

When Pablo came out of the bathroom, Tom said, "I guess you didn't bring Florence here. She would've screamed."

"I'm not proud of the place." Pablo rubbed his eyes. "Now that you're on to me, now what?"

"You're going to talk."

"Hey, sit down. Java?"

Pablo's housekeeping was enough to make Tom decline. Besides, yesterday he'd learned too much about poison. He shook his head and followed Pablo into the kitchen. The counter featured a bowl of spoiled fruit and a scattering of cafeteria-style dishes, probably nabbed, and so caked with food residue, Tom got an impulse to put them soaking. He resisted. "Hearst," he said. "What's his game?"

"Okay, he's my boss, but I don't talk to the guy. Not much anyway. How should I know what he's up to?"

"Sure. You just follow orders."

"You got it."

"And the orders were?"

"Get the lowdown on Tom Hickey, what he's snooping around after."

"Florence?"

Pablo made as if the brewing required all his attention. He stared at the coffee pot until it began to perk, then turned down the fire on the stove. "Hey, Tommy, listen."

"Let's don't pretend we're amigos, Pablo."

"That's the way you want it. Sure you won't have a cup?"

Tom glared.

Pablo poured his coffee and laced it with milk from a can. "Okay, here's the straight dope. I'm going one way down the hall, Mister Hearst is going the other. He gives me this long look, the kind makes you feel like your nose must be dripping. After we pass, he turns back my way and says, 'You there.' Well, there's nobody but me there. So I say, 'Yes sir?' He takes me up to his office, sits me down, and asks do I want to be a reporter. You bet I do. He says, 'Well then,' and he tells me keep tabs on you, and he says if he was the reporter, he'd get chummy with Florence. Didn't say I should or I shouldn't.'

"He knew her name?"

"Sure. Not a lot Mister Hearst doesn't know."

"He got you into Casa del Mar?"

"No problem."

"Teddy Boles and the others, they on Hearst's payroll?"

"Who?"

"The boys that worked me over?"

"Hey, I don't know where they came from."

Tom gave him a long, hard stare, yet Pablo didn't squirm.

"So this big shot who knows most everything, what's he know about Frank Gaines?"

"Don't ask me. Only place I ever heard about Frank Gaines was from Florence."

"And what you heard, you passed on to Mister Hearst?"

"Yeah, okay, I did reports. But you got to know, I wouldn't hurt Florence. She's a prize."

Tom stepped closer. "Maybe some years from now she'll be a prize. Right now, she's my little sister."

"Got it," Pablo said, as some coffee sloshed out of his cup.

"Drink it down," Tom said. "Then you're going to come clean about Hearst and the cover up."

"Cover up?"

"The lynching."

"Oh yeah. Hey, you know more than I do."

"Then get yourself dressed."

"What've you got in mind?"

"Where's Hearst this time of day?"

"They say he sleeps in, works late nights."

"Let's wake him up."

Wearing a look that meant Tom must be loco, Pablo shrugged and left the kitchen.

His jalopy was a Model T, pre-war, without the electric starter. It rattled over every rut and pebble.

According to Pablo, their best chance of catching Hearst in the morning was in Santa Monica at a construction site, the beach mansion Hearst was building for Marion Davies. "His doll baby's the only one can get him up early, so they say, and just yesterday she rolled in from New York. Bound to want to check up on the builders."

"Tell me about Jack Chavez," Tom said.

"Chavez, huh. I'm supposed to know him?"

"Hearst reporter."

"Oh yeah. That guy. He doesn't write much. A feature now and then."

"What's he got to do with Sister Aimee?"

Pablo swerved to miss a white cat. An oncoming Chevrolet's horn blew. Pablo leaned out the window and shouted in Spanish. The outburst appeared to relax him. He smiled and said, "You tell me."

"See here," Tom said, "I've got no reason to keep from treating you like a punching bag."

"That so? Well, I'm in a fix here, Tom. Mister Hearst pays my salary."

"Not anymore. You're bringing me to him. Means you failed him. You're as good as fired."

Pablo sighed. "Yeah, well then, Mister Hearst's got somebody planted at Angelus Temple, I hear. Chavez maybe. Could be more than one of them. See, Mister Hearst's got snitches planted all over, so they say."

"Who's they?"

"No sir. A reporter doesn't give out his sources. Not ever."

"You're no reporter."

"I aim to be."

Wilshire Boulevard ended at the bluffs of Santa Monica. With the wind at his back, Tom could've punted a football from the curb where Pablo parked his jalopy to the public pier. He shaded his eyes, looked beyond the pier and the Casa del Mar at Ocean Park Beach and imagined the mobs that overran the place in hopes that Sister Aimee would rise out of the sea.

He followed Pablo to the edge of the bluffs and along the path until they stood looking down at the foundation and some framed walls of what could become a ritzy hotel or beach club.

"No sign of Hearst," Pablo said.

"That's the mansion?"

"You bet. Mister Hearst knows how to treat a gal."

Up the street, a line of men paraded into a café. Rotarians, Tom thought, a suitable recommendation. He asked, "You run a tab for expenses?"

"Yeah, why?"

He pointed at the cafe. "Mister Hearst's treating to breakfast."

While they walked that way, Pablo said, "I don't know. He fires me, maybe I'm stuck with the tab."

"That'd be a shame," Tom said.

"I bet he'll pay up," Pablo mused. "Mister Hearst's no tightwad."

In the café, they sat beneath a stuffed swordfish. Along with his coffee, Tom ordered a steak, three poached eggs, hotcakes, and fresh squeezed orange juice. Pablo scowled and settled for oatmeal.

Tom said, "Tell me about Florence."

"Hey, you're her brother."

"When you took her out, where'd you go?"

"A club or two. Dancing. Fancy dinners. She can eat, I'll tell you."

"Drinks her share, does she?"

"Her share, I'd say."

"And when you put the moves on her, what else does she do?"

"Moves?" He raised a hand and held it halfway between them. "I won't tell you lies, Tom, that doll can give a fellow the heebie jeebies. But she's a good girl. Hell, you know that, don't you?"

"Go on."

"And smart. No Joe's going to pull the wool over that one. Something else you probably know. You don't want to cross her. We're in a club, some chit makes a crack about her dress, later on pokes fun at her hairdo. It's all I can do to keep Florence from grabbing the floozy and pitching her out the window. Fourth floor."

Tom pushed his plate aside. He knew about Florence's temper, where it came from and what it could mean. A reminder was hardly what he'd hoped to hear.

Pablo said, "You're not going to finish that steak, I'll give you a hand."

Chapter Thirty-nine

As Tom and Pablo sat on the edge of the bluff, legs dangling in the air, they didn't talk. Tom had nothing left to ask, and Pablo might've supposed silence was the safest strategy.

Tom checked his Elgin and began to doubt Hearst would show. He turned his thoughts to Sister Aimee and her disappearance. He hadn't studied enough to form an opinion about whether she'd gotten kidnapped or done a vanishing act. But as he believed she knew facts he didn't about the lynching and the cover up, he needed to decide before their next interview if she was honest or was herself the biggest liar in Los Angeles.

Even aside from the latest news about clues she'd left at some Carmel getaway, the case against her was a cinch to argue. No amount of searching turned up the shack where she claimed the kidnappers held her. Her decent condition when she'd arrived at the Arizona border saying she'd walked in the blistering heat all day indicated she was either superhuman or feeding them a tall tale. And as millions could attest, she possessed a supreme gift of imagination.

She was bombastic and a master of melodrama, but something so warm and soft showed through, Tom couldn't feature her sticking to her story under pressure of knowing her lies had cost two lives. A young fellow thought he saw her outside the breakers, and swam to his death in an undertow, and a diver lost his way in the undersea wreckage of the old Ocean Park pier.

Tom wasn't ready to convict her. Maybe this afternoon she would change his mind.

"Hey." Pablo nudged Tom and pointed at the approaching limousine.

The Phaeton, which passed them and pulled to the curb thirty yards ahead, hadn't quite stopped when a husky young man in slacks and the kind of long coat a reporter might wear sprang out of the front passenger seat. He opened the rear door and offered his arm to Marion Davies. The lady climbed out, brushing at her skirt. Hearst came right on her tail.

Tom hadn't seen either of them except in pictures. Although Hearst was about Tom's height and Davies was at least as tall as Florence, they looked smaller than he'd imagined.

Pablo called out, "Mister Hearst."

The couple turned and stared. She was a beauty, lithe and all blonde with luminous skin and rose tinted cheeks. Whoever mistook Hearst for her father would've needed to presume her grace came from the mother's side. He looked neither handsome nor powerful. But the way his sharp eyes roamed clued Tom that he saw, assessed, and drew conclusions in a heartbeat.

As they neared, Pablo said, "Mister Hearst, my friend Tom Hickey, maybe you heard the name. USC fullback."

Hearst only watched and studied. Marion Davies gracefully offered her hand, which Tom found warm and gentle.

"We came out this way on business," Pablo said, "and Tom happened to express what an honor he'd consider meeting you and Miss Davies in person."

Tom accepted Hearst's belated handshake. Their hands had barely touched when Hearst let go and turned to walk away.

"You want the truth?" Tom asked.

Hearst turned back.

"Truth is," Tom said, "I came to learn what you know about Frank Gaines."

The tycoon met Tom's gaze with something just short of a smile, the kind of expression often worn by a fellow answering a challenge he doesn't for an instant doubt he'll win. "Suppose you tell me what you think I know about this Frank."

"Sure," Tom said. "You know Frank Gaines got found hanged from a tree in Echo Park. And you know why your newspaper and the *Times* and the rest didn't print a word."

Marion used a small mirror and touched up her lipstick, while Hearst attended to Tom. "If we didn't report it, it didn't happen."

"Except it did."

"Then write your story. Give it to Pablo. Perhaps it will appear in the *Examiner* under your byline. Now if you'll excuse us."

"First let me tell you something you may not know."

"Another time."

"Honey," Marion Davies said, and petted his arm. "If there's something you don't know, I'd like to know what on earth it is."

Hearst frowned and Tom said, "You might not know it wasn't a lynching, only staged to look that way. And you may not know who did the killing, or why."

The man stood still, perhaps while the journalist in him, wanting answers, consulted with his conniving self. "And you know?"

"You tell me all about the cover up, I'll give you the murderer."

While Tom stood marveling at the nerve he'd summoned, Hearst took a minute to gaze at the choppy ocean. Then he said, "Write your story."

"Will do," Tom said. "Miss Davies, that's a lovely scarlet dress Milly made for you."

With the girlish smile her public adored, she said, "Oh, is it ready?"

Hearst whisked her off. Over his shoulder, he called to the chauffer and the stocky reporter, "Keep that fellow away from us."

Chapter Forty

When Pablo dropped him off at the corner of Sunset and Glendale, Tom meant to use the blocks walking to Milly's duplex to ease the burning in his chest. The last time he'd felt such a pain, he and the helmet of a Cal linebacker had collided straight on.

He meant to stride into Milly's presence and demand to know which Edenist poisoned Harriet Boles. Before her screaming reached its crescendo, he would assure her Teddy Boles murdered Frank, and convince her he'd found all he needed to prove she arranged the cover up by getting to Hearst through her pal Marion.

On his way up the hill on Fargo, he changed his mind. He wasn't afraid of Milly, he told himself, though he respected her ability to confound and set his mind spinning. Around anybody else, or facing a crowd, Tom felt able to think and choose his words before saying them. With Milly, he felt like a wicked, clumsy, dimwitted boy.

Besides, he couldn't separate Milly from Florence. Whatever happened to Milly happened to Florence as well. He imagined grief or fury knocking his sister out of the shadows of speakeasies and flirtations into far deeper darkness.

He returned to Glendale, caught the next streetcar downtown, transferred to the Central Avenue line, and rode to Jefferson.

On the sidewalk, he studied faces and eavesdropped for any clue about whether colored folks appeared more wary of a white fellow than before the *Forum* reported a declaration of war against the Klan.

At the barbershop he leaned against the wall just inside the door and waited while the barber shaved a man in spats and a worsted suit. All through the shave, the customer chewed a toothpick and scrutinized Tom.

The barber finished the shave, rinsed and stropped his razor. The customer slapped a dollar into the barber's hand, for a two-bit haircut and shave. He fetched a cashmere coat off the rack, slipped into it and went out, all the while eyeing Tom.

The barber said, "Your pretty hair do not look washed."

"Ask Socrates to come find me at the Smokehouse?" Tom handed over two quarters.

As Tom neared the Smokehouse Barbecue and the aroma got richer, he promised himself a decent meal. Otherwise he'd need to stab a notch in his belt, on account of Pablo's report about Florence's temper having ruined breakfast.

He entered the Smokehouse, sat at the counter, and picked up a menu. As he read, he calculated that soon, maybe tomorrow, he'd need to pawn his clarinet. He chose a snack instead of a meal. Two pork ribs and coleslaw. When it arrived, he began with the slaw and was soon breathing fire and hailing the waiter to beg for water, when Socrates appeared on the next stool.

The publisher said, "Smokey learned to cook in New Orleans."

"Good slaw," Tom gasped.

"You going to finish it?"

"Naw. Full." He shoved it in front of the publisher.

"I assume you brought me a story."

The water arrived. Lukewarm. Tom swallowed some, let the rest slosh in his mouth until he could speak without panting. "I'm betting the Klan didn't play much of a part, if any. How about calling your concerned citizens, suggesting they dismiss the tommy-gunners."

Socrates only raised his eyebrows, giving Tom to wonder if he might know more than the publisher did. "I've been putting some clues together," he said, with no mention of his fervent hope that what he'd fit together would prove dead wrong.

"You can provide evidence with which I could negotiate?"

"One thing I know about investigating," Tom said, "you don't let on what you've got until it all fits. What I'm asking for is a reason to hope time won't run out before then."

"Tom," Socrates said, like a landlord to a renter in arrears, "you're asking me to tell these citizens, who in all likelihood couldn't between them think of a single reason to trust a white man, to change whatever plans they may have on the basis of vague report coming secondhand through me provided by a white man about whom I know nothing except what concerns his music and his record as a football player. Give me the evidence."

"A Chevrolet parked across the street the night before they found Frank."

"Says?" Socrates reached into his vest for a note pad and pen.

"A neighbor." Tom checked his own notes and gave the woman's name and address. "Frank didn't die from the rope. He got stabbed first, hanged later."

The publisher's eyes lit. "Says?"

Tom shook his head, unwilling to risk trouble for Madeline's friend. "Sister Aimee's going to preach about the biggest liar in the city, the evening of the election."

"So I read. Does that make her part of the cover up?"

"It's something to think about," Tom said. "Look, suppose I say all you've got to do is tell me who saw Frank Gaines hanging and the cops take the body away and I'll find the murderer in two days. What'll you say?"

Socrates reached for a clean spoon and made short work of Tom's slaw. Then he said, "No names. A woman. Blonde and attractive."

Tom gulped. For a minute he stared at the counter. He shoved the ribs to Socrates. He stood and dropped a quarter on the counter.

As he walked outside, he told himself the woman didn't have to be Milly. She could be Marion Davies, or Mary Pickford, or any one of ten thousand Hollywood beauties.

Chapter Forty-one

The courthouse, Tom imagined, got designed as a Gothic structure in dark and solemn stone to make visitors feel reverent in the presence of high authority. He cut a path through the crowd of reporters, tourists and lost souls craving a glimpse of Sister, and hotheads demanding either her exoneration or her slow and miserable death in San Quentin.

He slipped past a marshal at the door but got halted by another at the base of a wide staircase. "Sorry, bub. Too much ruckus in the hall. Unless you've got a subpoena or your mother's the Pope, nobody gets up there today."

"Aimee's a friend of mine," Tom said.

"Half of L.A. thinks she's a friend of theirs."

"Go ask her. Name's Tom Hickey."

Either the man didn't follow USC football or he favored Stanford or Cal. "Not on your life. Now move along, bub."

Tom went peaceably. Outside, he asked a guy with a press pass slipped under his hatband, "Any idea what time the show lets out?"

The reporter said, "Most days, not much before 3:30, unless Sister faints again. You got anything for me?"

"News?"

"What else?"

Tom looked again at the press pass and decoded the top of the letters whose bottom halves the hatband covered. *Times*. He said, "You'll write what I give you?"

The reporter crooked his lips. "What's that supposed to mean?"

"Think about it, Shakespeare. You'll come up with an answer."

He walked away hoping he'd made the right choice by declining to steer the white public toward what the colored folks knew. One piece of wisdom life had taught him was, before you turn anything loose, calculate how it might come back to bite somebody you don't want bitten.

He'd thought about waiting on the courthouse steps and eavesdropping. But worries about Florence left him unfit to wait for anything. Besides, the Hall of Records was next door.

He stood in line while Madeline coached an old gal item by item through a request for a death certificate and spent minutes convincing the next fellow that she had no more access to the property map of some parcel in Massachusetts than he did, and that his best course was to inquire of Bristol county by telephone. The man huffed away.

Tom leaned on the counter. With his index finger hidden from behind, pointing toward the labyrinth, he said, "You see, Miss, Uncle Winslow staked a claim, way back, on a parcel down Compton way, and now the Canfield-Midway Oil Company says they own it, and they sent a gang to start drilling. I've got to stop them, and the lawyer won't budge without Uncle Winslow's deed."

"This *is* an *emergency*." She came through the gate at the end of the counter. "Follow me, please." To the three folks in line, she said, "Have a seat, won't you. This search might take quite some time."

Tom hoped the others hadn't noticed the twinkle in her eye. She led him to the first nook off the hall. "You wouldn't take advantage of a girl, would you, Tom?"

"Not if I can help it."

"Well, can you?"

"Maybe not, but first I've got a serious question. About Florence."

"Shoot."

"Our mother." Tom labored for the right words. They didn't come. "She had peculiar ideas. One of them, for punishment, she'd lock me in the dark. Naked, in a closet, with nothing in it but me, no clothes, no hangers."

Madeline's lip quivered. A tiny dark pool appeared in the corner of her eye.

"Florence was a good girl," Tom said, "and smarter than me, didn't cross Milly as often. She was twelve when I came home from somewhere and called for her. Milly was gone. I saw the chair wedged under the closet door handle. Florence must've heard me yelling, but she didn't call out. When I saw her, all still and curled up, I thought she was dead. I got her out, got her dressed, and we ran. Five years ago. As far as I know, she hasn't seen our mother since."

Madeline was gripping Tom's forearm and staring hard at his chest, as though trying to peer inside him. "Poor baby," she whispered. "Poor baby."

"Yeah," Tom said. "Now suppose, five years later, somebody lets on her mother's played some part in a murder."

"God no." Her wet eyelashes fluttered. "I get the picture. Now what?"

"Is it going to make her crazy?"

"Geez, Tom. Is she tough?"

"Thinks she is."

"How about this Milly? Does Florence talk about her? Ask about her? Dream about her?"

"Doesn't talk, doesn't ask. If she dreams, she doesn't tell me. The thing is, in some ways, she's too much like Milly for my comfort."

"What ways?"

"Vain. Restless. Wild. Hot-tempered."

Madeline let go of his wrist, then wrapped her arms around his waist and squeezed. With her cheek pressed into his shoulder, she said, "The hug's for Florence. Pass it on."

"How about one for me?"

"I knew it," she said.

"Knew what?"

"You wouldn't let me out of here unscathed." She squeezed again, even tighter.

After a minute, they released each other and Madeline led him out of the labyrinth.

Outside the courthouse, he stood toward the rear of the crowd thinking about his sister and Madeline until a loud woman nearby announced, "Some days they bring Sister out back."

He was walking toward the corner, from where he could run to either exit, when he heard the first shouts and cheers. He hustled to the front entrance, noticed at the curb the convertible he'd seen parked in the alley behind Sister Aimee's Bible school. To get through the crowd would require bowling over a dozen people, at least half of them women. Instead, he dashed to head her off at the car.

He wasn't alone. But as they approached, the crowd began to thin. Soon he knew why. Sister Aimee, though on her feet, looked so wretched, fatigued, and confused, even the hostiles and lost souls shied away. Tom imagined that if she'd looked the same when she crossed the border last May and gave the kidnapping story, nobody would've doubted.

The men who had backed Emma Shaffer yesterday held Sister up, and met with threatening glowers everyone who wanted a piece of her.

Tom stood aside and peered over the crowd that surrounded the formidable Shaffer, who answered every query in a monosyllable while she parted the mob as if by sheer force of will. She never so much as threw an elbow.

Sister was already seated in the rear of the convertible between the two men. Tom waited until the front door opened for Emma Shaffer. Then he knifed between two clumps of reporters and laid hands on her bony shoulders. "A moment of your time, please?"

The woman shot a glance toward the back seat and must've gotten an okay Tom didn't see. She nodded.

"Please," he said in a voice so desperate it chilled him, "tell Sister McPherson I'll be waiting under the hanging tree. If she could give me a few minutes, she might save a lot of people."

Chapter Forty-two

During the two hours he spent in the shade of the oak, Tom imagined different ways Harriet Boles might've died, and different possible connections between her death and the murder of Frank Gaines. He'd only started attempting to narrow them down when a whistle sounded. He looked toward the parsonage. A fellow waved him over.

Emma Shaffer met him at the foot of the half-circular stairs. "Only five minutes," she commanded as they climbed. When Tom entered the sitting room, he wondered if Sister Aimee would last five minutes.

Over the past few days, she had aged a decade. Her cheeks and forehead were pale gray, the thick hair damp and matted at the brow. Her eyes, he might've called timid. At least they lacked their usual readiness to flash or challenge. Yet she sat up straight to greet him and point to the settee across from hers.

"Emma said you needed me." Her voice was soft as a penitent's.

He remained standing, hat in hand. "I'll be brief."

"Please sit. Don't rush."

He sat. "Last time, I sensed that when you talked about Milly you implied more than you said. I got the idea that Milly did something more wicked than you figured I should hear about, at least from you. I mean, who'd want to turn a son against his mother?"

"Surely not I."

"Well, I'm asking for the whole truth, as you know it. Don't spare my feelings. The stakes are way too big for that."

She attempted a wan smile. "Lately everyone is asking me for the whole truth. You mention stakes?"

He told her enough about Socrates, Max Van Dam, and some colored folks out to hire tommy-gunners to support his concern that the Frank Gaines murder could lead to a blood bath, on both sides of the divide. The story carried him beyond the five allotted minutes. Emma Shaffer entered the sitting room but Sister raised her hand and fluttered her fingers. Shaffer backed away.

"Tom," Sister said, "you're a gifted observer of people. You see, I had a dream. I was sick, in the hospital much like the one at the end of my travail, in Douglas, Arizona. Milly came into the room, and a fright rushed through me. She gave me a bouquet. Though it was lovely, I knew very well it was no gift, but meant to adorn my grave. In my dream your mother was a great beauty, an angel. But not, I'm afraid, an angel of light."

Tom's hands had knotted into a single tight fist. A tremor climbed up his spine. "Do you remember what color the flowers were?"

"A deep, vivid purple, darker than violet."

Though Tom supposed her "dream" was actually a story based on what she knew, he saw no point in questioning. "Tell me about Kent Parrot? Is he behind the murder, or the cover up?"

Her eyes brightened a shade. "Why do you ask?"

"The parrot you preached to, the unrepentant sinner."

"My goodness, am I so subtle and creative as that? Tom, you give me more credit than I deserve."

If the grand jury summoned him as a character witness, he could assure them Sister McPherson wasn't much of a liar.

Emma Shaffer stood in the doorway. "Please, Mister Hickey."

Tom stood and made a little bow. "A guy in the Temple choir, his real name's Jack Chavez. *Examiner* reporter."

Sister thanked him. He went to the door, then turned and stayed watching her long enough so she said, "Yes?"

"Could you tell me in advance, who's the biggest liar in L.A.?"

All at once, she looked revitalized, with flushed cheeks and widened eyes. "I haven't told my own dear mother, my darling children, or precious Emma. All of you must wait until Tuesday. Do come early, or ask Emma to reserve your seats."

"Wouldn't miss it," Tom said as he backed out of the room.

On his way to the streetcar stop beyond the lake, he stood beneath the scarred branch of the hanging tree and made up his mind.

With a sizable wave of fear and trembling, he saw that his best chance of getting the truth was to squeeze it out of the biggest liar he knew.

Chapter Forty-three

All the way home and for an hour sitting in his dark parlor, Tom attempted to sabotage the apparent truth with doubts. He could've gone looking for Florence, but when he found her, he'd need to come clean. He couldn't go to Milly before he tried out his belief on Florence and saw how it changed her.

He turned on the lamp, fetched paper, a pen, and an architecture text. On the sofa, with the book and paper on his lap, he jotted ideas in a shorthand he'd developed during high school history and often used when writing notes for song arrangements.

Initials stood for people. Arrows pointed from murderer to murdered or boomeranged back to indicate suicide. He jotted possibilities in an order he realized amounted to wishful thinking. He meant to brainstorm, then read them over and rank them using whatever reason or intuition he could muster.

In the first scenario, Harriet killed herself. Teddy Boles blamed Frank for Harriet's death. So Teddy killed Frank. Then Milly, to save her man and avenge herself against Sister Aimee for ousting her from the congregation, convinced Teddy to hang Frank in Echo Park. But she repented and, through Marion Davies, enlisted Hearst to engineer the cover up.

Or, Harriet died from a miscalculation in her Edenist pursuit of the heavenly kingdom. Then Teddy blamed Frank and so on.

Or, another Edenist poisoned Harriet, perhaps because she knew and threatened to reveal the fatal result of a cultish rite or experiment. Teddy, bereft, enraged, and knowing of Frank's union organizing, rounded up a gang of Chandler's union busters and convinced them a colored Communist had killed a white gal. Teddy and the union busters killed Frank. One of them proposed laying the blame on the Klan with a staged lynching. But another, possessed by a trace of conscience, snitched to Chandler, who called Kent Parrot, who orchestrated the cover up to save Chandler's thugs from a murder charge.

But if Chandler called the play, Tom wondered, why would Hearst go along? Then he recalled that even tycoons who squared off as political enemies could have common business interests. And business was their game.

The scenarios he scribbled only had one item in common. Teddy Boles killed Frank. In all but one, Milly helped with the cover up.

He slammed the architecture book onto the sofa beside him. He groaned, heaved himself up, and plodded to the bathroom, feeling the need to vomit and vaguely wondering if Milly or another Edenist had broken into and doctored the leftover bean soup he'd forced himself to eat.

Afterward, he brushed his teeth and spilled tooth powder on his shirt. He peeled off the shirt and tossed it into the bedroom closet basket. Then he decided to lie down and wait a half hour before he went out to look for Florence. He kicked off his shoes and sprawled on the bed.

When he woke, Leo came into focus.

"Get ready," Leo said. "You won't like this."

He heard Florence weeping. He rolled off the bed, onto his feet.

"Whoa, Tom. Let me tell you before you get up."

Tom pushed back and leaned against the wall. Leo sat on the edge of the bed, rarely looking over while he spoke. "About ten, a guy calls to tell me Florence Hickey got picked up on a vice charge. Hold on, now. Here's how it went. A couple detectives go into the Top Hat, right upstairs, not a word nor a look to the other gals, they go straight to Florence. One of them, just for show, reads out Van Dam, warns him from now on, give the hookers the boot. Meantime, the other guy is dragging Florence. Only she's not cooperating, which gets her a tumble down the stairs."

Tom leaped off the bed. "Hear me out," Leo said. "Nothing's broken. Only, between the stairs and the car, she and the detective had another couple scraps. She's beat to hell," he whispered, "but I expect he got worse. And, knowing women, when you see her, I wouldn't make much of her looks."

"Can I go now?"

"A minute. See, it was a frame, pure and simple. The detective was Fenton Love. Now go on."

Tom rushed to his sister. She had moved a wooden chair into the center of the room. She sat with knees together and hands in her lap, the pose Milly used to enforce upon the girl while she yelled motherly threats or lectures.

"Stand up, babe," Tom groaned.

She was in his arms so soon, he barely got a look at the sequined dress, torn at the hem and waist, exposing most of her belly. He gazed down at a swollen bruise, big as a saucer, on what used to be an exquisite cheek.

Chapter Forty-four

Shortly after four a.m., while splashing his face at the bathroom sink, Tom decided to follow an impulse to visit Echo Park, now, close to the hour Frank's body got cut down and stolen away.

He checked on Florence, found her asleep with knees drawn up, a hand covering her cheek. He dressed and left her a note on the kitchen table. "Don't go to school. Wait for me."

He jogged the blocks to Wilshire, stopped beneath a street lamp, counted his money and hoped a dollar would get him all the way before daylight. He waved at three cabs before one pulled over.

The cabbie was dark and bald. When Tom directed him to Echo Park, he said, "Which side are you on?"

"You mean the kidnapping?"

"What else?"

"I'll pass," Tom said. "You?"

"Suffrage, that's the fly in the ointment. You let the gals vote, next thing they got a radio station and go filling empty heads with every whatnot comes to mind. You got a name, bud?"

"Tom."

"You see, Tom, women don't think in any kind of straight line, but in loops and circles that cover plenty of ground but don't end up anywhere at all. Am I right?"

"Could be."

"Thing is, they say something, don't matter how preposterous, damned if they don't start believing it. This Sister, that's why she lies so blasted well. Believes every word of it, she does."

He carried on about a magazine Pastor Robert Shuler put out, and Shuler's opinion that Sister Aimee was a crook and had been from the beginning, swindling the gullible and pocketing the scratch. "My wife, bless her soul, got hold of the magazine and next day ran down to the courthouse and punched one of Shuler's boys, right in the snout."

As he pulled to the curb alongside Echo Park, he said, "Vote, nothing. It's dangerous enough we let them learn to read. Hey." He pointed at Angelus Temple. "Suppose she gets to be our governor? Or president. Then what?"

"Couldn't tell you."

Tom handed over a dollar, no tip, and felt like a skunk even before the man's nose wrinkled at him.

As the cab pulled away, he walked out from under a streetlamp and leaned against the trunk of a willow about twenty yards toward the lake from the hanging tree. Dark hadn't begun to fade. A stormy cloud blotted the moon. Few stars appeared. If a body hung from the oak today, Tom would need to keen his eyes to make it out.

He remained in the darkness, squatted to make himself less visible, and swept his gaze back and forth from Angelino Heights past the Bible school, parsonage and temple to Glendale Boulevard.

When something white and shadowy moved slowly past the parsonage and into the road, Tom doubted he'd seen anything but an illusion. Then the shadow became a girl. About Florence's height, perhaps Florence's size, though her loose dress kept that secret. She had dark hair and long white arms. She entered the park and sat on bench about thirty yards east of the hanging tree.

The first hint of gray sky appeared as Tom approached the girl. She sat with head bowed and hands on her knees. Not until he drew almost close enough to touch her did she glance his way. She gave a tiny shuddering yip. Her hands made fists beneath her chin.

"Good morning," he said, in a rasp, though he tried to sound gentle.

"Oh. Yes it is."

"You like this time of day?"

"Oh, I do. It's my prayer time." Her small mouth quivered as if she were searching for more words. Tom guessed she was of the sort who appeased their nerves by talking. While trying to make a kind face, he observed her rosy cheeks and cornflower eyes set off by thick dark lashes. He couldn't detect a trace of makeup. She looked so pure, he sighed and thought about what Florence might've become had he managed to expel Milly from her memory and keep her away from the wolves.

"You pray a lot? Out here?"

"Oh, yes. Every single day."

Tom felt his heart leap. He hesitated to ask more, for fear of disappointment. He caught a breath. "Every day? Even when it rains?"

She treated him to a melodious laugh. "Sure, I do. I'm from Portland. Besides, I have a parka *and* an umbrella."

After he squatted to keep from towering over her, she said, "You look like Jesus."

"Huh?"

She pointed down where his fingers drew a pattern through the dewy grass. "You remember, the woman taken in adultery. Oh dear," she gasped, then blushed and turned her face toward the hill.

"Listen, can I ask you something important?"

As she turned his way, her chest heaved with a deep breath. "All right."

"Two weeks ago Monday, October eleventh. We were having a rainy spell."

"The rainiest day since Portland?"

"That's the one. You were here?"

"Oh, yes."

"Who else was here?"

"Well, two police cars. And a man, rather small, perhaps a negro. Or a very dark Mexican. He was sick. I suppose he was sleeping in the park. They do that. I'm learning Spanish. I've spoken to gentlemen who walked all the way from Mexico. Imagine."

"The police found the sick fellow?"

"Either the police or Joe, I believe."

"Joe?"

"He works for our blessed Sister, cleaning up and fixing things. He may come outside soon. He usually does."

"He was with the police?"

"Yes, he talked to them while they carried the sick man to the police car."

"Anybody else around?"

She squinted and folded her hands at her chin. "No."

"Did they come talk to you? Joe or the police?"

"They may not have seen me."

At first, Tom couldn't believe they would miss a girl in the all white Bible school uniform, like the nurse outfit Sister commonly preached in. Then he caught on. "What color's your parka?"

"Dark gray."

"You're an angel," he said.

She gave him a teasing smile. "Thank you, Mister Jesus."

"Tom."

"Mary Beth."

After he described the shift custodian he'd questioned a week ago, and she confirmed that was Joe, he said goodbye and hustled through the park, past the lake, and across Glendale Boulevard.

He arrived downtown with the first office workers and salesclerks and strode up Temple to the Examiner fortress, hoping the business operation of the newspaper didn't keep bankers' hours.

The front gate handle turned and let him in. But he hadn't gone many strides across the patio before a yawning guard stood, approached and requested his pass.

"Yeah, it's right here," Tom said and groped in one pocket then another while he kept walking, across the fountain and into the hallway, and along the glossy mosaic tile. By the time he reached the photo gallery, the guard had fallen yards behind.

Tom inspected the portraits. As the guard caught up, he laid a hand on Tom's shoulder. "Look here, chum. No pass, you're on your way out."

"Hold on," Tom growled, which bought him time enough. On the top row of photos hung Carl Calhoun, who looked younger without the handlebar mustache. "Joe the janitor," Tom muttered, as he fished in his pocket and handed the guard a quarter. "Buy yourself breakfast, amigo."

Chapter Forty-five

"Aw." Tom bit his lip to keep the next words from spilling out and offending the ladies around him. He'd just remembered leaving his scribbled theories on the coffee table.

At the end of the line, he bounded off the streetcar and ran the blocks to his cottage. He had his keys out before he entered Cactus Court. He unlocked and threw open the door, and leaned against the wall catching his breath. The notes were still on the sofa, which let him hope Florence hadn't seen them.

He eased open the door to her room and peeked, marveling at her ability to sleep in after being thrashed and charged with a wicked felony.

But the bed was vacant. He returned to the parlor grumbling about her going to school against his orders. He sat on the sofa beside his notes, and noticed another note on the floor written in Leo's boxy scrawl. He picked it up and read. "Still no Boles. Previous employer, Chandler shipyard. No evidence anti-union activity. Investigate later. Next stop, Echo Park. Talk to neighbors, use badge to loose tongues."

He thought of returning to the park, inviting Leo to join him for a talk with Carl Calhoun, alias Joe the graveyard shift custodian. But Florence came first. He needed to know whether she read his notes, to check on her wounds and comfort her better than he'd done last night, and to decide what he could tell her.

Besides, before he settled with Fenton Love, he wanted to get a more thorough account of events at the Top Hat.

He went to the kitchen for a slice of bread and an apple to eat on the way to Hollywood High School. He was reaching into the ice box for butter when a hard rap sounded.

When he opened the door, he met Oz. He stood aside. "Come on in."

"No need." Oz looked timid, hardly his usual state. He kept shifting his weight right to left and back. "Just bringing a message from the boys. Thing is, a Mexican fella got him a hotel in Rosarito Beach, not far past Tijuana, he booked the band for Saturday."

"Tomorrow?"

"Sure did. Fella goes by Manuel. And what he told Rex is, we half as good as folks say, he means to book us Saturdays on and on."

"Swell," Tom said. "What's that mean?"

Oz nodded. "You reading me. Thing is, what the boys got in mind, we *all* going down there tomorrow, else Rex going to take over for you. For good, is what it means."

Though Tom had seen the punch coming, it knocked the wind out of him. "Says Rex?"

"What all us say. You got a day, Tom." He nodded again, backed off the porch and turned up the walkway.

Tom stood a minute, groping for an idea that might keep him from losing his dream, before he stepped off the porch and shuffled up the walkway. Instead of dodging the cholla, he swung his leg back and kicked the villain, which flew past one cottage and landed beside Señor Villegas' porch.

Tom followed the cholla and strode past it to his landlord's door. When Villegas appeared, Tom asked to use the telephone.

Rex didn't answer until after a dozen rings. Then he said, "What kind of degenerate calls a guy in the middle of the night?"

"The degenerate whose band you're about to snatch."

"Hey, somebody told you I want it, he's all wet. I want to play, Tom, that's all. Somebody's got to lead. It's me, so be it."

"Who's this Manuel?"

"Tijuana big shot. Got wind of us from some nephew called Pablo. What's got the boys jumping, this hotel works out, we don't only get Saturdays, we get Fridays at Manuel's cousin's speakeasy down on Balboa Island. You hear what I'm saying. Friday Balboa. Sleep it off, motor on down the coast to a posh hotel in the land of sultry señoritas. Sunday, motor on back just in time to rest up for the grind. What could beat that, short of the Coconut Grove?"

Tom swallowed hard. "Do it."

"Huh?"

"It's all yours."

"Think it over, Tom."

"I just did. I've got a sister."

"Boy," Rex said, "that's a fact. I'd call her a sister and a half."

Tom set the telephone receiver in its cradle.

He wanted to go find Pablo, this minute. Shake the truth out of the pretty boy. Find out whether Manuel from Rosarito was on the level, or just another stooge in Hearst's employ. Decide if the Rosarito booking was no more than a ploy to lure Tom away.

But Florence still came first, after he used the Villegas telephone to set up a meet with Socrates. Maybe the Hearst, Milly, and Carl Calhoun connections would convince the man to stall the citizens and their tommy-gunners.

The directory was on the marble table beside the phone. Tom found and dialed the number of Sugar Hill barber shop.

The barber answered.

"Tom Hickey here. I'm on my way, need to meet with Socrates."

"You be coming to the wrong place," the barber said.

"What's the right place?"

"City Jail. He been a guest of the police since last night."

Chapter Forty-six

Tom decided his sister was safe enough until school let out. Socrates, in jail, wasn't safe for a minute. You don't write the truth without making a host of enemies amongst the liars.

Tom felt like a different, more desperate man than yesterday. Now, he figured his mother as an accessory to murder. He longed to avenge the wrongs done to his sister. If anyone but himself stood a chance of preventing a bloodbath, he couldn't guess who it would be.

The one advantage he could recall of growing up with Milly, his good manners, failed him. He'd waited in a line five deep, rapping his knuckles and checking his Elgin every minute or so. When he reached the desk officer, the fellow excused himself and began shuffling papers.

Tom reached over and slapped the papers flat onto the desk. "I'm here to see Mister Kent Parrot."

The officer was a puffy fellow with a black streak on the temple of his mouse brown hair. All the people in front of Tom, he had treated with admirable patience. "Is that so?"

"It is."

"On what business."

Tom felt like saying, I'm planning to toss him through the window into the street, in traffic. "Murder. Tell him my name's Tom Hickey. Played football for USC, like he did."

The officer's eyes rounded. "Follow me," he said.

He opened a gate, led Tom around desks whose occupants watched his moves. From their faces, he guessed he'd spoken his name too loudly, and that what they knew of him wasn't all about football.

The officer led him to a wing beyond the common room and to an unmarked door. He told Tom to wait outside, rapped on the door and entered. Tom moved closer and tried to listen, but whatever was said inside got drowned beneath gab and shouts from the common room.

When the officer came out, he left the door open and nodded in that direction. Tom entered, crossed the room in a couple strides, and planted himself in front of glossy teak desk behind which stood a tall, solid, dark haired man with a square face, a navy blue pinstriped suit, and a lighter blue silk tie tacked to his shirt by a king-sized diamond. He offered his hand and a curious smile. While Tom reached across the desk and they shook, the man said, "I never did quite grasp why you left the school, the team."

"Other obligations."

"Busy fellow, aren't you, Tom?"

"You ought to know."

"Have a seat." Parrot motioned to a pair of chairs beneath a side wall adorned with photos of Governor Young, President Coolidge, Mayor Cryer, and Chief Davis, all of them stern.

Tom remained standing. "Sir, if you want to waste your manpower following me, that's your business, and I don't mind. But I'd appreciate if you'd get word to Detective Fenton Love, tell him if he's of a mind to assault or harass my sister again, he'd be wise to kill me first."

Parrot nodded. "Anything else?"

"Matter of fact, though it's hardly my place to advise a person of your stature, it's my sense that jailing a publisher on account of his reporting could be the end of you."

"A threat, Tom?"

"No sir, a warning. I believe it's been proven by our forefathers that you can only push folks so far. And when you and the news gang cover up a lynching and then step on whosoever speaks the truth about it, about the time it backfires and the shooting starts, one of those fellows on the wall is bound to go looking for a scapegoat. I wouldn't be surprised if you're it."

"This jailed publisher would be?"

"Name's Socrates, of the *Forum*."

The man reached for a pen and jotted the name. "Crusader, are you, Tom Hickey?"

He considered that a real question, and one he needed to answer for himself. He gave himself moments to ponder. "Only if it looks like I'm the one guy willing to do what needs to get done."

"Admirable." Parrot leaned his elbows on the desk. "And nothing I say or do will convince you to go home, play your instrument, and leave police work to the police department. Correct?"

Another real question, Tom thought, which deserved a serious answer. Though he felt not the least suicidal, at some point in his rather brief life he'd decided that if a guy starts letting people push him around, he might not be able to stop.

"You could call a murder a crime and act accordingly," he said. "Or you could have the police kill me, I suppose. Gun me down, like they did to Sid Fitch and his boys."

"They were criminals, Tom. You're not. And now you've said your piece?"

"Almost. Since we're not exactly teammates but close enough, I'm going to ask if you'll look me in the eye and tell me there was no lynching."

The man's game face slipped into a mild frown. "To the best of my knowledge, there has been no lynching."

"Damn," Tom said. "Sir, you're a mighty fine liar."

Parrot smiled. "You're welcome to your opinion. Be that as it may, I'll take your advice about the publisher under consideration."

"Thank you, sir," Tom said.

As he walked outside, he heard the streetcar and ran to catch it. He rode up Temple, transferred to the Sunset line, and arrived at Hollywood High toward the end of third period, unless they had changed schedules since he graduated. Protocol required a stop at the office to ask for a student helper to fetch his sister out of class. He decided not to waste the five or ten minutes.

He left his hat behind a bush and strutted down the hallway, impersonating a high school boy, and stopped at Room 12, where he'd dozed through most fifth periods of his senior year. Not that he didn't appreciate literature, or Mrs. Rigby. But he'd worked nights and needed a nap whenever the opportunity presented.

As he entered the room, he saw they were writing. Mrs. Rigby looked up from her correcting. Fresh and attractive as four years ago. She stood and came to meet Tom at the door.

"A friendly visit?" she asked.

"Next time," Tom said. "This one's an emergency."

"Oh?" She looked truly puzzled.

"Florence needs to come with me."

"But Tom, look around."

He did. A full classroom of students watched him. "No Florence," he said.

"True, and what's more, according to the daily report, she hasn't been in school at all today."

Chapter Forty-seven

Milly, Tom believed. After Florence saw his notes on the sofa and broke the code, she went to Milly on her own.

Outside the high school, he dashed across Sunset and strode east, too anxious to wait. He hadn't gone a hundred yards before he recognized the danger in going to Milly's alone.

She would be waiting, backed by Teddy Boles and his shooters or other men she'd lured to her side, a skill she'd long ago mastered. He needed a gun of his own, and a clearer head than he could count when facing his mother.

He needed Leo, who might still be around Echo Park. Tom was about to dash back across Sunset and catch the bus, ride it up Highland to Hollywood Boulevard where he could transfer to the streetcar line. A horn's beep stopped him. A truck pulled to the curb beside him. Alamo Meat. The driver leaned out the passenger window and asked, "Where you been, Tom?"

He hardly knew the driver, a young fellow so plump and doughy looking, a butcher had nicknamed him Muffin. Muff for short, and the nickname stuck.

"How about a lift?"

Muff frowned. "I would, except I'm running behind."

"Yeah, and I'm trying to save my sister's life."

"Gee, no kidding?"

Tom reached for the door handle. "Do I look like I'm kidding?"

Muff leaned back. Tom climbed in. "To Echo Park, is all."

"Only I'm on my way down Central. I don't make the drops before the lunch crowd, Mister Woods is gonna hear about it."

"Mister Woods is going to hear if you don't give me a ride."

Muff sighed. "You're a favorite of his, aren't you?"

"Maybe I am," Tom said, with a twinge of gratitude because the boss hadn't spread around the bad blood between them.

As the truck pulled out, Muff asked, "Want to tell me about your sister?"

"No."

"Sure, that's none of mine. Say, where you been all week? You didn't quit, did you?"

Tom nodded while eyeing the westbound autos in case one of them might be Leo's Packard.

"Where you working now?"

"I'm not."

"You didn't quit, did you?"

"Turn up here and take Wilshire down to Glendale."

Muff slowed and made the turn. "You got money in the bank?"

"Not a cent."

"Oh, the orchestra. That's why you quit. You're going to make a record?"

"Yeah, that's it," Tom said, to keep the fellow from rubbing in grim facts. Which were, supposing he could rescue Florence, bring some killer to justice, and give a few big shots a sleepless night or two, he still was broke. With no job, no band, and with a sister who still needed him.

They turned onto Glendale Boulevard, and he saw a Packard. But the driver had a bony, dark face. As they neared the park, Tom peered all around and across the lake. No Packard. He groaned in fear for his sister, beset by dread as if he'd just fumbled the ball that would decide not just a game, but everything.

Then he spotted Leo by the lake, puffing a cigar and tossing something to the ducks. "Here," Tom yelped. "Pull over."

Chapter Forty-eight

Milly's door was locked. Tom pounded with the side of his fist. He waited a few seconds and glanced at Leo, who nodded. Tom leaned back, raised his foot high, and attacked the door just beside the knob with the sole of his shoe. The lock held, but the molding tore away.

"Stay back," Leo said, and put his free hand on Tom's shoulder. He lifted his Colt .38 Special to waist high and entered the house with Tom on his heels. They stopped before the entrance to the hallway. Leo leaned around the corner and peered. Tom held still and listened. What he heard terrified him.

He dodged around Leo and dashed up the hall, past the first doorway and into the second room on the right. Milly's bedroom, he knew, because it smelled like a blend of mothballs and lavender.

A chair-back was jammed under the closet doorknob. He kicked the chair so hard it crashed into a dresser against the far wall. He started to reach for the knob but stopped. Because his sister wasn't hollering his name or anything sensible. She was singing.

Oh, a grasshopper sittin' on a railroad track
Sing Polly wolly doodle all the day
A-pickin' his teeth with a carpet tack
Sing Polly wolly doodle all the day.

When Tom opened the closet door, she didn't miss a beat or move from the back corner into which she had wedged herself.

He slung dresses and hangers over his shoulder until he could see her. Bound at the ankles. Again at the knees. Her arms at the wrists and elbows.

Her legs were bare. The yellow skirt was hiked up around her waist. A smell more pungent than perfume or mothballs wafted out into the bedroom. Without looking back at Leo, Tom said, "I've got her. You can go look around."

He ducked and entered the closet, leaned and wrapped his arms around Florence. She melted into his arms, still singing,

> He sneezed so hard with the whooping cough
> Sing Polly Wolly Doodle all the day
> He sneezed his head and the tail right off
> Sing Polly Wolly Doodle all the day.

He carried her to Milly's bed and lay her on top of the orchid quilt. "Mama," she whimpered, "what if I need to go pee pee? Why can't Raggedy come with me. Oh Mama, I'll be a good girl. I'm freezing, Mama. When you come back I'll be a block of ice, you wait and see."

"You're okay, babe," Tom said, "Mama's gone."

Whoever bound her used a knot like a double figure eight. It required such patience to unravel, Tom thought of calling for Leo to work on her feet while he loosed her hands. Only Florence appeared in no hurry to get free.

But the instant he'd loosed the cord around her ankles, she pitched off the bed. She landed on her knees and grabbed a handful of the dresses Tom had slung out of his way. She stood, fell, and crawled a few steps before pushing herself up and hobbling out of the room and across the hall. She slammed the bathroom door behind her.

Tom stuffed dresses into the closet, shut the closet door, and went to the living room where Leo stood gazing out the back window at Milly's garden.

"You'd think it's springtime," Leo said and rubbed his nose. He turned and sat in the stuffed chair beside Milly's sewing machine. His hand swept around, calling Tom to notice the jungle of ferns, trailing vines and flowers. "Makes a guy want to go live in the desert. She all right?"

"Maybe," Tom said. "Milly didn't put her in there."

Leo raised his eyebrows.

"Fancy knots," Tom said.

"Maybe she's taken up boating."

"Florence wasn't naked. Milly didn't put her there."

He listened to her sing the fee fie fiddle-ee-i-oh part of "I've Been Working on the Railroad," another piece, like "Polly Wolly Doodle," Charlie Hickey used to cheer them with. Often after one of Milly's whippings or tongue-lashings.

When her song turned to moans, Tom rushed to the bathroom door and knocked. "You okay, Sis?"

"Okay?" She croaked a laugh so sinister, he worried she might be toying with Milly's razor.

"Are you decent?"

"Decent?" Again, she moaned.

Blindsided by an eerie fear that somehow Milly had taken charge of his sister's brain, Tom didn't bother to use his foot, only dipped his shoulder and crashed into the door. As it flew open and slammed the sink, Florence screamed, as though possessed, "Hey, bud, get out of here."

He turned his eyes to the floor, backed a step and waited.

"Is that you, Tom?"

"Yeah. Can I look?"

"Okay."

She stood with her back against the tub, wrapped in the yellow rose shower curtain.

"Need anything?" he asked.

"Well, panties or something."

She cast her eyes down, wept until tears dripped onto the floor, then turned, bent into the tub, and started bath water running. She sat on the edge of the tub and wrapped the curtain tighter around her middle. "Good thing Milly wasn't home. She would've stripped me, wouldn't she, Tom? And to do it, she would've had to kill me, wouldn't she?"

"Get your bath," Tom said. "Make it nice and hot."

He backed out and went to Milly's room, rifled through her dresser until he found underwear that didn't have a pattern of flowers.

In the living room, Leo sneezed, rubbed his nose, and sneezed again. He reached into a side pocket of his coat, pulled out a cigar, slipped off the band and lit up. "Nothing like a Havana to clear the air."

Motioning for Leo to follow, Tom went to the front porch. Leo came out carrying a book, which he laid on the porch rail. "What now?"

"Depends on Florence."

"We take her to my place. Vi's the best nurse since Miss Nightengale."

"From here on out," Tom said, "my sister's giving the orders." As he stepped inside to check on her, he mumbled, "Providing she's able."

The bathroom door was open. Florence, in the panties Tom had chosen and brought, stood adjusting her bra and drying her hair with a towel. When she turned toward her brother, she said, "Take me to Mama."

"You sure?"

"Yes," she snapped. He noted the fierce glint in her eyes and looked away. The eyes made her a ringer for Milly.

He waited while she brushed her hair and slipped into a white sleeveless dress covered with tiny gardenias. Then he ushered her out front. Always before she'd greeted Leo with a hug. Today she didn't shake hands, say hello, or thanks, or give him a smile.

Tom said, "I don't figure Milly'll be coming home soon." Leo nodded and stubbed his cigar on the porch rail.

"The man," she said, "what's his name?"

"Teddy Boles?"

"That's it. Teddy Boles told me they were going far, far away."

"Not yet," Tom said. "Milly wouldn't go to Pasadena without packing her suitcase full of dresses, potions and perfume."

"We could stake the place out," Leo said.

"While Socrates rots in jail and nobody else is likely to stop the tommy-gunners from strolling into some klavern?"

The way the others stared at him made Tom remember he'd been working alone and tight-lipped. He said, "First, where do we start looking?"

Leo reached over his stubbed cigar and picked up the book he'd set there. "What do you know about Sherlock Holmes?"

"I know he's not here," Tom said, "so you'll have to do."

Leo held up the book. "*The History of Spiritualism*," he said. "By his Lordship Arthur Conan Doyle." He opened it to a page marked by a newspaper clipping. "Here's some hoopla about a gal that talks to the dead. And here," he held up the clipping, "is headlines. This same gal's here in town, and tonight she appears at the Knickerbocker to lecture about ghosts and such and choose out of the audience a crew that's allowed to assist her in a séance. See, tomorrow at midnight, the onset of Halloween, she's going to summon Valentino's ghost, if it takes her all night, all day, and right up to the witching hour."

Chapter Forty-nine

In the Packard, after Tom related all he knew about Socrates and the tommy-gunners, he watched Florence in the back seat. She wrapped wisps of her hair around her finger, as if the task were serious business. He was deciding not to ask her to revisit the events that landed her in the closet when she said, "What'd Mama do?"

"Let's ask her."

"You think she killed somebody."

"Maybe."

Leo drove using one eye, while the other shot glances at Florence. "Mind telling me what sent you to Milly's place?"

"Tommy left notes so I was helping." She returned to curling her hair. After a mile or two, she said, "Or, you know, she's mean all right, I remember that much, but still she's my mother. I should give her a chance to prove Tommy's wrong, shouldn't I? But she wasn't home. Tommy, is Teddy Boles a killer?"

"Maybe."

"He didn't act like one."

Tom said, "Isn't he the guy that tied you up?"

"Okay." Her fierce eyes drilled Tom, as if she didn't find much distinction between him and Teddy Boles. "And he said if I didn't let him, he'd have to knock me out and do it anyway, and I asked, well, are you going to make me strip, like Mama did. He said, 'She did?' I don't think he knew. And he said he was going put me in there for safekeeping."

She turned sideways in the seat, and gazed out the window. When she turned again toward Tom, she looked bewildered, as if she'd fallen asleep in Los Angeles and awakened in Shanghai.

"Safe from what?" Leo asked.

"That's what I said, a couple times, but he wouldn't tell me."

Leo followed Sunset to Hollywood Boulevard, and drove west along the base of the hills to the Knickerbocker.

Only last year, Tom remembered, his sister came home in a fit of ecstasy from having seen Valentino here in the lounge dancing the tango. Now, months after their heartthrob died in a shamefully prosaic manner, from complications of an ulcer, millions of women still mourned.

Tom only caught a glimpse of Raleigh Washburn. His station out front of the hotel was encircled by men probably using a shoeshine as an excuse for a respite from the melee inside.

The crowd awaiting the chance to partake in the Valentino séance made the place reminiscent of Angelus Temple, only the Knickerbocker congregation wore jewels, feathers, lace, silks, and hand-woven shawls from the orient. But finery couldn't disguise desperation. Even among the prosperous, Tom spotted more than a few lost souls.

Leo blazed a trail through the lobby to the front desk. Instead of waiting in line, he flashed his badge. He showed it again to the clerk, a svelte young man with oiled and perfumed black hair. A spit curl danced on his forehead with his every move.

"Room for three," Leo said.

"But I fear not," the clerk said. "You see, we booked the entire weekend day the lecture and séance were announced. You'd be amazed at the number of, shall we call them believers, and I only refer, of course, to those with the means to partake of our superb accommodations. You see." The clerk leaned closer as if to give Leo a prized secret. "Each of the good ladies dreams that, should she fail to be one of the chosen, Signori Valentino will return from the great beyond but find his sense of direction skewed by the journey, and appear by mistake in her own boudoir."

Leo pointed to a leather bound volume on the counter beside the clerk. "That the book?"

"Yes indeed."

"Open it, to today."

The clerk's face pinched into a censuring frown, but he complied. "You can see for yourself, every line is taken."

Leo reached out and placed the tip of his index finger on a mid-page line. "What's this name?"

"Oh, I can't *tell* you."

Leo grabbed both sides of the book and stared at the clerk while he turned it around to face him. "George Whitney," he said, "as I thought. George wants to cancel."

The clerk's eyes moistened while he slid the book out of Leo's grasp and folded it shut. He gave a swift bow and retreated, opened a door, entered an office, and shut the door behind him.

Tom was about to suggest they could forget the room, plan on intercepting Milly and Boles in the lobby or lounge and marching or dragging them out to the Packard. But the clerk returned, smiling. Tom imagined he told the manager all about the tough cop, with an even bigger guy and a wild-eyed doll backing him, and the manager knew better than to cross the minions of Two Gun Davis.

The clerk scratched George Whitney. After Leo signed for Room 216, he spent a minute or so scanning the registrants for a Milly, or Millicent, or a Boles. Over his shoulder, Tom looked for Milly's flowery handwriting.

"No dice," Tom said.

Leo closed the book and slipped the clerk a five.

As a football player, Tom had roomed in a few swank hotels, but none with a bed so long, wide, and soft as what the Knickerbocker's Room 216 provided. The quilt was blue satin, finely embroidered. Persian tapestries decorated the walls.

"I'm paying for all this," Tom said to Leo.

"Going to sell your soul to the devil, are you?"

"I've got prospects."

"Sure."

Tom expected his sister, a lover of the elegant, to lounge on the bed. But she passed it by, went straight to the window, parted the satin curtains, cranked the window open wide, and peered down at Hollywood Boulevard, where a cop with a bullhorn shouted orders the crowd ignored.

Tom signaled Leo to join him in the hallway. He left the door open a couple inches so he could watch Florence. "Don't let her jump out the window."

"You think she's apt to?"

"Look at her eyes. Maybe we should keep her away from Milly."

"Your call."

"Yeah. I'll see what kind of help we can find." He turned and walked down the hall, considering and rejecting his idea that Raleigh would make a reliable lookout. Not only was he surrounded by customers, his job required looking down at shoes.

Tom was on the stairs when a bellhop hustled past. "Whoa," Tom said.

The bellhop's looks might've won him a role as an aging jockey. "At your service, Chief."

"Keep an eye out for a blonde, pushing forty but still could double for Marion Davies with the lights down. She might be with a curly haired guy, thick neck and a tiny right ear. Come to 216, tell me what room she checks into, I've got a sawbuck waiting for you."

"I'm your man," the bellhop said and hustled down the stairs.

On his way back to the room, Tom wondered how he could hope to keep an eye on Florence in the heat of the game, once they caught up with Milly and her man. An idea came. He asked Leo for his car keys.

"Nothing doing."

Tom said, "You'd rather run an errand, it's all the same to me. See, I've got a bellhop on the lookout for Milly, but he's in and out, up and down. What we need is a scout, somebody Milly won't recognize."

"Let me make a couple phone calls."

"How about, you go down to the Hall of Records, into the archives, ask for Madeline. Tell her what's up. Maybe she'll help out. And once the fur starts flying—." He pointed at Florence.

With Leo gone, Tom joined his sister at the window, where she stood like a mannequin. He supposed she was either gazing into darkness or dreaming herself into a prettier, safer world.

He craned his head over her shoulder and watched a shaft of rainbow light sweep east to west. "Egyptian having a premiere?"

Florence only glanced his way.

"Sis," he said, "what do *you* see out there?"

She moistened her lips. He waited, then touched her shoulder, and sat on the edge of the bed, an arm's length away.

She turned just far enough so the drapes shuddered. "Tommy, why does Mama hate us? I mean why did she hate us even before we ditched her?"

Years had passed since Tom vowed to quit asking that question. "Mostly, she's good at hating."

"We were bad kids, weren't we?"

"Not you, babe. But I gave her reasons. For a while, I believed when she said it was me drove Charlie away. Then I remembered she was almost as crazy before Charlie disappeared."

"Where'd he go, Tom? Why'd he leave us?"

"Let's make a deal," Tom said. "After we get through this business, we'll start looking for him."

She came out from behind the drapes and gave him a sweet smile, which didn't soothe her wild eyes. "You and me both this time? "

"You bet. Team Hickey."

She leaned, pecked his cheek, grabbed his hand, pulled him up, and hugged him tighter and longer than a guy wants to get hugged by his beautiful sister. When she let go, she darted back to her post at the window.

The door rattled and Leo called out. Tom let him in. As he entered, he said, "This scout of yours is some looker. Let's hope she won't get too occupied fighting off the piranhas to follow instructions."

"I'm betting on her."

"Say, Flo," Leo said. "Did you know your brother's got himself a redhead?"

Chapter Fifty

Florence didn't respond. Tom split his time between pacing the cramped room and perching on the bed near his sister. She appeared to keep watch even after he assured her Madeline and the bellhop were all the lookouts they needed. Leo killed time pestering Tom.

"Where'd you meet this gal?"

"Never mind."

"What do you know about her?"

"Plenty."

"She want to be in the movies?"

"Maybe."

"I don't know, Tom. Piece of work like her can send a guy straight to the poor house."

"I'm headed there anyway. What's with all the chatter?"

"You'd rather I brooded, like you?"

"I'm not brooding."

"Oh? What are you thinking about?"

"Milly."

"Don't. Think about something pleasant, an ice cream soda, a voyage to Catalina, or the redhead. Something that won't sap your juice, all of which you'll need when Milly shows, if Milly shows."

Tom tried to expel Milly from his mind, and failed, until a knock brought him to his feet. Florence leaped into his way and stood facing the door. He crawled over the bed, went and looked through the peephole. Nobody. He eased the door open.

The bellhop saluted, then glanced at a slip of paper. "Room 142. A tough looking guy and the Marion-Davies blonde, like you said." He stuck out his hand.

Tom turned to Leo. "I need a ten."

Leo delivered. The bellhop pocketed the bill and said, "Your babydoll, she's in the know. I put her staking out the hall." He started to leave but glanced past Tom and ogled Florence. "Some guys get all the fluff."

Tom closed the door. "Now who calls the shots?"

"You're the boss," Leo said. "I disagree, I'll let you know."

"Then here's how it goes. I run out and send Madeline up. She stays with Florence while we pay a visit. Soon as we've got things in hand, we send for the girls."

Florence had come to life. Her head lashed back and forth. "No sir. No you don't."

"Sis," Tom said, "Argue all day, I'm not letting you stumble into a gun battle."

He left the room, hustled down stairs and saw Madeline at the far end of the hallway. In case Milly or Boles stepped out of 142, instead of going to Madeline, he beckoned her.

The smile he hoped for, he didn't get. Madeline looked to be in dead earnest. She came close. "Tell me something, fella. Suppose you catch the villain, put him where he belongs, is that the last I see of you?"

"Depends."

The scowl made her look part gypsy. "Depends on what?"

"On what you feel about seeing a guy who wants to take you to the Biltmore but his billfold says cafeteria."

The scowl morphed into a smirk. "Depends."

"On what?"

"How you feel about the beach, moonlight swims, yesterday's rolls, apple butter."

He took the liberty of stroking her hair. She leaned her head on his shoulder, but only for an instant. "Enough, Casanova. We've got business, I hear."

He briefed her about his sister and the closet, and told her he suspected Boles as the killer and Milly as the brains of the cover up. After he gave her his plan and a couple hints about managing Florence, she said, "Yeah, and promise you'll stay alive?"

"When the shooting starts," he said, "I'll jump behind Leo."

"No need, the way he talked about you, he'll jump out in front of you."

Tom felt a bit weepy. "Get a move on. Room 216."

While he waited for Leo, he scouted the hall and noted the darkest crannies, one in the shadow of the stairs, the other in a corner of the far end. The wait lasted so long, he thought Florence must've pitched a fit. Another minute, he would've run back upstairs. But Leo came into the hall, out of the lobby.

"Tell me the name registered to 142," Leo said, "I'll give you another sawbuck. You miss, you wash my Packard."

"Marion Davies."

Leo reached for his billfold and grumbled, "Lousy cheat."

"What do you think?" Tom asked. "Do we go in, or wait them out?"

"I don't go in or let you go in without Samuel at my side." He patted the lump in his sport coat. "I see another gun out, doesn't matter if it's Milly, I shoot." He reached for Tom's chin and gave it a tap, so their eyes met straight on. "Suppose I shoot your mama. You going to blame me?"

"Not likely."

"I'm betting Florence will."

"Let's wait them out," Tom said.

He left Leo by the stairs and hustled to the far end. Long minutes passed between the arrival of each dowager, flashy dame, gent with starched shirt, or party of swells. Every guest, Tom believed, eyed him with suspicion before proceeding into a room. Nobody entered 142. Tom began to worry that 140 or 144 might feature adjoining doors. He began hoping Teddy would appear on his own either on his way to run an errand or to escape a tirade from Milly.

When they came out together, his every muscle quaked.

Chapter Fifty-one

He bent into a half crouch and crept toward them, watching Teddy's head until he closed to ten yards. Then he launched himself into a sprint and dove for the man's waist, his hands out and set to pin Teddy's arms to his sides, keep them away from any weapon.

Boles saw him soon enough to turn. Tom's head drove straight into his belly. As Teddy folded, he tried to lunge and recover the small revolver that slipped out from under his belt and landed on the carpet beside the room key that dropped from his hand.

Tom drove and slammed Teddy into the wall, grabbed his shoulders, and yanked his head down. A knee to the jaw sent him reeling and left Tom free to snatch up the gun and key. He grabbed Teddy by the scruff of the neck, jabbed the gun barrel to his temple.

Leo had Milly on the carpet. He was pressing a wadded hotel face towel into her mouth, which muffled her banshee cries. Down the hall beside the staircase, the bellhop stood talking to a couple of ancients. Telling them the attack was a rehearsal for some moving picture, Tom hoped.

When Leo got Milly to her feet, tipped back, gagged, and thrashing against his chokehold, Tom passed him the key. He unlocked the door and kicked it open. Tom entered first, walked his man to the stuffed chair and shoved him down into it. When Teddy opened his mouth, before he got a word out, a quick shake of Tom's head stopped him.

"Here's the rules," Tom said. "Any screaming, we knock you out and take you to Leo's car. We drive to a place way down Central, the back room of the Smokehouse Barbecue, and we invite a group of concerned citizens to meet you. These folks believe the Ku Klux Klan lynched Frank Gaines, and they're about to take revenge, send tommy-gunners to some klavern. We don't want to see that happen. So what we do is, we tell them they blamed the wrong murderers. Then Leo and I say adios. You don't."

Milly was still on the floor, face down, getting bound hand and foot with the ropes Teddy used on Florence. When Leo finished, he picked her up and held her like a groom approaching the threshold. Then he tossed her onto the bed. "Doesn't weigh much more than a chicken." He brought the remaining ropes to work on Teddy and said, "Best cooperate, pal."

Teddy glowered and held still just long enough to retain a speck of pride, before he reached out. After Leo had him suitably bound, he relieved Tom of Teddy's Mauser. He shoved it into his coat pocket and brought the Colt out of his Sam Browne. He showed it to Teddy. "Mine's bigger than yours. Big enough, a shot in the toe might kill you."

Tom went to the door and opened it just enough to scan the hall both ways. He hustled down the hall, up the stairs, and to 216. Madeline met him, with Florence at her heels, leaning forward as though to take a dive. Much of her hair stood on end, as if she'd brushed it backward. Her mouth had hardened into a ravenous look even wilder than her eyes. "Mama?" she asked.

"Got her. You going to be okay, babe?"

Florence put her hands on Madeline's shoulders. "Can she come?"

Madeline nodded but Tom said, "You'd better go home."

"Why's that?"

"Never mind Leo being a cop. He's off duty. We're lawbreakers here."

"I've got a soft spot for desperadoes."

"Any idea what it might get you?"

"Like wasting the blush of my youth in a prison cell? Quit the nagging, will you? Let's go."

Tom gave in and led the way, holding Florence first by the shoulders, then by the hand. From the time he knocked on 142 until Leo opened the door, tiny whimpers issued out of her. But she hitched herself up tall and marched ahead of her brother. Before she even glanced at Milly, she strode the width of the room to Teddy. Then she cocked her leg and delivered a mighty blow with the pointed toe of her Italian shoe. He howled.

Leo raised the Colt. "Hush now. Remember the Smokehouse."

Florence had already gone to the foot of the bed. She stood and stared at Milly as though at a gruesome exhibit.

Milly spat out the last of the gag on which she'd gnashed since Leo set it. She rolled onto her side, one hip aloft. Her daisy-patterned blouse had lost a button, which created a visible a swatch of yellow slip and ivory breast. Her delicate face with its big aqua eyes expressed innocence in mortal danger, as if she were auditioning for a melodrama. She gave her daughter a long, wounded gaze. Then she said, "Florence, dear, look what they've done to me."

Florence said, "Be quiet, Mama."

Leo came alongside her, holding the desk chair. He turned to Tom, who stood with Madeline between the dresser and the closet, which was just inside the door. "How about we take it from the top?" He walked the chair to the side of the bed from where he could glance over Milly at her lover. "Where's it all start, Miz Hickey?"

"I'm no Hickey," she said.

"You're not Miz Boles, I'm betting. Again, where's it all start?"

"What are you talking about?"

"You and Teddy, Harriet and Frank. I hear you all go back a long way, back to Azusa Street?"

"What if we do?"

"One thing, I want to know how Frank ended up with Teddy's wife."

"Frank stole her away. He was a charmer."

"So you caught Teddy on the rebound?"

Tom suspected, from his mother's wily, shifting eyes, she was going to play for Florence. Maybe she believed she just might turn the tables on her evil son and walk out of the room at her daughter's side, reunited.

"Teddy and I didn't find each other until years later."

"How many years?" Leo asked.

"Seven or eight."

Teddy muttered, "Two, the first time." She cocked her head his way, no doubt shot venom with her eyes.

"Meantime," Leo said, "you and Harriet stayed friends, seeking heavenly bliss with the Eden crowd. Gypsies, are they?"

Milly tossed a haughty smile her daughter's way. "I rarely met with the Edenists. Harriet was the devotee."

Though Tom knew a wise fellow wouldn't intervene, a suspicion had come with such force, he acted on it. "Question." He approached the foot of the bed. "I hear Frank and Pastor Seymour could be twins. Both of them gentle, strong, kind and all. I remember you were stuck on Pastor Seymour."

Milly gave a little hiss and looked away.

"Did you ever meet up with the Pastor later, after you left the mission? Ever sit down to tea or coffee, say four years ago?"

She must've caught his accusation, the way she stretched out and curved her lips, got ready to spit on him if he'd only lean closer. But soon she resumed the haughty pose. "I don't talk to Judas."

"Don't call Tommy names," Florence commanded.

"Oh? Then you don't agree he ruined my life when he stole away with my precious beauty, my only little girl."

"You know why."

"I most certainly do not, unless it was out of jealousy. You were your mama's little girl and the Judas never loved me. He's the image of the devil who left me with nothing, left me on my own to raise two babies."

For a minute, Florence peered at her mother and leaned ever farther Milly's way until she had to brace herself with a hand on the bed. All the while, Milly lay still, her face a portrait of long-suffering woe.

When Florence straightened, she turned and gazed at Tom. She gave him a smile, but her eyes didn't lose a trace of their wildness. Once again, she peered at Milly, then at her brother. "Tommy," she said, "let's rip her clothes off and put her in the closet."

He left his post against the wall, went to Florence, and pressed her head against his shoulder. "Good idea, babe. Maybe we'll do that. Only later. First she's got to talk."

Milly called out, "Goldilocks," once Florence's nickname. "Can't you see the truth about these heartless creatures who use us and cast us off. They only care about our beauty, to stare and paw and show us off to the fellows. To them, we're things. They say they'll protect us, but look." She jabbed a finger in Teddy's direction. "He never loved me, even in a man's miserable way. I just couldn't compare to his Harriet. Sweet, patient, buxom Harriet."

"So Teddy couldn't let Harriet go," Leo said. "I guess he must've hated the ground Frank Gaines walked on."

"You don't know the half of it," Milly shouted, and Tom thought, she's lost her mind and can't even see the trap.

Again Milly speared a finger at her man. "I told him a hundred times, it wasn't Frank to blame, but her, and Teddy himself. Him more than her. He didn't treat her any better than Hickey treated me. She got out of line, he slugged her."

Florence broke away from her brother and yelled at Milly, "Charlie never once slugged you."

"You don't know," Milly said.

Leaning between them, Leo asked, "Teddy knocked his wife around?"

"Sure he did. Why do you think she ran to Frank, and had every right to? Frank was a kind gentleman while her husband was a moocher, a brute, a gigolo."

All through her rant, Teddy had sat as though suffering through the thousandth performance. Now, he said, "I never been any gigolo."

"So, Teddy," Leo said. "you figure Frank got tired of Harriet. Found a younger doll, or one who could buy him things. That why you killed Frank?"

"I didn't."

"Sure you did. And who could blame you, after the law called Harriet a suicide. Nobody was going to serve justice unless you did."

Teddy sighed. "I didn't."

Tom passed by Florence. Another step put him looming above Teddy. "Tell me who was with you in the Chevy?"

Teddy's eyes rounded. "Chevy?"

"Parked across the street from Frank's place."

"What're you talking about?"

Tom felt his sister's hand on his shoulder and he noticed her watching Milly.

"She knows. Look at her face." Florence climbed onto the bed and crawled to beside Milly. "Who was with Teddy when he went to kill Mister Gaines? Come on, Mama."

"Goldilocks," Milly pleaded.

"Stop it," Florence yelped.

Then Milly spat.

Tom stood waiting, part of him hoping his sister's claws would fly and blood would spill. But Florence, without so much as wiping her face, turned to her brother and spoke softly. "Tommy, let's clean out the closet."

"Sure," he said. "We don't need her. We'll get the truth out of Teddy."

Instead of going to the closet, he watched his sister while she grabbed a clump of Milly's linen skirt, a pattern of yellow rose petals, and yanked. The skirt tore away. As Florence reached for the bright yellow slip, Milly yelped, "I'll tell you. Why should I cover for him?"

"No reason," Leo said. "Let's hear it."

"Every blessed day, he couldn't stop telling me Frank killed his darling."

"Hey there," Teddy said. "If you're going to spill the beans, make it the truth."

"Which is what?" Leo asked him.

"Truth is, she was the one hollering that Frank killed my wife."

"Liar," Milly shouted.

"Yeah, yeah. About that Chevy. After a while, I came around to believe her. So I gather a couple boys, from where I used to work at the shipyards."

"The guys you introduced me to at Casa del Mar," Tom said.

"Yeah, sure. We stopped by Frank's place, figuring to get the truth out of him."

Boles was staring at Milly as if he feared her more than anything they could do, as if she could send him to hell. No doubt she'd shown him a foretaste.

Leo rolled his hand, and Teddy said, "The way Gaines told it, if somebody killed Harriet, his guess was Milly. I got mad for that crack. I socked him. He got right up and said, 'Let's go see her, maybe I can prove it.' So we brought him over to my place."

"And you killed him there?" Florence demanded.

But Teddy had clammed up. He didn't say a word until Leo flipped his Colt, held it by the barrel and passed it to Florence, who was still on the middle of the bed. "Hand it to Tom, will you."

She did, and Tom, holding the barrel, lifted it to a good angle from which to crack Teddy's head.

"Remember the Smokehouse," Leo said.

"What do you want?" Teddy yipped.

"Who killed Harriet?"

"He did. Frank. Sure he did."

"Why?"

"Maybe she was going to leave him."

"Maybe she was cheating on him," Tom added.

"Yeah, maybe she was."

"Like she cheated on you?"

"Sure," Teddy grumbled.

"But you didn't go and kill her. You might've felt like it, but all those years, you let her get away with it. Because you loved her. But not Frank. He didn't have the guts. Everybody thought he was a saint, but he was a coward, and a killer."

"You got it."

Tom leaned closer. "So you killed him."

Once again, Teddy clammed up. Only this time he gave Tom a look that had to mean go ahead and whack me, I'm done talking.

"Want to know what I think?" Florence asked. "I think Frank got it right. I think Mama did poison Harriet."

All but Florence stared at Milly, who lay gaping as though at a world gone berserk.

"Why so?" Leo asked Florence.

"Well," she said, "That's exactly what I would've done, if I had a man that kept loving a cheat like Harriet, when he ought to been loving me. And, see, I'm Milly's daughter."

"Well you're a liar," Milly shouted.

What his sister said so distressed Tom, he made his way back to the wall beside Madeline, who reached for his hand and gave it a squeeze. Her second squeeze worked some magic. Allowed him to think.

He said, "Outside of you two—" He pointed at his mother then at Teddy. "—I'm the only one who knew both Frank and Milly enough to believe one of them over the other. And Frank was nobody's liar." Staring at Milly, he felt something inside him begin to collapse. He reached back and again found Madeline's hand. "Think about it, Boles. Milly could be the biggest liar in L.A."

Teddy had been gnawing his lower lip, and now a line of blood ran down his chin, while he stared at Milly and shook his head, and lifted his bound wrists to prop his chin with his folded hands. "She stabbed Frank," he said.

Milly screamed, "What else could I do? Frank grabbed for the knife. He was going to kill both of us, Teddy and me."

Teddy sat shaking his head. "No. He didn't do anything. I'll bet he didn't even kill my wife."

Chapter Fifty-two

While Milly lay exuding disdain as if nothing anyone but her said made any sense or in any way mattered, Tom sat slumped against the wall. His mind felt like quicksand only hot. Madeline stroked the arm that hung limp at his side. Florence knelt in the middle of the bed, staring at her mother as though in awe and clawing at the satin quilt.

Leo said, "Frank's dead. Now who dreams up the lynching?"

"Who do you think?" Teddy had crooked his head back to face the ceiling. "The brains of the outfit."

"Milly."

"Sure."

"Don't go telling me she trucked him there and hanged him on her own."

"Naw, that was me and a couple of the same boys roughed up Tom. You think I'm giving out names, you're gonna find out different."

"Could be the fellas at the Smokehouse will ask you that one, but it's not a concern of mine. Not now. The cover up. Milly the brains of that one?"

Every eye in the room, except Tom's, fixed on Milly's disdainful gaze.

"Beats me," Teddy said.

"Hmm," Leo turned to Tom, studied him, began to speak, then shook his head and turned back to Teddy. "Maybe she repented, and called her friend Marion."

"Why would I repent?" Milly screamed. Then she rolled over and buried her face in one of the pillows. The scream must've horrified Florence because she jumped sideways, dove off the bed, and crawled to her brother and Madeline, who parted to allow her between them.

Now the girls, on the floor against the wall beside the closet, held each other and stroked each other's hair. Tom heaved to his feet and offered each of them a hand. He helped them up and ushered them out to the hall.

Florence appeared barely able to stand. Her eyes were no longer so wild. Now they were bleary. The last time he'd seen her anything like this, she had snuck off, gone to the Top Hat, and met a creep who invited her to the Palomar to see Paul Whiteman. When they arrived at the hotel, she discovered Whiteman had never played the Palomar nor was he scheduled to. But the creep had a room there. She gave him a goodbye punch in the ribs and then hiked, barefoot, as her shoes weren't for walking. All the way home, she got whistled at, propositioned, belittled, and chased.

The way she looked when she arrived home that night wasn't only exhausted and outraged but bewildered. And now, when she looked the same only doubled, Tom worried any second she might slip away into some permanent nightmare.

"Now what?"

Madeline said, "How about we get away from this spooky hotel, take a walk someplace you two can talk it over."

Tom agreed. He knocked. When Leo came to the door, he said, "The girls need some air."

"Time you get back," Leo said, plenty loud enough for Milly and her man to hear, "I'll judge if they should go to the Smokehouse."

Tom and the girls walked arm in arm, him in the middle, past the staircase and into the lobby. The lecture was about to commence in a ballroom at whose entrance a mob stood, waving, shoving, yelping pleas at the two guards who held them back.

Raleigh had packed up and left for the day. A couple of dejected matrons occupied his shoeshine station.

Across Ivar Street and up Hollywood Boulevard, the Hickeys and Madeline passed hustlers offering gems, thrills, solace and the like to surly fellows leaning on posts. Other fellows slumped in parked cars waiting for the lecture to conclude and their wives to come bore them with tales from the beyond.

With a girl on each arm, which earned him some jealous glares, Tom walked until they found a vacant bench at a bus stop. Then they sat holding hands.

"What do you think?" Tom asked his sister. "Could Teddy be lying?"

Though Florence seemed most intrigued by passing cars, she turned and said, with quavering assurance, as though to convince herself, "Mama stabbed Mister Gaines."

"What about self-defense, Frank reaching for the knife? You think Teddy lied when he said not so?"

"Why would he?" Florence asked.

"Say, to get back at Milly for all her lies and accusations."

"She probably says mean stuff every day."

"So Milly killed Frank," Tom said, "and maybe Harriet." And, he thought, maybe Pastor William Seymour. And just maybe Charlie Hickey. He squeezed both girls' hands too hard.

Florence whispered, "Ouch."

Madeline leaned and kissed his cheek.

"Yeah," he said, "Mama's a murderer." He watched Florence turn as if to stare again at Hollywood Boulevard, only her eyes were shut. Then tears came in a flood. She let them roll off her pale cheeks and fall onto her lap. Twice, she tried to speak but gave in to sobs. At last, after a mighty shudder, she said, "We can't turn our own mother over to the police, can we, Tommy?"

"Not for murders the cops say didn't happen."

Madeline said, "Maybe you can get her into an asylum."

"Probably not without a police say so."

"We can't let her go on killing people, can we?" Florence asked. Then she fell on Tom, wrapped her arms around him, and wept with abandon, while a motor coach appeared as if out of nowhere and took on the half dozen passengers Tom hadn't noticed gathering around them.

When the motor coach pulled away, Florence put her lips close to her brother's ear, so even Madeline couldn't hear. She whispered, "What if we need to kill her?"

Chapter Fifty-three

In the hotel lobby, the mob around the ballroom doors had multiplied. Chauffeurs and reporters squeezed between princesses and dowagers in custom outfits pricier than Milly's creations. Some of their jewels sparkled as bright as the crystal chandelier. If not for a platoon of wandering guards, a pickpocket could've earned a king's ransom.

When Leo opened the door to 142, Tom said, "Cut them loose."

"Both of them?"

"Teddy served his time, living with her." He glanced in Milly's direction.

"And her?" Leo asked.

Florence pressed herself against her brother's side, stood on her toes, and whispered, "Tommy, we really aren't going to kill her?"

"No, Sis. We're not going to kill anybody. You know why?"

"No. I mean, I'm not sure."

"Because we're Charlie Hickey's kids, not hers."

"But she killed Mister Gaines. And maybe Teddy's wife."

He turned to Leo and crooked his head toward his mother. "Get her out of here."

Leo used his pocketknife on the ropes. For a minute or so, Milly sat rubbing her ankles and staring vile accusations at each of the others. Then she rolled off the bed, stumbled, and rushed out of the room as if from artillery fire.

While Leo freed Boles, Tom said, "You want to stay out of the Smokehouse, here's the deal. You'll keep an eye on Milly, don't let her run off."

"Yeah. Hey, no hard—"

"Shut up. Where do we find you?"

With a newly freed hand, he pointed to the pencil and stationery on the nightstand. Tom fetched it. Teddy jotted the name and address of his brother in El Segundo. "She can have the duplex. Hell, it hasn't been my place since the day she moved in. What're you going to do to her?"

Tom glared a warning.

Teddy passed along the address then stood and limped to the restroom. When he came out, he limped to the door, then stopped and peered over his shoulder at Florence. He shook his head and might've soon begged her forgiveness.

"Get lost," Tom commanded.

When the door closed behind Boles, Leo asked, "What now?"

"I say we talk to Kent Parrot."

"Oh? You think the boss might arrest a gal who's got Hearst's pet on her side for a murder he prefers to maintain didn't happen, you've still got a heap to learn about the ways of the world."

"Give me a better idea."

While he waited for an answer that didn't come, Tom checked his Elgin. A few minutes past 9:30. If Friday night traffic didn't stall them, he thought, they might reach Sugar Hill Barbershop before it closed. "I'm guessing a barber on Central would know how to get the word out, maybe buy us a day or two."

Leo pointed to the phone. "You know how to use one of those gadgets?"

"Give me a lesson, smart guy." He reached for his notebook.

"With all your occupations," Leo said, "you ought to be getting a telephone, as soon as one of those prospects of yours pays off."

Florence, who sat beside Madeline on the bed watching them, didn't second Leo's advice. Because his sister regularly begged and wheedled for a telephone, he knew she'd gone far away.

The barbershop phone rang until Tom gave up on it, after Leo said, "See here, if the tommy-gunners are going to visit the Klan, it'll be during a meeting. Meeting time's probably over for today, and tomorrow's won't likely be till evening. I say we all could benefit from sleep."

Tom agreed. Madeline concurred. Florence said nothing.

On their way out of the hotel, Tom saw Milly, at the edge of the mob trying to bully her way in. She nudged a fellow with her shoulder and jabbed a reporter with her elbow. The sight made him feel as if a tackler came hard and drove a helmet straight in, below the belt.

Chapter Fifty-four

In the Packard, Leo suggested they stop in Chinatown for dinner. The others stared as if he were telling jokes at a funeral. Tom found opening his mouth to talk a struggle. His sister sat with arms wrapped around herself, as if they held her stomach together. Madeline hadn't touched either of the Hickeys since they left the hotel room. When Leo pulled to the curb in front of Bruno's grocery, she didn't say goodbye, only gave a little salute.

Between there and Cactus Court, Leo attempted to console the Hickeys. "Don't forget, Teddy's nobody's star witness. Could be Harriet was suicide, Frank self-defense."

"Could be, all right," Tom said, for his sister's sake.

Leo parked, jumped out, ran around, and helped Florence to the sidewalk. "You going to be okay?"

Florence didn't answer, but made a face as though astonished he would ask such a question.

"How about you, Tom?"

"Sure," he said. But he owed Leo the truth. "I mean, how the hell do I know?"

Florence would've stumbled into the cholla Tom hadn't demolished, but he caught and deflected her. In the cottage on the sofa, she curled her knees up to her chin. "Tommy, is our mama really evil like that Roman emperor Nero? Or is she just crazy?"

Tom asked himself if there was a difference.

"What makes her like that?"

He shrugged. "Give me a couple days to think." He went to the kitchen and fixed them a snack of soda crackers, canned tuna, and apple slices. They left most of it on the plate.

In her bedroom, Florence didn't turn on the radio. Tom lay in bed listening for any sound. He heard some moans. Several times, he thought her heard her get up and went to check. Every time, she appeared to be sleeping, although once she jerked with little spasms. He sat on her bed and sang, just above a whisper, two Stephen Foster songs. "Beautiful Dreamer" and "Aura Lee." He wasn't much of a singer, but they were all he could offer, the most peaceful melodies he knew.

Back in his room, after another hour or so of listening, he slept until the first gray light seeped under his shade. He drank coffee on the porch while he wrote on the backside of sheet music blanks a somewhat orderly report, all he'd gathered about the deaths of Harriet Boles and Frank Gaines.

Leo arrived before seven. "Boss Parrot's an early riser," he said.

A mild Santa Ana rustled the palms. When Florence came out in a green and white summer dress, a pattern of vines like ivy, Tom thought of asking her to change. Not because the dress showed too much leg, back and shoulder. Because it looked like Milly.

But other matters occupied him. All the way downtown, he wrestled with Florence's question, what made Milly who she was. He could've simply said vanity, that she was one of the crazies, too proud to make peace with broken dreams. Except he believed the truth went deeper. That was the problem with truth. You never quite got to the bottom of it.

He tried to recall anything she'd told them about her childhood, aside from the fact that her parents were immigrants from Bohemia and Austria, her father ran off to the Klondike after gold, and her mother died of a broken heart. Hardly an original story among Californians.

Leo parked behind the Hall of Justice in a space reserved for detectives. He led the way through the common room where only a few detectives and uniformed cops scribbled or typed or leaned on their desks. Instead of knocking, he waved at a fellow in uniform and pointed to the door. The man hustled over, knocked softly and listened then opened the door a crack. "Sir, you got a minute."

Tom didn't hear an answer, but the cop entered the room. "Detective Weiss is out here, wanting to see you. Him and Tom Hickey and a gal." The cop stepped out and ushered the three of them into the office.

The way Parrot sat, tall, chin high, forearms at ease on the armrests of his rolling chair, he looked like royalty awaiting petitioners. As they entered, his eyes trained on Florence and followed her every move.

"Please, have a seat," he said, in a voice far more toney than he'd used on Tom alone.

Florence seated herself beneath the portrait gallery. Tom went to the big teak desk, reached for the stapler, used it, and slid one copy of the report, which he had started last night, finished this morning, across the desk to the man. Then he sat in the chair next to Florence's. Leo stood by a window looking out while Parrot gave a few seconds to each page of the report. Either a fast or careless reader, he soon looked up. "Quite a tale."

"News to you?" Leo asked.

Parrot didn't answer. "This Millicent, she a relative?"

"Do you mean to charge her?" Tom asked.

The man stood and went to the window as if to learn what had caught Leo's attention. But he didn't look out. He returned to his desk and again sat tall and straight. "For what? A suicide? Or the natural death of a colored fellow who's already been planted?"

Tom rose, went to the desk, reached across and retrieved his report.

"Where's it go now?" Parrot asked.

"Depends. Socrates, or if he's not available, how about Fighting Bob Shuler."

Parrot's face broke into a smile, then a hearty laugh. "First thing Shuler'd do is figure a way to blame it on Aimee McPherson. Next, he'd use it to start a race war. That what you want?"

"What I want is Socrates."

When the boss opened a drawer on the right side of his desk, Tom wondered if he'd taken all the complaints and demands he could abide and now a gun would speak for him. But the items Parrot took from the drawer were several issues of the *Forum*. He held them up and asked, "Who's his backer?"

"Huh?"

"No ads. Gets his money from the Bolsheviks." He let the broadsides fall onto his desk. "You still want him?"

"Yes sir, whatever he is."

"You've got him. Give me a couple days."

"Why's that?"

"Red tape."

"Until after the election?"

Parrot motioned for Tom to approach, and although Leo and Florence were present, he spoke as though in strictest confidence. "I'll tell you, as a teammate, what the people believe doesn't matter. What does matter, is how they vote. Tom, don't get the wrong idea. We have no intention of harming this Socrates, or even silencing him. We're not cruel people."

"Who is *we?*" Tom asked.

"Whoever you think we are. We're not out to hurt people, as are the Bolsheviks."

"Yeah," Tom said. "You're only out to make money, I hear."

"If you think it's that simple, so be it." Parrot stood, went to the door, and opened it. He politely aimed a finger at Florence then at the exit. As she passed him, he called out, "Mitchell, take care of Miss Hickey while I have a word with the fellows."

He shut the door behind her. "Tom, you should know I've informed Detective Love, if anything befalls Tom or Florence Hickey, he's out of a job. I suspect he doesn't care. He's the kind, if we turned him away, he'd go right to work for Ardizzone or Charlie Crawford. Weiss can tell you about him. Am I right?"

"Yeah," Leo said, in a voice Tom would've called murderous coming from anyone else.

Chapter Fifty-five

Leo drove them to Sugar Hill Barbershop where Tom delivered his report, asked the barber to read and act on his conscience, and to pass it along to Socrates as soon as the publisher got free.

Ever since they left Kent Parrot, Leo had neither spoken nor glanced any way but straight ahead. On the drive home from the barbershop, Tom asked, "What's eating you?"

"I'm fine," Leo grumbled.

"Why'd you clam up?"

Leo shook him off.

Maybe, Tom thought, they both were equally steamed at Parrot because he wouldn't call a murder a murder. Still, one way or another, he supposed, the truth would burn them all. Boss Parrot as well as Leo and both Hickeys.

At home, he asked Florence to use the Villegas phone and call the Egyptian, claim she was sick.

She gave him a withering look. "One of us needs to bring home the bacon."

After she walked out in her harem girl outfit, Tom attempted to read the beginning of a book about Marco Polo, hoping it might carry his mind far away. It accomplished something even better, put him to sleep until dusk. Then the front door rattled. Socrates, he hoped. Instead, he found Vi, her puffy face grim and hands clutching her dress at the hips. "Are you busy?"

"What is it?"

"Leo started drinking as soon as he got home. Why, Tom?"

"Did he tell you about Milly?"

She reached for his hands. "Tom, I'm dreadfully sorry."

"Yeah." Letting go one of her hands, he walked to the porch steps and lowered himself. She sat beside him. "He tell you Boss Parrot won't budge?"

"Yes, he did."

"Maybe he's done being a cop and doesn't know how to not be one."

"But today," Vi said, "it's something more. Shortly after he came home, he took a phone call and chased me out of the room. All day, he's been chasing me out of the room, making phone calls. A call, he pours a drink. Next call, he pours another. And he looks so angry, savage I could call it, he was frightening Una. I took her to a neighbor."

"Who's he talking to?"

"He won't tell me." She lowered her eyes as she turned his way. "I picked up a few words. Fitch. His bootlegger friend, the one the police gunned down. O'Doul, who may be a fellow detective, first name Donald. And something about love. You don't suppose—"

"Let's go see him."

"Yes, please. Will you drive?"

"I don't have a car."

"No, I stole Leo's Packard." Vi shuddered. "I didn't want him to leave before I came back with you. I hope I didn't break all the gears."

Tom drove, defying the speed law while Vi, in the shotgun seat, kept her eyes pinched closed and squeezed the door handle as though preparing to fling it open and jump.

They found Leo at the kitchen table in the dark, staring at a half full tumbler. He glanced up at them. "Did you wreck my Packard?"

"I'm sorry," she said. "I just went and fetched Tom."

"What if I needed the car?"

"Did you?"

He looked at the wall clock and squinted to bring it into focus. "Another half an hour or so I would've." He patted the table across from him. "Sit down, Tom, as long as you're here. Vi's going to allow us some privacy."

Tom complied. Vi disappeared.

Leo pointed to the tumbler. "Drink that, will you? And you catch me going after another, sock me good and hard."

Tom pulled the tumbler his way and tasted the smooth whiskey. "Canadian?"

"Came on a sailboat from Vancouver. Sid picked it up on the backside of Catalina."

"Let's hear it," Tom said.

"Hear what?"

"Tell me."

He met Tom's eyes and held them, which appeared to require an effort of will. "You'll get it out of me. Might as well spill it. Drink up."

Tom gulped a mouthful.

"Here goes. A couple of Sid's boys, the ones took over the business, are set to make a drop at a house on Cosmo, off Hollywood, next block toward downtown from Cahuenga. Chief's sending four of us to meet them."

"So you're not fired?"

Leo shook his head.

"Davis sends you gunning for your pal's boys?"

"That he does."

"Does he know about you and Fitch?"

"What all he knows, I couldn't say. Only he knows plenty."

"Good God," Tom muttered. "You're going?"

Leo spread both hands flat on the table and lifted himself a few inches. "I got my reasons," he said, in a voice that warned Tom against arguing.

Chapter Fifty-six

In the back seat, behind Detective O'Doul, Tom wondered why Leo hadn't much objected to his riding along though when he asked for a gun, Leo refused.

He didn't expect to get the gun. Long ago, while Leo coached him about the difference between boys and men, between dreams and real life, he'd claimed pulling a trigger was to shooting a person what playing toss was to throwing a touchdown Hail Mary pass in the Rose Bowl. The first time out, at least, a guy would be lucky to hit the target, never mind the bull's eye.

Because Leo and O'Doul discussed nothing, Tom presumed they'd settled plans by phone. O'Doul brought the tommy-guns and laid them on the seat between himself and Leo. They'd driven a mile or more before the detective asked, "Why'd you bring the kid along?"

"Can't shake him," Leo said.

O'Doul turned just far enough. "Hickey?"

Tom nodded. "O'Doul?"

"You got it." The detective turned back toward the front and asked, "You doing all right, Weiss?"

"Splitting headache," Leo said.

As they passed the new Warner Brother's Theater, Leo said, "Tom, get down low."

Because he recognized the car in front of them, he obliged without question. The Packard pulled alongside the tan Nash.

O'Doul stuck an arm out the window and waved the Nash over. Leo passed, pulled over, parked, and backed up.

Both detectives climbed out, for a meeting on the sidewalk with the driver of the Nash. With both the side windows open, Tom listened to Fenton Love crabbing, "Vitale's a louse. Busted his arm, did he? Fell out of a tree, did he? I tell him, 'Can't use the Thompson a pistol will do.' Chump says he's no good left handed. He's yellow, is what."

"Nobody replacing him?" O'Doul asked.

"I made a call, sure I did. Davis says, 'We got plenty of business tonight. You three boys can handle it.' I tell him, 'Sure we can.' How about it?"

Leo said, "Fenton, you go up here." He must've pointed but Tom couldn't see. "Park, sit and have a smoke until you hear gunfire. See, we'll come in shooting, from down there. The Selma end of the block. They'll be attending to us, you creep in and hold them while we come running."

"Sure thing, I'll hold them," Love said, and croaked a laugh.

The detectives returned to their cars. As the Packard pulled away from the curb, Tom said, "Love's a partner of yours?"

Leo made the turn onto Wilcox. "Sit up, if you want."

He drove to Selma, made a left, and parked at the T-intersection, straight across from the foot of Cosmo Street. He climbed out and peered at Tom through the open rear window. "Get out, if you want. But stay behind the car." A tommy-gun hung from a strap at his right side. He reached inside his coat and pulled out his Colt. "*Only* if the whole deal goes wrong."

He gave Tom the gun, reached into a trouser pocket, and handed over the key to his Packard. "You hear me yelling, jump in and start it up."

After the detectives crossed Selma and entered Cosmo Street, Tom climbed out and followed, holding the revolver at his side.

Cosmo didn't have streetlamps. A clear sky, a half moon, and the lights from inside a few houses allowed him to see silhouettes. He stood beside a eucalyptus and watched Leo and his partner making their way up the block, using parked cars for cover.

Then he saw Leo's weapon rise, and heard it fire, while bullets sparked out like tiny flares. Tom ducked behind the eucalyptus.

For a minute, tommy-guns, some closer than others, fired dozens of bursts. About half way up the block, a motor sputtered to life. A Chevrolet swerved out of a yard and raced in Tom's direction. He squeezed against the tree, in case bullets ricocheted his way off the car. But the shooting was over. The Chevrolet turned onto Selma and sped east.

Tom waited as long as he could restrain himself, then left his cover and ran the way the detectives had, pausing behind the same parked cars, until he saw that a man was down.

Leo and O'Doul stood gazing at Fenton Love, who was stretched out long at their feet. Blood seeped from his neck, dribbled out of his torso and arms, and poured from one of his thighs. His homburg lay beside his right hip as though meant to collect alms. A quake passed through him, head to feet.

Leo used his shoe to nudge a tommy-gun farther away from Love's hand. "Shame."

O'Doul said, "Yeah, Chief's gonna raise hell."

Chapter Fifty-seven

By morning, Tom had absolved Leo of murder. Though he'd no doubt wanted to kill Fenton Love on account of the Sid Fitch massacre, he hadn't. Besides, he must've killed the man on orders from above, and to protect Tom and Florence, and to serve everybody Love would've wronged. Like cops pledged to do.

Tom asked his sister to dress in something without flowers, and to wear a sun hat. While she fussed over her outfit and makeup, he walked to Abuelito's Grocery and bought a hunk of cheese to eat with their soda crackers and apples, about all they had left in the kitchen.

Though Tom understood a sensible fellow wouldn't spend most of his last few dimes on the streetcar and a rowboat, he suspected Florence needed a taste of peace and normalcy.

Since Leo had promised to stop by with any report about Milly, Tom left a note on the door, giving their destination and predicting they would return mid-afternoon.

They arrived at Echo Park and secured the boat before the first service at Angelus Temple let out, at which time a line would form at the dock. While Tom rowed and Florence navigated, guiding him past other boats, obstinate ducks, and clusters of lily pads, he wrestled with thoughts about Milly.

He'd advised Florence to think about most anything except their mother. As usual, she paid his advice little mind. Setting a half eaten apple on her lap, she said, "Tommy, do you think evil is in our blood?"

He stopped rowing. "Let's suppose evil's a family trait. Maybe we've got nothing but evil ancestors, all the way back to Adam, or monkeys. The question is, what're we going to do about it."

"So, we ought to do what?"

"That's a tough one. Like I said before, give me a day or two."

They didn't need to ride the streetcar home. When they docked the rowboat, Leo came around the line and met them.

"Milly's staying put."

"You've seen her?"

"Found a place uphill from her duplex. It gave me a view right into her back yard. Not an hour ago, she was puttering in her garden."

As they strolled around the lake toward Leo's car, a Mexican boy came running their way. He ran up to Tom and handed him a small manila envelope.

"What's this?" Tom said.

The boy gave a look as if he'd encountered a nitwit. "Is a letter."

"Where'd you get it?"

"A lady. Gave me a quarter."

"You see her?"

The boy looked all around. "No, she gone."

"What'd she look like?"

"Not so good."

Could be Emma Shaefer, Tom thought as he lifted the flap of the envelope.

The boy said, "Don' you give me another quarter?"

Since turning over a quarter would've left the boy richer than Tom, he said, "Scram."

The letter was typed on stationery cadged from the Knickerbocker. "Your mother will come to the tar pits tomorrow at 7 a.m. She expects to see you there, alone." No name, but he knew the handwriting all too well.

Chapter Fifty-eight

Tom wished he could count the times he'd gotten visited by nightmares about the tar pits. He'd gone under the black goo so many times, though he couldn't remember so much as actually sticking a toe in the crud, he could feel the sensation more clearly than walking in rain or a dip in the ocean.

Florence warned him not to go and Leo backed her. He didn't tell them he meant to learn whether Milly killed their father, no matter what method the interrogation required. He only persuaded them by promising he'd watch from a distance, make sure Milly hadn't brought a gang of thugs to pitch him over a low fence into one of the pools with the bones of saber tooth tigers.

He broke the promise. Whatever equipped him to play fullback also refused to let him shy from walking straight into the park and around the pools. He watched his periphery and listened for footfalls behind his back. He circled every pool at least twice, and kept watch on every visitor, even couples with children. He stayed until 8:30 a.m., watching and wondering how many human bones might be in there with the tigers and mastodons.

He only left then because he'd deciphered what the note from Milly meant. The message came clear: She was still able to take back his life at will, and she always would be.

A half hour later, he stood in line in the Hall of Records archives. One hand held his hat. In the other was an IOU he'd jotted for dinner and dancing at the Casa del Mar.

Until he reached the front of the line, Madeline didn't let on she saw him. Then she said, "Aw, you're the fellow called about some deeds?"

"Yes, ma'am."

"Follow me, please."

Once she'd got him alone in the labyrinth, she stayed beyond arm's length. "What do you need, Tom?"

"Nothing. I mean, company."

"Uh huh."

"I mean your company."

"That so?"

He handed her the IOU. She smiled and shook her head, which made her wavy hair bounce. "Casa del Mar is a pricey joint. Think you can pay up before I grow old?"

"Every morning I'll meet the newsboy, scour the help wanted page."

"You do that."

"Meantime, one of these evenings, how about we harmonize on a few tunes."

She allowed a pensive moment. "You like strings?"

"Do I ever?"

"I know a couple guys who swing on guitar and fiddle, like Joe Venuti and Eddie Lang."

"Tell you what," Tom said. "How about we work the kinks out of our act before we call in the strings?"

She gave him a soft, pretty laugh. "I know what you're up to. Listen, Tom. If you get hungry, come by my place. Bring Florence, if she's hungry too."

He was hoping she'd give him a peck on the cheek as she passed. She didn't.

All the way home, on top of his other concerns, he felt like a charity case. So he searched the cottage for something to sell, other than his clarinet. He thought of Florence's radio, then felt like a bandit for even considering.

He brought out the Selmar clarinet, for which he'd spent almost two years saving his pennies and trading up. He played

"St. Louis Blues" and "Crazy Blues," then packed the instrument into its case. When he visited Madeline, he would play his bamboo flute.

He was on his way out of the court when Leo's Packard pulled to the curb. He leaned out the passenger window. "What'd Milly have to say?"

"She didn't show?"

"Hmmm. What do you make of that?"

One of these days, Tom would explain. Now he said, "What do you make of it?"

"Well, here's a clue. This morning, no sign of her. So I went to the door. She didn't bother to lock up. I spent a half hour scouring the place, not counting the times I ducked outside to get out of range of those lousy flowers. I can tell you the closet and dressers are empty. So I asked around. Neighbors saw a couple colored fellows sizing up the neighborhood, dressed in flashy suits. You say she didn't show at the pits, I'm betting, sometime during the dark of night, either she went for a ride with the coloreds, or she headed for parts unknown. Where are you going with the licorice stick?"

If Tom could've thought of a reasonable lie, he would've used it. Nothing came. "Pawn shop."

"The devil you are." Leo reached for his wallet, emptied it, and tried to hand Tom a stack of ones and fives.

"Nope."

Leo said, "Thing is, I want a clarinet, I'm offering more than some pawnbroker will, and I'm a whole lot more likely to let you borrow it, if you promise to treat it right and stop by once a week to give me lessons."

Tom hated taking the money. But he had a sister, probably as hungry as he was. He handed over the case, pocketed the bills, and double-timed to Abuelito's. He bought a whole chicken, a heap of vegetables, bread, butter, a sack of rice, and a tin of strawberry jam. He was cooking when Florence came home.

She sniffed, dashed into the kitchen, gave him a wild embrace and chanted. "Yum, yum, yum."

When she asked what occurred at the tar pits, he said, "Milly didn't show," but left out his conclusion.

Half way through dinner, she said, "Say, I haven't eaten this well since you stuck your nose between me and Pablo."

"Hunger keeps you trim and fit," Tom said. Then he passed along Leo's news about Milly.

Her eyes hooded. She made fists then let go and shoved her plate aside. "Tommy, are we going to track her down?"

"Suppose we do. And suppose we catch her. Listen, yesterday you asked, what do we do about this evil blood of ours."

"And you didn't say."

"Well, the way I see it, some folks stake everything on their dreams. When they don't come true, they go looking for answers why. Sometimes the answers are true, sometimes they're lies or just screwy. You find the wrong answer or none at all, it's tough to keep from getting bitter.

"See, bitter people can't keep from hating. When you hate enough, killing comes easy."

"What'll we do?" Florence asked. "Don't dream?"

"Dreaming's okay. Some kinds. Only, while we're out chasing our dreams, suppose we keep our eyes and ears open, look for what's beautiful. Sights, sounds, people. And when we find them, suppose we remind ourselves to be thankful just because they're around. I'm betting, as long as we keep ourselves thankful, we won't be killers."

"Milly loves beautiful things like flowers."

Tom had to grope for an answer, but soon enough one came, with the warm feeling of truth. "Only if she grows them herself," he said. "If she doesn't have to thank anybody."

Chapter Fifty-nine

November 2, 1926, was the first election in which Tom could vote. That morning, he recalled Boss Parrot saying, "What the people believe doesn't matter. What does matter, is how they vote."

He thought he'd sooner pass up voting than vote wrong. Meaning he needed advice from someone who'd studied the issues. The only trustworthy advisor who came to mind was in jail until after the election.

While he leafed through the *Forum* copies he'd borrowed from the library, he remembered one he hadn't chosen. A voter's guide.

An hour later, in the library, he discovered more than he'd sought. A handwritten draft of a *Forum* from the day Socrates got jailed. Tom imagined the sly publisher deposited such a draft every time he wrote one. He knew if he tried to expose the wrong stuff, the wrong people would hear, and act.

```
October 28, 1926
For the people:
    This reporter offers apologies for his
belated word on the election of Tuesday
next. Some truths which in retrospect appear
obvious, in discovery elude the diligent.
    May of this year, the people voted to fund
a new railroad depot on the Plaza, which, as
was revealed in the August 6, 1926 Forum,
will further enrich Mister Harry Chandler
and his California Club brethren, due to
their ownership of surrounding properties.
```

Public concerns about the expense and aesthetics of elevated trains, heated by the vituperation of the *Times*, turned the voters away from their own best interest.

Better we had chosen to side with progressives' customary enemy, the Southern Pacific railroad, and relegate the depot to renovation in its current site. From that location, the railroads, electric and otherwise, could establish new lines, below ground, surface and elevated, to suburbs and outlying cities, through rights of way they hold.

New lines from the Plaza site will prove far too costly, as the elite will set the price. Clearly gross economics, also known as greed, has ceded the future of our city to drillers and refiners of oil; manufacturers of automobiles; and developers of tracts in areas to be chosen by city planners whom all concede are pawns of said oilmen, manufacturers, and developers. At the head of whom stands Harry Chandler.

Once again, we the people have been swindled. Need I argue that all of us who toil with muscle or mind to feed, clothe, and house our families, are better served by trains than by automobiles we can only afford by denying ourselves moments of leisure and thereby denying our children the care and attention upon which they thrive.

Although the future appears set in asphalt, this reporter will lodge his protest by casting a no vote on each of the several propositions meant to fund new roadways or alleviate traffic congestion.

Until public transportation to all our citizens is assured, he will so vote and urge his readers to follow suit.

Tom voted accordingly.

Chapter Sixty

Tom and Florence arrived an hour early for the Angelus Temple service. As they entered the crowd and stood attempting to discern where the line began, Tom felt a tug on his arm. For an instant, he imagined the ghost of Fenton Love. Then he heard the soft, stern voice of Emma Shaffer.

"Sister requests a moment with you. Both of you."

They followed the woman, who parted the crowd and led them past the reporters and swarthy fellows standing guard, into the parsonage and up the winding stairs to the sitting room.

Sister Aimee, already dressed for the performance, rose off her settee and reached her arms out wide. She embraced them both at once.

"How are you faring?" she asked.

"Okay," Tom said. Florence, as shy as he'd ever witnessed, only cracked a demure smile and nodded.

"Sit, please." Sister Aimee returned to her settee.

When the Hickeys were seated across from her, she said, "You two have faced trials most of us couldn't imagine and prevailed. I'm awed and grateful."

Florence said, "Tommy's the best."

"You know about Milly?" Tom asked.

"I do."

"Want to tell us how you found out?"

"I'd rather not," Sister said. "I do have something to offer that may assist in putting all this horror behind you. It's this.

Fenton Love adored your mother. Before she chose Mister Boles, and perhaps afterward. Your mother is a remarkable woman. Troubled, yes. Insane perhaps. But her power to captivate and persuade is rare. Certainly her beauty plays a part." She paused for a deeper study of Florence, who blushed yet didn't avert her eyes. "You are truly stunning," Sister said. "A masterpiece. Might I ask a favor?"

"Oh, yes," Florence said.

"Use your beauty for good."

"Okay," Florence whispered, then lifted her voice. "I'll sure try."

"After your mother chose Mister Boles, Fenton's loyalty became ever more directed toward me. He even presumed to invite me on outings. I suppose his ardor, or my rejection of him, might have led to extreme behavior. And now, I'd best prepare for the service."

They all stood, and Tom said, "I don't suppose you'll give us a preview?"

A smile appeared and broadened until it charged her face with a pearly glow. "You of all people should know the answer."

Emma Shaffer appeared and led the Hickeys downstairs, out a back door, across an alley, and through the stage entrance to the sanctuary. She directed them to their reserved seats, on an aisle in the first row of the mezzanine balcony. Then she hustled away.

Tom and Florence took their seats and waited. While Florence observed the crowd in its rush to find places, Tom thought about Fenton Love, who probably hoped to win Milly away from Boles by foiling her wicked son's plan to expose her.

A minute after Tom's Elgin informed him the polls had closed, Sister Aimee floated down the ramp in her nurse outfit with its cape gliding behind, to tell the world who, among a legion of candidates, was the biggest liar in Los Angeles.

Tom doubted Sarah Bernhardt could've heightened the performance with voice and gesture any more dramatically than did Sister Aimee. She detailed the greatest of Biblical liars. Eve, Pharaoh, Joseph's brothers, and Jezebel. She chronicled the supreme liars of secular history, from Ghengis Khan through Charles Darwin.

She worked the congregation into such ever deepening suspense, when she gave the punch line, announced that the biggest liar in Los Angeles was none other than Satan himself, Tom and Florence were hardly the only ones who let out audible groans. Several hundred folks joined them, Tom estimated. He supposed ten times that many groaned under their breath.

But afterward, as he and Florence strolled across the park beside the lake, he decided Sister got it right.

He thought back to a philosophy prof lecturing about a German whose name Tom's overloaded mind couldn't recall. The German claimed the key to what drove people was an unquenchable will to power.

Maybe, Tom thought, the devil was a demon from a fiery domain. Maybe he was the will to power, or some other need or delusion humans got possessed by. If you didn't try to define the devil, you couldn't argue with Sister.

In some way Tom didn't understand, Milly, the Klan, Reverend Shuler, probably Hearst and Chandler, maybe Sister Aimee herself got smitten by the devil and acted accordingly. No doubt the devil got into Fenton Love.

As they waited for the trolley, Tom began compiling his own list of the city's great liars. Besides the devil, it included every reporter who wrote to do Hearst's bidding or to promote the profiteering of Chandler and his cronies, and every booster who, for money, pitched California as the promised land.

Chapter Sixty-one

As far as Tom could remember, the last time he'd slept until nearly 10 a.m. was before they ran from Milly. He brewed coffee, fixed bread with butter and jam, and was carrying his breakfast outside when he found the *Forum* wedged into the crack between his door and the jamb.

A note jotted above the headline read: "Tom, you need a brother, we go out on the town. Ernestine send her love. Oz."

```
November 3, 1926
For the people:
   An Unlikely Champion
   Franklin Gaines may now rest in peace, con-
sidering his mortal life well accomplished,
his goodness proven out by the loyalty of a
friend. While the wicked go unmourned, at
Franklin's passing a young white man expressed
his devotion by exposing the murderer at a
nearly unimaginable cost, which this reporter
is not at liberty to reveal.
   The hero of our report, possessed by cour-
age and conviction, by plunging into pitched
battle against the police and the oligarchy,
uncovered the truth of the Franklin Gaines
murder.
   The killer was one Millicent Hickey, a
white woman. In a fit of passion resulting
from a love triangle with its roots in the
Azusa Street revival, Hickey murdered Gaines
```

```
by stabbing. Subsequently, she masterminded
hanging Gaines from an Echo Park tree in an
effort to degrade even further the reputation
of Sister Aimee Semple McPherson, against
whom she harbored a poisonous grudge.
```

Tom wasn't given to weeping, yet he sat on the stump outside his cottage, and devoted some minutes to wiping his eyes.

Clerks and salespeople jostled and collided along Temple Street and up Broadway, hustling to join the line outside the Boos Brothers' cafeteria. Tom cut into the Hall of Justice parking lot, on his way to Boss Parrot's office.

"Hickey," a deep voice called.

Tom wheeled and saw Parrot standing beside a Chrysler Touring convertible. As Tom approached, the boss asked, "Come to see me."

"Yeah. Can you give me five minutes?"

"I'm late for a meeting."

"Where is it?"

"Brown Derby, up Wilshire. Have you been there?"

Tom shook his head. "It's on my way home. Give me a lift?"

Parrot rolled his hand, motioning toward the passenger seat. Tom went around, climbed in and sunk into cushioned upholstery that matched the lime paint job. "Some auto," he said. Then he waited for Parrot to talk, to question or maybe confess. But the man only drove, his expression cordial yet earnest. Tom supposed matters of great import had nudged the lynching, cover up, election and all out of his mind.

"You read today's *Forum?*" Tom asked.

"I did. You have an ardent admirer, as well you deserve. You're a rare one, Tom. If you ever need work, look me up."

"And the *Forum* you jailed Socrates over, so it wouldn't get out until after the election. You read that one, no doubt, in the author's own hand."

"I read them all. In my position, it's essential."

"So the cover up was about the election?"

For several blocks, the boss appeared to ponder. "Tangentially, perhaps. After all, Tom, one could speculate Sister Aimee controls at least a hundred thousand votes, should she care to exert her influence."

"Doesn't she stay out of politics?"

Parrot looked over and smiled. "You'd be mistaken to predict any move of McPherson's, as she repeatedly warns us, by subtle means such as the announcement of last night's sermon topic. Did you attend?"

Tom nodded. "Now it's over and done, tell me, did she call for the cover up?"

Parrot made a smooth turn onto Wilshire, then jammed the brakes. He was a careful driver. Once the traffic got moving, he said, "No, in this case, your instigator was Fenton Love."

Just the name caused Tom's pulse to rise and a knot to grip his belly. But relief overcame all that. Something in him needed to absolve Sister Aimee. Maybe knowing the truth about Milly had shaken his faith in everybody. He might've needed a piece of it back. "Love got to the police," he said. "What about Carl Calhoun, the Hearst reporter, alias Joe the custodian? What kept him from blowing the cover?"

"Ask Calhoun. My guess would be a roll of bills or a death threat. Fenton was capable of providing the one and making good on the other."

A laughing gaggle of coeds caught Tom's attention. They came prancing out of the art institute bequeathed by Harry Chandler's infamous father-in-law. One of them waved. Tom sighed. "What about Chandler? What kept the *Times* quiet? Kept Chandler from scooping his rival?"

"Who says Harry knew?" Boss Parrot looked over with a fatherly expression. "Tom, nobody knows everything."

A trio of slick, hearty fellows stood outside the Brown Derby waiting for the boss. Tom recognized the faces, probably from news photos. He didn't know their names. Or wish to.

He accepted Parrot's handshake, then turned away and let the swells be.

Chapter Sixty-two

Leo arrived before Florence left for school. He handed her an *Examiner,* Tom a *Times.*

"If you want me to be sorry," he said, "I sure am."

The front page of each newspaper featured a small article on the same topic. The *Examiner* headline read, "POPULAR SEAMSTRESS SUSPECTED DROWNED." The story reported that Millicent Hickey, a seamstress employed by film stars, went to Ocean Park, accompanied by a friend, Elva Lister. To the very same beach next to Ocean View Hotel from which Sister McPherson disappeared last May 18. Leaving her friend on the beach with a magazine, Mrs. Hickey dove into the first of a set of waves. By the time the last wave broke, she had vanished.

Mrs. Lister dashed to the shoreline and called out for some minutes, then ran to the Ocean View Hotel and asked a desk clerk to summon the police. Until dark, a lifeguard boat had patrolled the coastline for a mile each direction. Finding no sign of the woman, the sheriff's department deemed her a victim of drowning. A sheriff's spokesman assured reporters the body would likely wash ashore.

While Florence read, she backed to the sofa and eased herself down. She finished the article, folded the paper on her lap, and appeared to stare out the window that overlooked the Ornelas' vegetable garden.

Tom said, "Just like Sister Aimee."

"Want me to look up this Elva Lister?" Leo asked.

Tom went to sit beside his sister and looped his arm around her shoulder. "What do you think, babe?"

"She drowned," Florence said. Each of her wide blue eyes shed a single tear.

An hour later, on a westbound Wilshire coach, she said, "Tommy, do you think Sister Aimee got kidnapped, or is she lying?"

"Beats me."

"Come on. What do you think?"

He watched a man hacking at a golf ball, trying to knock it toward the seventh green of the Los Angeles Country Club where he'd spent a summer caddying, and wished for the means to cloister Florence somewhere green and orderly. "I'll make a guess, as long as you promise not to tell anybody."

"Promise."

"Suppose Sister thought, 'I'm done, I can't be a mother and preach twenty sermons a week and contend with choirs and board members and take in motherless babies and run a Bible school and feed the poor.' Suppose she thought, 'Dear God, I was on the road twice as long as Jesus ever was. I've traveled farther than Saint Paul, reached as many lost souls as Martin Luther and Charles Wesley put together.' Suppose she believes she can't go on, and so she cooks up a scheme. She'll disappear. Start a new life, say on the shore of the Snake River. A year or so down the road, she'll figure a way to take back her kids."

"Did she tell her kids?"

Tom shrugged. "Anyway, they've got Grandma and the indomitable Emma Shaffer to console and care for them. So she plays the vanishing act. But after a couple weeks relaxing, she comes around to her old self. She misses the kids, the adoration, the feeling of being called to a mission. She realizes she can't become anybody other than who she is. So she cooks up the kidnapping story. And it's true. To her way of thinking, it's true. Just like the Bible."

"You lost me."

"I mean, what's true is the story behind the story. Take Jonah and the whale. Suppose the real Jonah didn't go into a real fish. What's it matter, if the pain and anguish the guy felt couldn't be described better than to say a big fish ate him?"

Florence looped her arm around her brother's. "You've got strange ideas, Tommy."

"That's what college will do for you if you let it."

From the end of the line they walked along the bluff, then down the path Hearst and Marion Davies had used to inspect the progress of their mansion.

On the beach, they carried their shoes. Tom rolled up his cuffs. They walked ankle deep in the icy tide.

They walked under the public pier upon which tourists frolicked, lost souls sought their hearts' home, and crazies wished for a tidal wave.

As they passed through the shadow of Casa del Mar, Florence said, "Tommy, what you guessed about Sister Aimee. I mean, if Milly was copying Sister, does that mean she's not gone for good?"

Raising a beautiful sister might be hard, Tom thought, but he'd bet raising a smart one was considerably harder.

He didn't answer for some minutes, until they arrived at Ocean Park beach. Then he peered out to sea through the mist and saw only one small dory. The dozen or so folks on that stretch of beach all appeared to be fishing or picnicking. None were looking for Milly.

She was alive, Tom believed. She was roaming the world like a hungry lion on the lookout for someone to devour.

But he said, "No, babe, she won't come back like Sister did. She's gone."

To receive a free catalog of Poisoned Pen Press titles, please contact us in one of the following ways:

Phone: 1-800-421-3976
Facsimile: 1-480-949-1707
Email: info@poisonedpenpress.com
Website: www.poisonedpenpress.com

Poisoned Pen Press
6962 E. First Ave. Ste. 103
Scottsdale, AZ 85251